They danced

"You should do this more often, Miss Briggs. You are a very graceful woman."

"Now you're mocking me," she said with momentary unease.

"I'm not, Lila," he said sincerely. "I'm not."

"Well, I don't care," she declared as she gazed up and saw a dart of moonlight reflected in his eyes. "This is wonderful."

"Yes, it is."

Her hand was delicate in his and, when he smiled down at her, Lila's eyes crinkled with delight and she threw back her head, gazing briefly up at the stars.

"I've never felt this way before," she whispered.

Don't miss Jill Metcalf's other
Diamond Homespun Romances . . .
Spring Blossom and *Autumn Leaves*

Praise for *Spring Blossom*:

"A sweet, gentle romance."   —*Rendezvous*

"This hero is incredible!"   —*Heartland Critiques*

"Well done. Ms. Metcalf writes with a true feel for her characters' emotions. This is a very pleasurable read."
                                    —*Romantic Times*

Diamond Books by Jill Metcalf

SPRING BLOSSOM
AUTUMN LEAVES
LILA'S DANCE

LILA'S DANCE

JILL METCALF

DIAMOND BOOKS, NEW YORK

This book is a Diamond original edition,
and has never been previously published.

LILA'S DANCE

A Diamond Book/published by arrangement with the author

PRINTING HISTORY
Diamond edition/October 1993

ISBN: 1-55773-951-X

Diamond Books are published by The Berkley Publishing Group,
200 Madison Avenue, New York, NY 10016.
DIAMOND and the "D" design
are trademarks belonging to Charter Communications, Inc.

PRINTED IN THE UNITED STATES OF AMERICA

10 9 8 7 6 5 4 3 2 1

For Mike
—You can't choose your family, so the saying goes. But, if I could choose, I'd sure choose you. You've been outstanding, brother!

And Barb
—I've always been so very happy that you and Mike chose each other. You've been as close as any sister could be, dear sister-in-law . . .

This one is for you both
With love always
Jill

LILA'S DANCE

CHAPTER 1

 THE OUTSIDE OF THE WEATHERED THREE-ROOM cottage looked calm. Inside, chaos reigned supreme.

 Outside, fourteen-year-old Tommy Briggs pulled at weeds now and again, maintaining some sort of order about the small yard. Inside, Tommy's eighteen-year-old sister, Lila, demanded order but rarely achieved that high goal. Some occasions were more orderly than others, but those were short-lived.

 Lila snapped a clean, worn sheet across the second bed in the small room and tucked the edges under the mattress. "Beth," she said to her ten-year-old sister, "run into the kitchen and give the stew a stir for me. Careful of that stove, now," she added as a gray wool blanket fell into place. Rounding the end of the bed, Lila tucked the corners of the blanket under the corn-husk mattress before moving with quick efficiency to the other bed, where she

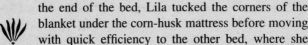

scooped the small boy up in her arms. "There," she crooned to four-year-old Sammy. "We've got you your own nice clean bed, darlin'." She smiled at five-year-old Annie before turning her back and walking to the newly made bed. She had two sick children on her hands in addition to cooking for her father and the four other healthy children. Cooking and cleaning and washing clothes and trying to maintain a small house took up the better part of Lila's days and nights.

In her attempts to keep this illness from striking the others, Lila had tucked each child into separate beds in one room. The other boys would have to sleep in the kitchen for a night or two, she decided. And her father, Jonathan, would sleep where he might; if he managed to stumble in before the rooster crowed.

She didn't need two sick children.

But Lila's stride was barely broken by this added burden. It simply meant less sleep and more running from room to room. Her love of the little ones did mean, however, that worry lines had become evident across her forehead.

She tucked Sammy's small body under the clean bedding and smoothed his brow with a work-worn hand. Both children had fevers, but Sammy had been moaning and clutching his belly since she had first discovered that he, too, was sick. "Doc Fraser's coming, baby," she said as she dipped a cloth in cool water and wrung it between her hands. "Young Jon's gone to fetch him." She stroked Sammy's brow with the cool cloth. When the child moaned again and rolled onto his side, Lila scooped him up and sat on the side of the bed, rocking him as she looked across the room at Annie. "You two didn't eat those crabapples, did you, Annie?"

The five-year-old girl felt miserable and weak and she wanted Lila to rock her, too, so she merely shook her head and whined a soft denial as she snuggled into the pillows.

"Where is Doc?" Lila questioned softly as she rocked back and forth and Sammy mewled.

Daniel Stone stretched out his long legs in order to keep up with the gangling youth who was leading. The boy had assured Daniel he would not need his horse as they had to walk only to the edge of town. Near the smithy, the boy had said. Well, Daniel supposed that if he took this walk often and at this pace, he would remain fairly fit.

"What did you say your name was?" he asked the boy.

"Jon. Jon Briggs. My father is the blacksmith. That's where we're goin'. We live next to the smithy."

Daniel nodded and his gaze returned to the street ahead.

"My sister, Lila, says the two young ones is pretty sick," Jon volunteered. Jon was fifteen and helped his father in the smithy now. He had for the past year, giving up his schooling to learn the trade. But he left the running of the house to Lila; everybody did.

And if Lila said Annie and Sam were sick, they were right sick.

They came upon a weathered wood-sided, single-story cottage. As they turned into the yard, Daniel's eyes scanned the darkened wood, almost black with age. The roof that covered the front porch seemed to dip precariously at one end, and he carefully stepped up onto the wooden step, eyeing the floorboards of the porch for breaks in the wood; a broken leg would interfere with his work for weeks.

Jon charged through the flimsy wooden door and hollered from the only common room the small house possessed. "Lila?"

"Here!" a feminine voice called.

Daniel followed Jon to the right and entered a small bedroom, which contained two wide beds and a single commode. The walls were of unpainted wood, and no rugs covered the floor. One bed was occupied by a small girl, whose eyes seemed to grow larger as she looked at him. On the other bed sat a pretty young woman, rocking an even smaller child. Daniel turned in her direction.

Lila stared at the man with obvious surprise before turning a glaring glance at her brother. "Where's Doc Fraser, Jon?"

"I'm Dr. Stone," Daniel said quietly as he approached. "Dr. Fraser is tending a patient out of town."

Lila's brows arched severely above her brown eyes as she openly inspected this unknown man. He was tall, appearing very tall from her perch on the side of the bed. His hair was closer to blond than brown, and his eyes were a pretty, bright, sunny-day, sky-blue. It was the kindness in those eyes that began to convince her it would be all right to allow this man to look at the children. If she watched his every move, that is. Still . . . "You're sure you're a doctor?" she asked suspiciously. "You seem kinda young."

Jon thought better of getting involved in this conversation and ducked from the room to return to work.

Daniel managed to hide his smile as he stared down at her. "I assure you, Miss Briggs—I assume you *are* Miss Briggs—that I possess the proper medical credentials."

"Well, Doc Fraser always seemed *old*," she said softly, clutching Sammy to her breast.

Daniel did smile at that. "I'll do you a favor and be certain he never knows you said that. Now, what's wrong with these children?"

He was asking *her*? "Well, that's why Jon went to fetch you," Lila said logically. "I don't know what's wrong with them."

Daniel had been in the act of bending over the young woman to look at the boy she held, but now he straightened to his full six-foot, one-inch height. He stared into her eyes trying to determine if her comment was meant as a bit of sarcasm, but her large brown eyes appeared honest enough, and he decided to take her words at face value. She *didn't* know what was wrong with these children. It was as simple as that. He had to remember he was no longer dealing with people from high society who flaunted contempt and cloaked their true thoughts in double entendre. "Point taken, Miss Briggs," he said lightly. "Let's lay this boy down so I can have a look."

Sammy whined like a sick puppy when his sister's arms disappeared from around him.

"All right, young man," Daniel said softly as he bent over the bed, "let's have a look at you."

Lila backed away a step, moving down the side of the bed; she wanted Sammy to know she was staying close.

The young doctor had a good face, and as she watched, his hands appeared sure and gentle, but she didn't know him, and he would have to earn her trust when it came to the care of these children.

Daniel examined the child's eyes and pressed a palm across the small forehead. "What's your name?" he asked.

"He's Sammy," Lila volunteered.

Daniel nodded his head but maintained his concentration on the boy. Turning to the black bag he had dropped on the end of the bed, Daniel reached out for it, causing the young woman to dance back another step to remove herself from his path. He wondered if she was naturally jittery or if nervous energy had her hopping out of his way.

Lila watched as he pulled the tubular stethoscope from his bag and shook her head. "It's his belly that's hurtin' him," she said quietly. "'There's nothin' wrong with his heart."

Exasperated by the note of disgust he had detected in her tone, Daniel straightened once again and turned on her.

"Miss Briggs," he admonished.

Lila's gaze instantly dropped to his dusty black boots in chagrin. "Sorry," she muttered. She moved away then and sat on the edge of Annie's bed.

"Who's he?" the small girl whispered.

"He's a new doctor," Lila said, lightly stroking wisps of fine brown hair from the feverish brow. "I think he's here to help Doc Fraser."

"Is he goin' to hurt me, Lila?" she asked in a small voice.

"No, darlin'. He won't hurt you."

Daniel noted the tone of comfort in the elder sister's voice; she spoke with the softness of a mother's concern. He raised Sammy's worn nightshirt and gently touched the boy's tender belly. He received an instant reaction from the child for his efforts.

Lila jumped to her feet and raced across the room when Sam cried out. "You're hurtin' him!" she blurted.

Daniel's frown returned as he probed the firm abdomen. "What has this boy eaten today?" he asked, allowing Sammy to roll onto his side and curl up into a small ball. He turned to face Lila then, his eyes questioning as he towered over her.

"He had some bread and honey for breakfast," she said, thinking back. "That's all, I think."

"You're sure? When did this fever come on?"

"Annie's been feeling poor all day," she said. "But Sammy only started complainin' just before I sent Jon to fetch you."

Daniel turned silently away from her and approached the other bed, smiling now to reassure the frightened little girl. "Hello, Annie," he said softly and sat on the edge of the bed. "My name's Daniel. I understand you're feeling a bit off today."

"But you're a doctor," she whispered reverently. "Shouldn't I call you *doctor* something?"

"Well, my last name is Stone. You may call me that if you wish. But I like Daniel better."

"Daniel," she said, smiling timidly.

Lila watched him work his magic on the tiny girl who was normally afraid of everything and everybody. He peered closely into the child's eyes and felt her forehead, talking to Annie all the while.

"Do you have a sore tummy, too?" he asked.

Annie shook her head.

"You just feel hot, then, sweetheart? You don't hurt anywhere?"

"No," she said shyly.

Daniel rested his elbows on his knees and knit his long fingers loosely together. "Do you know if Sammy ate anything he shouldn't, Annie?"

Annie's large brown eyes dared a quick look at her sister, who was now seated and stroking Sammy's back in circular motions. When she looked up at Daniel again, Annie was decidedly worried. "Lila will be mad," she whispered.

Daniel turned his head briefly, noted that Lila was watching and listening carefully, and then smiled at the child, lightly stroking the back of her hand. "I don't think Lila will be angry, dear. I think she would like you to tell me whatever you know so I can help Sammy."

There was a moment's hesitation before Annie sighed as if she carried a tremendous burden. "He was pickin' at Lila's dough," she said unhappily.

Daniel's hand stopped moving over her much smaller one as he questioned, "Dough? Do you mean bread dough, Annie?"

She nodded.

The doctor's head turned toward Lila then. "You've got

bread dough rising?" he asked quietly.

Lila's dark brown eyes appeared enormous as she peered from Annie to the boy at her side. "Oh, Sammy, you didn't! I've told you . . ." She rushed from the room then.

Daniel followed, his long-legged gait easily catching up with her. He watched her fling a thick brown braid back over her shoulder as she crossed the room to a small wooden table set to one side of the blackened iron stove. She lifted a clean white cloth which covered four pans of rising dough.

"I can't tell for sure how much he ate," she said miserably. "The dough's been risin'."

Daniel peered at the four pasty-white loaves. "He ate enough to make his belly ache," he said.

"I only left him long enough to hang the wash," she said frantically, dropping the cloth back into place before staring up at him, hoping for understanding.

She got it.

Daniel reached out and touched her upper arm in a comforting gesture. "No one is accusing you, Miss Briggs." He smiled at her, giving her arm a reassuring squeeze. "Children do these things, and it won't be the last tummyache that boy will experience. If you'll boil some water to make peppermint tea for Sammy, he'll be better in an hour or two. Do you have peppermint?"

"None."

"I have some in my bag," he said easily, dropping his hand to his side. "And I think the fever is simply a springtime ague. If you keep the children warm and have them drink plenty of water, they'll be right again in a day or so."

Lila seemed to relax a little, but worry continued to crease her brow.

Daniel had noticed still another child hovering near one

end of the long table that occupied a large portion of this room. She appeared to be about ten, and as he looked from her back to the young woman by his side, his curiosity got the better of him. "How many children are there in this family?"

"We're seven," Lila supplied.

"And your mother?"

"Dead since Sammy," she said forthrightly. "Mama had three babies in her last three years. I think that's what did her in."

That wouldn't surprise Daniel in the least, considering the woman already had four children before birthing three with barely a rest in between. He had seen it happen before.

"There should be some way to stop that sort of thing," Lila suggested with quiet intensity.

Daniel's brows arched upward in surprise. "I beg your pardon?"

"There should be some way a woman can be with her man and not have babies popping out one after another like buds on a tree in springtime," she said.

Daniel stared at the intelligent, inquiring brown eyes, and realized this young woman was simply seeking information; in the same manner she would seek information about any subject, he suspected. She was forthright, to say the least. "As a matter of fact, there is, Miss Briggs," he said in answer to her question. "Is this something you feel you should discuss with me?"

"Well, if you doctors have got the answer," she said in a peevish tone, "why don't you tell women about it so they know?"

"We *do* share the information with any woman who seeks it," he returned in like manner; *exasperating* was a word he would definitely use to describe her. "My question was directed to you, personally. Do you have a reason to seek this information *now*? For your own protection?"

Lila visibly started when his meaning took hold. "Lord, no!" she squawked as her cheeks pinkened. "I haven't got time for *that*!" She moved away and thumped a kettle on the stove to boil.

Brazen? Painfully honest? He wondered.

Spontaneous, he decided. And a little spontaneity was refreshing. It was a shame at her age that she didn't have time for *that*; or for at least the courting that preceded *that*. She was pretty, in a very petite way. Small-boned with delicate features in her face; a face that was quite obviously fatigued. She had a woman's figure, with narrow waist and well-proportioned bosom. He guessed her to be perhaps twenty; past time for starting her own family. Instead, she seemed to be in command of this small house and her six siblings. "How old are you?" he asked, taking a step toward her.

Lila turned and caught Beth staring at them, doting on their every word. "I don't see that my age has anything to do with Annie and Sammy needin' your help," she said warily.

"It could have something to do with *you* needing my help, Miss Briggs," he said, halting in front of her. His gaze quickly scanned the room again. The furnishings, for the better part, were simple, many homemade. But the room was tidy and clean.

"I'm not doin' anything to get any babies!" she said defensively.

Daniel shook his head and smiled. "We've had done with that conversation, Lila," he said. "I understand what you've told me. I was referring to the amount of work you must do here with little help. We've not met before, but I would hazard a guess that your face is drawn and tired from overwork. Is that so?"

"I kept Beth from school today to help me," she blurted, a little shaken suddenly that his attention seemed to have turned to her when there were two sick children in the next room.

"I suspect that doesn't happen with any degree of frequency."

"She needs to be in school. I don't want her growing up ignorant."

"I'm certain that won't happen," he said kindly, smiling briefly at the younger girl. "I'm simply suggesting that you devote some time to caring for yourself. You've taken on a big responsibility here."

Lila took offense and squared her shoulders as her eyes narrowed. Could he be suggesting she was not capable of the task? "Any woman worth livin' would do what I'm doing," she said hotly.

Daniel examined her face for a moment before nodding his head in understanding. "Yes, I suppose you *would* see it that way," he said softly. "I'll get the peppermint," he added and turned away.

Lila frowned, studying the wide shoulders as he disappeared into the bedroom. She wondered what he had seen with those big, blue eyes. She wondered why she cared that his attention had been drawn to her. She wondered about the uncomfortable warmth that crept up from her neck to her hairline.

Sammy's painful tummy began to ease after the second cup of peppermint tea, but Lila remained awake all night soothing and sponging the feverish children with cool water. When Annie began to sneeze, Lila breathed a sigh of relief, now understanding the source of the fever. Although, unfortunately, *this* sickness would probably spread to the other children; she had been through this before.

During the long night, Lila decided quite firmly that

Doc Fraser should be the one to return to check on the children the following day. She didn't want Daniel Stone in the house; his blue eyes saw too much, and he was too judgmental by far. Who was he to suggest that she couldn't take care of one small house and six children? And a drunken father, she added as she lay on top of the covers beside the sleeping Annie; dawn was not far off, and she could not sit upright another moment.

"Papa will find his own way home," she whispered. He'd been doing it for four years. Lila fell instantly into a deep sleep.

Earlier that same evening Daniel Stone joined Edmond Fraser for dinner at the older doctor's home. Daniel had a small house of his own, but he had not taken the time to see it properly furnished during the month he had been in Frankfort. There were a lot of things he had not taken the time to complete; like equipping his kitchen. That is why an invitation to eat with Edmond was always welcome. Edmond had a wife who could cook as well as a Parisian chef.

"So your family has resided here a number of years?" Daniel asked the older man before forking a tender piece of lamb into his mouth.

"Yup. My father came to Kentucky all on his own and settled in Frankfort in 1800. He was twenty years old at the time and had a burning need to enter politics." Edmond chuckled, remembering. "So he picked the state capital and jumped in like he was a naked boy swimming in the creek against his mama's wishes. Made a fair name for himself, too. One of the only honest politicians I ever knew."

"Edmond!" Rachael admonished, frowning. "We've known some *fine* political families."

Her flare over his remark only caused Edmond to chuckle

again. " 'Course we have, darlin',' " he drawled. "That's not to say *fine* and *honest* run together, Rachael." He turned his attention once more toward their guest. "She hates it when I talk that way."

Daniel smiled and nodded, waiting.

Edmond shifted in his chair and continued his story. "I came along about ten years after my father settled here." He nodded sagely as his thoughtful stare returned to his wife. "It doesn't seem possible that was sixty years ago," he said softly. "I don't feel *sixty*!"

Rachael Fraser smiled and gave the back of her husband's hand a gentle pat. "You don't act sixty either, dear," she reassured him. And then her complexion darkened as she wondered how Daniel might interpret her statement.

Daniel smiled secretly as he realized, from the woman's stricken face, that Edmond was an *active* husband. He chose, gallantly, to relieve her embarrassment by changing the subject. "I visited the Briggs family today while you were out," he informed Edmond.

Dr. Fraser's thoughts turned from reminiscences to business. "Don't tell me there's sickness in *that* family?" he asked with obvious concern.

"Nothing serious," Daniel said, reaching for his wine. "I suspect the two youngest will have sniffles and sneezes by morning."

"Good," Edmond said with a satisfied nod. "Young Lila has enough on her hands without having serious illness to contend with."

"I thought so, too," Daniel agreed. "Young Sammy had been nibbling on some rising bread dough, though. That gave her a scare when he started moaning with the belly-ache."

Edmond smiled. "He's fractious, that one."

"I regret that I didn't take time to stop and talk with Mr.

Briggs," Daniel added after sipping his wine. "I should have assured the man that his children would be all right."

"Jonathan?" Edmond grunted. "He'd be too thick-headed from rum even to know that they were sick. You're best to deal with Lila, I assure you, Daniel."

"That horrible man," Rachael said softly while studying her food.

Daniel looked from Edmond to his wife and back again. "There is something wrong within that household, then?" he asked Dr. Fraser. "It seems that young woman has sole responsibility for her six siblings."

"She's a mere girl!" Rachael put in indignantly.

. Daniel frowned as he turned his attention to her. "A woman, surely, Mrs. Fraser. Young perhaps, but she must be all of twenty, perhaps a year or two more."

"I don't know that she's reached her eighteenth birthday," Rachael explained heatedly. "Lila has cared for that family since she was a child, when her mother, God rest her weary soul, passed on."

"Rachael," Edmond warned softly.

His wife turned angry eyes in his direction. "I'll never understand why you don't try to do something about that Jonathan Briggs and the way he keeps those children."

Edmond was instantly sorry he had spoken. Wiping his mouth with a napkin, he draped the cloth across his lap and sighed before looking at his wife. "What would you have me do, Mrs. Fraser? The man keeps food on the table—"

"And little else," she said tightly.

"Rachael . . ."

"Edmond . . ."

"Excuse me," Daniel said lightly, getting up from his chair. "I think since I've started the battle, I'll dismiss myself before the war breaks out."

The Frasers looked up at him in utter dismay and then

Edmond began to chuckle. "Sit, sit, sit and have some coffee," he said, waving a hand. "My dear wife is a crusader of sorts, and while I agree with her position, there is little I can do about this particular matter. It occasionally causes . . . ah . . . debate between us."

"I can see that," Daniel said, grinning as he sat down. "I'll be certain not to raise this particular topic again."

"I'm sorry," Rachael said, embarrassment causing her soft voice to quiver. "I have little tolerance for drunkards, you see." The woman stood then, stacking their now empty plates and moving past her husband. She hesitated beside his chair, bent, and lightly brushed his forehead with her lips before disappearing into the kitchen.

"Rachael is a good woman," Edmond said softly to his young partner. "But she has this tendency to want to correct all the world's evils. In addition to always believing the *best* about absolutely everyone."

Daniel nodded, stroking the stem of his glass with a forefinger as he considered whether or not to broach the next topic that had been on his mind. "Lila Briggs asked me today about preventing babies," he said quietly.

Edmond's upper body snapped back in his chair. "What?!"

Daniel's dark blue eyes sought the older doctor's. "I believe you heard me, Edmond."

"I did, but I don't believe it."

"At seventeen . . . or eighteen, as it would seem, she's old enough to be . . ."

"Of course she's old enough," Edmond said shortly.

"She admonished me for not sharing such information with women generally," he continued with a smile. "She assured me, however, that the information was not required by herself."

Edmond relaxed. "That's just as well. If that girl turns out to be half as prolific as her mother, we'll have an epidemic of babies on our hands in no time. Did you know her mother lost six children in addition to the seven who lived?"

"Thirteen?" Daniel questioned. Large families were common in these days when medical practitioners were unable to prevent high infant mortality rates, but thirteen pregnancies bordered on lunacy.

"Knowing that might explain to you why the girl would ask such a thing," Edmond said wisely.

"Knowing that makes me think I should have told her," Daniel returned.

CHAPTER 2

 THE RAVAGES OF THE WAR BETWEEN THE STATES had not left the town of Frankfort unscathed. Like Kentucky, Frankfort had been sharply divided during the war and had seen her share of torn families. Lila knew many a man who had yet to speak to a brother or a father because they had fought on opposite sides. There were painful memories fed by opposing views and too many disfigured men as reminders. Lila understood the suffering the community had survived and had watched many of the people grow strong together as they sought to rebuild their lives. She prayed that those still ravaged because they harbored old grievances would soon find a way to make peace with their own kin.

 And that is why she considered her own lot in life to be not too burdensome for her slim shoulders. After all, her papa had returned a whole man, able to work and put food on the table. As a matter of fact, he had returned often from the war, having never been posted far away. Her mother's almost constantly pregnant body had been evidence of that.

Lila deeply regretted the loss of her mother, but she could not resent her father. Jonathan had deeply loved his Sarah, and Lila was mature enough to speculate on how that love would be manifested between any couple who cared as deeply as her parents had. It was a woman's lot in life that God wanted her to have the babies, she had decided long ago. But now, having boldly questioned the new doctor in town, she knew that she would personally not be so free in meeting God's desires with such frequency. At least not in this way. *He* must have been delighted with Jonathan and Sarah's efforts, however.

Now Lila knew something her mother had not. Well, she would see to it that she *knew* before taking up with some man she thought she loved. If she ever had the time to look for a man. And she had plenty of time to learn about "protecting" herself, as Daniel Stone had so delicately put the matter. The children were too young to do without her just yet. It would be some years before she could break away to go seeking a life of her own. In the meantime, Lila had her little dreams.

Twisting away from the board supported by two chair-backs, she banged a heavy iron on the stove to reheat and reached for the second iron there. After spitting on her index finger, she gingerly tapped the base of the iron and heard the satisfying sizzle that indicated the presence of the required heat needed for ironing the heavy cotton bed sheets. Brushing a heavy hank of hair off her forehead with her wrist, she stooped over the spread sheet and skillfully applied the iron, moving quickly so as not to leave a yellowed imprint on the cotton. This was the chore she hated most each week, and as summer moved in, the task would become almost unbearable.

Her eyes focused briefly on the window, judging the time; the hour was growing late, and her preparations for dinner should begin very soon now. "One more sheet," she muttered quietly. "And then I'm makin' a cup of tea." She was tired today, having slept only a few hours in the sickroom. She wondered if she should allow the boys back into their beds tonight and thought better of it; one more night on the kitchen floor wouldn't hurt them, and it might prevent the rest of them becoming ill. Experience had taught her that sneezes and coughs could spread through this family quicker than dandelions could spread across the lawn. "If you could call that a lawn," she said outright.

A knock at the door caused her to sigh wearily, but Lila moved around her makeshift ironing board and, sweeping her annoying hair back with shaking fingers, moved across the room. When she pulled the door inward, she was surprised to see Daniel Stone standing there.

"Oh! Hello," she said, peering quickly at the roan horse that was tethered outside. "I wasn't expectin' you."

Daniel saw the purple smudges under her eyes and frowned. "I thought I told you I would be back to check on the children today."

Lila's hands rose and fell to her sides in a motion that was clearly one of capitulation. "Oh, you may have." She sighed, standing back to allow him access. "Sometimes my memory is as short as Papa's."

"Your father has a bad memory?" he asked. "Why is that, do you think?"

Sighing, Lila frowned up at him. "Is there a medical question for *every* statement, Doctor?" she returned.

Daniel grinned in the face of her exasperation. "Point taken, Miss Briggs. I apologize."

She nodded in an abrupt fashion that he assumed meant she had accepted his apology.

"I was about to make some tea," she said, moving toward the old stove. "Would you like some?"

"Thank you."

"You can check on Annie and Sammy if you like," she said over her shoulder. "They were sleepin' well a few moments ago."

"No more tummyache?" Daniel questioned before moving toward the bedroom.

"Gone," she said simply.

By the time he returned to the kitchen, Lila had placed cups and a large brown teapot on the table and was cutting cake in a pan. The instant she heard his footsteps, however, she raised tired eyes to watch him. "They're fine, aren't they? Except for sneezes and sniffles?"

Daniel nodded and sat down opposite her. "They'll be underfoot again in a couple of days."

"That's certain enough," she said lightly and pushed small squares of cake off her knife and onto a plate. "I'll be lucky if the others don't come down with it. The boys are pesky when they're feelin' sick."

"And what if *you* should come down with it?" he questioned softly.

"Me?" she asked in surprise as she poured their tea. "I never get sick."

"Tap wood."

"What?" she asked, a cup suspended between her hand and his.

"Knock wood to keep that statement true."

Lila shrugged and rapped her knuckles on the table. "A superstitious medical man," she teased. "Who would have thought?"

Daniel surreptitiously scanned the room, noting the mountain of laundry yet to be ironed. "Do you ever do anything except work?" he asked abruptly.

Lila was affronted by his tone. "Certainly," she returned shortly.

"Such as . . . ?"

"I don't know that it's any of your business, Dr. Stone."

Daniel stared at her a moment, regretting his hastily spoken question. "I apologize again, Miss Briggs. I seem to offend you with some frequency."

With another weary sigh Lila shook her head. "It's me," she said. "I'm normally not so touchy."

"You're tired, no doubt," he said expansively.

She nodded.

"Anything else?"

Lila shook her head and laughed. "Lordy! Having you here is truly a challenge! Livin' with you must be purely impossible. You take doctorin' too seriously, *Doctor.*"

Daniel settled back against the straight chair and stretched his long legs beneath the table as he smiled, chagrined. "Not really, Miss Briggs. I simply have an interest in my patients."

"I'm not your patient, Doctor."

"Daniel. My name is Daniel."

"Well, if you think I'm going to be so familiar with a man of medicine, you've got another *think* coming," she said firmly.

"How about a friend, then?" he probed. "Wouldn't you call a friend by his Christian name?"

Her eyes rounded and her back straightened. "Are we friends?"

"We could be," he said.

"Why?"

"Why not?"

Lila thought about that and shrugged. "All right."

Daniel's smile broadened, and he held his right hand across the table to her. "Good! Lila," he said pointedly.

She took the hand, liking the sound of her name the way he said it. She smiled in return. "Daniel." His hand was large and warm as it wrapped around hers, and Lila could feel the strength in his fingers, even though he did not squeeze her hand overly much. She looked at her small hand buried within his grasp and raised sparkling, teasing eyes. "You wouldn't happen to be related to the one who brought Goliath down to size, would you?"

Daniel removed his hand and laughed.

Lila sipped her tea, watching him over the rim of her cup. He had a wonderful smile, showing strong white teeth, and his eyes crinkled at the corners when he laughed. She liked being with him, she decided in that moment. Even though he could be irritating with his mind always turning to doctoring-type thoughts, she liked him. He had the shiniest hair she had ever seen, and his features were handsomely refined. His wife surely must be pleased, waking up and looking at that face in her bed every morning. Lila would have taken bets that he had a beautiful body to match the face, as well. It was difficult to tell under his coat.

"I understand there's a party at the school Saturday night," he was saying. "Will you be there?"

Placing her cup on the table, Lila shook her head but managed to maintain a reasonably genuine expression. "I have other plans."

"That's too bad," he said sincerely. "We could have shared a dance or two."

"Next time," she returned and reached for the teapot.

Daniel held his palm up to halt her. "I would like to, but I have to be on my way."

He rose and Lila did likewise, moving slowly behind him as he walked to the door.

He turned there and smiled down at her. "If you have any more problems with the children, just send one of the boys along for me. They should be fine in a day or two, however."

Lila nodded, and then a sudden thought caused her to gasp and race back into the room.

Daniel was clearly puzzled as she reached for a tin and pulled it down from a high shelf.

"I almost forgot," she said as she approached with a few coins in her hands. "Thank you."

But Daniel shook his head and refused her offer of payment. "I would prefer if you would offer to cook a meal for me sometime," he said. "I don't get a lot of home-cooked meals, and I have a strong suspicion you are an excellent cook."

"Well . . . sure," she said, clearly surprised. "You could come Sunday. I always cook special after church."

"Sunday supper, it is," he said, pleased. "If you allow me to supply the ham."

"That won't be necessary," she returned, her pride stung by his offer. They could certainly afford to feed one more mouth quite adequately, and she resented his suggesting otherwise.

"You don't understand," he said, rotating the brim of his hat through his fingers. "You would be doing me a favor by taking it. I have so much given to me that I can't always use. We could have chicken if you prefer. If you're up to killing and cleaning it."

Now she understood and felt foolish. "Why not bring one of each?" she said quietly; she would clean and cook the chicken and send it home with him. After her unkind thoughts about him, it seemed the least she could do. "And your wife is most welcome," Lila added.

Daniel's eyes darkened before he said, "No wife, Lila. Just me."

He waved briefly to her before turning his fine horse toward the center of town.

Lila returned the gesture and wondered who had caused the pain she had just seen in those beautiful blue eyes.

CHAPTER
3

 FRANKFORT RESIDENTS LOVED TO PLAN PARTIES and dances for every occasion. Aside from political affairs, it was one of their favorite means of socializing with their neighbors; those in town and those from nearby farms. Spring planting was behind everyone now, and it was time to celebrate.

Lila often dreamed of the dances. It was one of 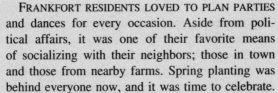 her most cherished things to think about, and she could always visualize the scenes from previous dances she had witnessed. The gentlemen, looking fine and spit-polished, would guide their ladies around the floor with ease. The women always appearing so graceful as their skirts flowed around them 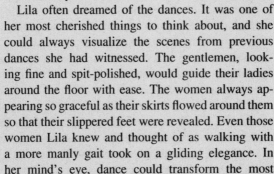 so that their slippered feet were revealed. Even those women Lila knew and thought of as walking with a more manly gait took on a gliding elegance. In her mind's eye, dance could transform the most ungainly of creatures into a feminine wonder. It was a scene she breathlessly anticipated several times a year.

And one she watched from *outside*.

She was grateful that the evening was warm as she'd had to cut the sleeves from her calico dress once the material at the elbows had worn through. And her bare feet distinctly disliked the earth if it was too cold. But the warm sun of the day had not only warmed the earth but had filled the air with the wonders of all things growing and the fragrances of the nearby river.

She had taken a wooden crate from her father's smithy and carried it to a place below one of the high windows of the schoolhouse. After carefully positioning her box, Lila stepped up and had an excellent view of the party within. The window she had chosen at the rear corner of the building was not subject to the light of the many lamps and lanterns that had been lit inside, thereby reducing her chances of being revealed in a most mortifying situation.

Children were caught sneaking peeks of adult affairs, she thought. She was too old to be doing this.

But she couldn't seem to help herself.

Daniel Stone escaped the warmth of the large schoolroom and stepped into the cooler night air. Being an eligible male in this town had proved a bit uncomfortable as doting mothers pushed unmarried daughters into flirting with the young doctor. At the reasonably mature age of thirty-two, Daniel was still not quite comfortable with flirty women and had never been. So he had escaped for a much needed breath of air and a cheroot.

He struck a match on the doorjamb and lit his small cigar before descending the steps and sauntering across the front of the building. It was when he turned the corner that he saw the dark shadow of a person, obviously a woman, by her skirts, peeking in the window.

Lila had been forced to wait until the younger children were all asleep before escaping the house. As a result, the party was well under way by the time she took up her position. Homer Fielding's fiddle was well-warmed, she decided, and Teddy Shoemaker was having to struggle to keep up; he'd break his bow-string if he weren't careful. Harmon Fielding, Homer's brother, was playing his Jew's harp with a gusto that made her smile. "He'll twang the teeth right out of his head," she whispered with a light giggle.

"A travesty, to be sure," a deep, male voice whispered beside her.

Lila started, gripping the edge of the windowsill to keep from falling off her box as her startled eyes darted downward. "Daniel Stone!" she admonished in a hushed tone.

"Lila Briggs!" he returned.

"Well, he can't play his harp if his teeth are gone!" she snapped.

Daniel laughed softly and reached up to help her down. "Quit playing and get down here before you fall."

"I never fall."

"Oh, ho! You've done this before!"

"Of course," she admitted primly.

"Explain to me why you are doing this?" he said, smiling down at her now.

"I like to watch the dancin'," she said easily.

"But you could watch from inside," he said logically. "You could join in, if you prefer."

"I don't *prefer*," she answered smartly. "Explain to me why you are out here," she added.

"I needed some air and a smoke," he drawled, crossing his arms over his wide chest. "You simply like to watch?"

"If you mean the dancing, the answer is yes."

"I think there is more to this than you're confessing."

Lila cast him a saucy glance. "I wasn't aware that you had become the town marshal, Doctor."

"Ooow, aren't we cheeky tonight."

His teasing hit its mark, and Lila realized she was treating him badly. "I'm sorry," she said softly.

"Apology accepted. *If* you tell me why you're out here instead of inside enjoying yourself."

"I can't leave the little ones for very long," she said, hoping he would accept her explanation.

"No. That's not it," he said resolutely with a shake of his head. "You have Jon or Tommy to watch the children."

"They can't be trusted," she returned.

"They could if you were willing to trust, I imagine." He lowered his arms, reaching out and taking one of her hands in his. "Tell me why you're out here, Lila," he said with such gentle persuasion that she found herself completely disarmed.

"I just like to watch the dancers. It always looks so lovely . . . it's a dream I have."

"A dream?" he prodded gently. "What kind of dream?"

"I don't know," she said, shrugging with embarrassment as she watched the white smoke from his cheroot drift high above them. "A dream that dancin' makes every woman lovely." She shrugged, laughing lightly in embarrassment. "I suppose I dream that I would look lovely."

Something anchored around Daniel's heart and tugged. "You are lovely, little friend. Don't you know that?"

Her head moved in his direction, and her eyes were large with dismay that he might think she could be fishing for compliments. "Oh, I don't mean in appearance," she blurted. "I mean . . . I think I *look* all right. It's just that . . . I don't know . . . the women always look so graceful and the men so dashing when they're dancing. It's something that's far beyond everyday life."

Daniel thought he was beginning to understand. "Something that is better than everyday life, Lila?"

Her head bobbed frantically, acknowledging that he understood at last.

He tugged on her hand and half turned away, dropping the cheroot to the ground. "Come with me."

Lila resisted, leaning back and pulling against his more powerful force. "Where?"

"Inside," he said simply.

"No!" she whispered frantically. "I can't."

"Of course you can," he said, turning back to her. "You are a part of this community. The party is for everyone, I understand."

"Not for the likes of me, Daniel. You don't understand." Her eyes pleaded for him to think about what he was suggesting. "Daniel," she said softly, "I don't even have shoes."

He heard her clearly then; heard the pride in her voice as if she were admitting only to the fact that she did not possess shoes. *That* fact alone made her unfit to join in the festivities, nothing else. Lila Briggs and her family were poor, perhaps, but she considered herself as good as anyone else in town. And so she should, he thought. He was beginning to think she was quite the remarkable young woman.

Pained by his stupidity, Daniel raised his face toward the evening stars, thinking, thinking . . . how to ease her way. He had decided her dreams were worth his consideration, and after a moment he smiled down at her again, closely examining her from head to toe.

He stared at her for such a very long time that Lila braced herself with various ready-made returns that would heat his ears if he dared to mock the poorness of her appearance.

But then he spoke.

"I see soft, beige satin slippers on tiny feet," he said quietly, taking her hand and placing it on his shoulder. "And a gown of matching color, trimmed with lace, here." He lightly touched the neckline of her calico dress. "And the lace at your wrists falls in gentle folds, just touching the backs of your slender hands. The waltz is beginning, Lila," he whispered, taking firm hold of her right hand in his. "Will you dance?"

"I can't," she whispered, mesmerized by his oration.

He tipped his head slightly, listening to the strains of the music through the open windows. "This is *Lila's dance*," he said simply and stepped easily to his left.

He guided her slowly at first as she hesitated over the steps of the dance, but soon she was gliding across the clearing at the side of the schoolhouse.

No highly polished dance floor bathed in a thousand lights could have made her feel more breathless as Lila followed where he led. He had his own kind of grace, this tall man of medicine, and he looked down at her as if they were the center of attraction at some grand ball. "I can't believe I'm doin' this," she said breathlessly.

"You are," he returned, admiring the rosy blush of happiness that had kissed her cheeks. "You should do this more often, Miss Briggs. You're a very graceful woman."

"Now you're mockin' me," she said with momentary unease.

"I'm not, Lila," he said sincerely. "I'm not."

"Well, I don't care," she declared as she gazed up and saw a dart of moonlight reflected in his eyes. "This is wonderful."

"Yes, it is."

She was small but not so small that dancing with her was not pleasurable. And Daniel Stone found this dance *distinctly* pleasurable. She had a natural grace, and dancing on her toes as she was, her chin just matched the height of his shoulder. Her hand was delicate in his and, when he smiled down at her, Lila's eyes crinkled with delight and she threw back her head, gazing briefly up at the stars.

"I've never felt this way before," she whispered gaily.

The music stopped then, but Lila's lightheartedness did not. "You've danced with many women," she said. "I can tell."

"A few."

"Lovely women, Daniel?" she asked curiously. "Beautiful women with beautiful clothes and loads of experience?"

Daniel's brows arched in surprise. "Experience?"

"At dancin'," she explained.

Now he felt foolish. "Oh! Yes. Some."

"I knew you had," she said happily. "It was so easy to follow you."

"Because you have a natural grace, Lila. That's why."

The intense look he gave her in that moment rocked Lila to the soul. Her heartbeat quickened, and she placed the palm of her hand over that place on her chest as she suddenly became nervous and backed away from him. "I have to go now," she whispered.

Daniel nodded. "All right, little friend," he said softly. He wondered if he had been so in awe of his first dance. And perhaps his first partner? Probably not, for he couldn't remember.

"All this dancin' has made my heart hurt," she breathed and turned to run from him.

Frowning in concern at what he may have inadvertently done this night, Daniel wondered about the *hurt* in her heart. "*Is* it from the dancing, Lila?" he whispered as she disappeared into the darkness.

God, he hoped that was the case.

* * *

Lila raced home, then tiptoed through the house. She stripped and washed and donned a white nightdress, all without waking Beth and Annie, who slept in one bed and shared her room.

Lying down at last, she stared at the ceiling, grinning with joy, tingling with new sensations, and sighing at the thought of the very first dance she had ever shared with a grown man. It was probably too bad Daniel Stone had been the man, she decided. A man that looked that good just had to distract a girl's thoughts away from the wonderful sensations of the dance, of being whirled about and moving in rhythm to another person's body.

"I can hear you breathin' heavy," Beth whispered through the darkness.

"I've been runnin'," Lila returned.

"Is that why you're sighin' and makin' all those funny noises?"

"I'm not *sighin'*," she whispered back.

"You are, Lila. What've you been doin'?"

"Oh, Beth, I danced tonight. Really danced."

Beth reared up and propped herself on an elbow, trying to see her sister's profile through the darkness on the other side of the room. "With a *man*, Lee?" she asked in awe. "You mean you went to the school and went to that party?"

"Well, not to the party," she confessed, but her voice reflected anything but disappointment. "We danced out under the stars," she added dreamily. "It was so wonderful. The music was driftin' through the open windows, and he held me so nice, Beth. I could feel the heat of his arm around my waist right through my dress. It was better than a stove-warmed blanket for comfort, I'll tell you."

"Who's *he*?"

Lila rolled onto her side facing the wall, wanting to hold some of this night secret within herself. Wanting to protect it in her memory, away from the opinions of others. He had called it *Lila's dance*, and she wanted to keep it hers. "Just a nice man," she said softly. "Go to sleep now, Beth."

But for Lila it was hours before sleep would come; she was made far too dizzy by her dance-dreams.

Sunday was no different from any other day for Lila Briggs. Aside from being a little more hectic in the morning, perhaps. Sunday morning the Briggs family, with the exception of Jonathan, washed and spruced and dressed in their best—and their older sister always had their clothes clean and pressed. Sunday meant moving double time for Lila in order to help the young ones get ready for church. Sammy was always a trial; they all wore shoes for church, and Sammy hated the heavy, sturdy boots.

Lila tightened the suspenders over his narrow shoulders and gave the shoulders of his shirt a smoothing. "There," she said, smiling at the small boy whose brown hair insisted on falling forward on his forehead like a girl's bangs. "Get your shoes," she said.

Sammy bolted and headed for the front door.

"Sammy!" She laughed, having played this game with him before. Lila jumped from her chair and raced after him. She caught him before he could scramble down the stairs from the porch. Lashing out with an arm around his waist, she scooped him up against her hip.

Sammy tipped forward and saw a black boot hit the bottom step. He looked up, just as Lila straightened. "Hi, Doc!" he said gleefully.

Daniel smiled. "Hi, yourself."

"Don't you call him Doc," Lila corrected. "His name is Doc Stone."

Sammy, who was still more horizontal to the floorboards than vertical, allowed his head to drop forward. "Can I get down now, Lee?"

Lila set the boy on his feet and then nervously wiped the palms of her hands together. "Sorry for the greetin'," she said, smiling at Daniel now. "We should say hello proper."

"I consider an exuberant 'Hi, Doc' a fairly good start." He held up two potato sacks, one in each hand. The one in his right hand was moving. "You're certain you don't mind dealing with this chicken?"

Lila laughed lightly and relieved him of both sacks. "I've been *dealin'* with live chickens for a long time . . ."

"Daniel," he reminded her when she hesitated. His eyes skimmed down the length of her pretty yellow dress; the color did wonders, setting off her lightly tan skin and her rich, chestnut hair. "You look very pretty, Lila," he said.

Lila actually flushed as Sammy bumped against her thigh. Compliments from gentlemen were rare. "We're goin' to church," she said, looking down at her brother. "If I can get the shoes on this boy."

"Maybe I can help," Daniel offered, holding out a hand to Sam. "I was heading that way myself. I would enjoy the company if you would permit me to walk along."

Lila stared up at his fine good-looking face; as if she would say no after last night. When she looked at him, she thought she could still feel his arm around her waist, still feel his warmth from having her hand tucked so neatly in his. "Of course," she said around a nervous lump that had planted itself in the middle of her throat. "Come inside for a moment while I put this chicken in the pen out back."

Daniel entered into a world of screeches and laughter as the child he knew as Annie raced from a bedroom and around the long table in the kitchen. She was being chased by a boy not much older than herself. "Hi!" she said happily and wandered over as Daniel sat on a wooden bench and pulled Sam up onto his lap.

"Hello. You're feeling much better I assume?"

The older boy ran smack into her back. "Yy . . . es! Get away, Edward." She smiled up at Daniel then. "I'm lots better."

"That's good," he said, returning her smile. "Would you happen to know where Sam's boots might be?"

"Sure. I'll get them!" she crowed.

Edward propped his elbows on the end of the table close to where Daniel was seated. "Sammy hates shoes," he said seriously.

"Well, I suppose barefoot is more comfortable."

Sammy was playing with his suspenders. "If I pop these, they hurt," he said sagely.

Daniel grinned down at the boy on his lap as Sam's head craned around. "I imagine that's true."

"But if I don't wear 'em, my britches fall down."

Daniel playfully tested the waist of the boy's pants. "Yes, I can see you could have a problem."

Beth emerged shyly from the bedroom and smiled at Daniel.

"Hello," he said.

"I've got 'em, Daniel!" Annie crowed and placed a small pair of well-worn brown boots in his hand. It did not take close inspection to realize that the shoes had known several owners.

Daniel looked at the children around him as he placed one boot on the floor and started pulling the other onto Sammy's small foot. "Now, I know Sammy and Annie," he said, reaching around the slim shoulders to pull the bootlaces tight. "Why don't you tell me your names and how old you are?"

"I'm Edward and I'm six. I go to school now."

"I'm Beth and I'm ten."

"Ah, Beth," he said apologetically. "Of course, Lila told me your name when I first came here."

"That's okay," she said graciously. "There's a lot of us to remember. Jon doesn't go to church with us anymore, 'cause he's bigger and does what he wants, and Tommy's out back trying to talk Lila into lettin' him stay home."

"How old is Tommy?" he asked for conversation's sake as he put Sam's second boot in place.

"Tommy's fourteen. But he's scared of makin' Lila mad still. He'll get over that soon," she added with a voice of authority.

"I can't imagine Lila getting *mad* at any of you."

"Lila knows what's right and what isn't and she makes us do right," Beth continued.

Daniel smiled and set Sam on his feet. "Yes, I can believe that."

The object of their conversation entered the kitchen from a back door, an unhappy, tall young man following in her wake.

Daniel supposed Tommy was going to church.

"Is everybody ready?" she asked, scanning her small crew critically.

Daniel rose and extended his hand to the boy he guessed to be Tommy. "Daniel Stone," he said.

Tommy took the proffered hand, his spirits lifting a bit with this sign of manly acknowledgment. "Tommy. Tommy Briggs."

"Well, Tom. Shall we escort these fine ladies and gentlemen to church?"

Tommy looked a little taken aback at this attention from the doctor but managed, "Sure."

Tommy volunteered to lead Daniel's horse at the back of the small procession and the smaller children ran and skipped ahead. Lila nervously fingered the edges of her mother's black leather Bible as Daniel walked silently beside her, his hands clasped behind his back. She rarely had difficulty speaking with people, but with this man she suddenly found herself tongue-tied.

"Do you like livin' here?" she blurted at last.

Daniel nodded, his eyes following the children who would run ahead and then race back. "Very much."

"Where'd you live before here?"

Daniel's eyes darted her way, and then he smiled. "I lived in Boston."

"Boston!" she gasped, noting that there was something a bit sad about his smile. "A big city like that? You must miss Boston."

"There's a lot to be said for small communities like this one, Lila. I don't believe I miss Boston at all."

"But all your family and friends must be there."

"I'm making new friends," he said easily, flashing her a genuine smile.

"I'd go crazy bein' away from my family," she said thoughtfully as her eyes darted from child to child.

"Yes, I imagine you would," he said. He understood this much about her.

"Don't you miss your family?" she asked, frowning now with concern.

"I've no family left, I'm afraid. I was an only child and my parents weren't young when they had me. They've both passed away."

Lila placed a small, gentle hand on his forearm, causing them both to stop and turn. "I'm sorry, Daniel," she said softly, her expression hurting for him.

She had such a heart, he thought. She just naturally reached out to everyone. "Thank you. It's been a very long time, and the pain dulls somewhat with time."

"But the missin' doesn't," she whispered.

Daniel found himself staring into her big, brown, tender eyes and turned, feeling unsettled as he walked on. "We're going to be late," he said.

Lila hop-skipped to catch up with him. "Well, I bet Doc Fraser is glad you're here!" she said, cheerfully trying to lighten the mood. "He's got too many people to look after by himself."

"He's a fine man, Dr. Fraser." And in that instant, instinctively, he felt he should tell her. "I'm meeting him and his wife at church."

Lila's light mood dissolved in an instant, but she wouldn't let him know that. Of course, he wouldn't be sitting with the Briggs tribe when he knew the Frasers so much better. "That's good," she said with apparent ease. "Just look at all the fine friends you're makin' here, Daniel."

His eyes darted to hers, but she refused to look in his direction. Yes, he was making a lot of fine friends.

But last night he had danced with an angel.

CHAPTER
4

 IT WAS AGREED THAT DANIEL WOULD ARRIVE early at the Briggs house for supper that day. Sunday was the one day that Lila provided only two meals; she cooked a hearty breakfast before church and at four o'clock an even heartier supper.

 When Daniel arrived he could smell the delicious odors of roasting chicken and baking ham even as he stepped onto the decrepit porch. He paused there, thinking he had not smelled anything so wonderful since the days when he was a boy in his mother's kitchen.

 His knock on the front door was answered by a big man. A man of stature with the appearance of one who oft abused his body. His face was bloated and veined, his nose red, and large purple-tinged pouches stood out beneath his eyes.

Daniel instantly understood the additional burden Lila had to bear.

"Doc Stone, I presume!" Jonathan blustered.

"Mr. Briggs," Daniel returned, extending a hand.

"Welcome to my home," the man said expansively and stepped aside, allowing Daniel to enter.

"I appreciate the opportunity to join your family for dinner," Daniel said, for want of anything better to say.

"Oh, that Lila would have half the strays in the county here," Jonathan said airily. "And that's fine. She does the cookin'."

Daniel winced silently.

"Papa!" Lila admonished as she moved forward to greet their guest. She had decided to continue wearing the yellow dress, her best, but had protected it with a shoulder-to-hem white apron. "I'm glad you could come, Daniel," she said graciously, motioning him into the room. "We're about ready to eat."

"How about a tot o' rum?" Jonathan asked cheerily.

Lila raised disapproving eyes. "We're goin' to sit to supper, Papa."

Jonathan was not so far gone that he had forgotten his manners. "Oh, well, then. Later, perhaps."

Daniel was feeling distinctly guilty for having invited himself here. Lila obviously had enough to contend with and did not need additional pressures.

But she smiled easily and directed him to one end of the table. "Take your coat off, if you like, Daniel," she said as she moved toward the stove. "It's warm in here."

Daniel draped his black coat over the back of his chair and sat, looking the length of the table to see Jonathan take his place at the opposite end. "You have quite a marvelous family here, Mr. Briggs," he said.

Jonathan's chest seemed to rumble a bit before he could

answer. "They're a good lot, I admit. My Sarah always did sprout good'uns."

Daniel shuddered inwardly, his heart going out to Lila, who must no doubt expend as much energy looking after this besotted man as she did on all of the young children in her charge. He looked around the room and found Beth helping her sister load up plates and bowls with food. Tommy sauntered in from the back, as did Edward, but the others were missing.

Jonathan was not so drunk as to miss that the doctor was counting heads. "Jon's off sparkin' some gal he's taken a shinin' to and the little ones is in disgrace."

Daniel looked toward Lila, who had turned from her carving of the large ham. "Annie and Sammy? What have they done?"

"I should have known when they were quiet," she muttered, turning back to her task. "I should have checked even though I was busy."

Daniel could barely prevent a grin, wondering what the two small children had done. "You're not going to tell me?" he asked.

Lila whirled from the stove, brandishing a large knife. "Those two decided they were big enough to handle a two-man saw," she said with obvious disgust. "They tested their strength by cuttin' the pole to my clothesline near in half!"

Despite his good intentions, Daniel laughed.

"It's not funny!" she said. "The next wash I try to hang out there is goin' down in the dirt."

"I'm sorry."

"I'll fix it, Lee," Tommy said quietly.

Daniel thought there just might be a second volunteer, but Jonathan appeared not at all interested in the problem; the man was busy studying the toe of his boot.

"I've half a mind not to let those little ones up to the

supper table," Lila muttered as she placed a large platter of ham before her father.

No one believed she would do that. Including Daniel, who knew her the least.

Daniel's gaze followed her as she wiped her hands on her apron and crossed the room. He smiled when she opened a bedroom door and looked inside. Two very quiet little people emerged, looking up with wary concern as they passed in front of their sister.

Sammy was the first to spot the outsider in their midst and wandered over to a place beside Daniel. "Hi, Doc," he said in a soft voice that was completely out of character.

"Hello, Sammy. What's new?"

"Oh, not much." The child sighed, approaching the bench that ran the length of the table. "I bin locked in the bedroom pretty much all day."

Daniel stood, having watched the boy struggle to get up on the high bench, and lifted him. "I understand you've been up to some mischief," Daniel whispered.

The small head bobbed, and Sammy's bangs fell into place. "Lee said as I should think about what I done."

Annie had wandered over to the table, and Daniel lifted her to the bench opposite her partner in crime.

"Hello, Annie," Daniel said as he returned to his chair and looked from one child to the other; they were a much subdued pair from what he had seen earlier in the day. Daniel wondered briefly what role Jonathan played in the disciplining of these children. After a brief reflection, he assumed the man left this, also, to Lila.

Sam and Annie played the role of chastised children for an appropriate length of time, Daniel thought. Lila appeared satisfied that her form of punishment was enough to make the children understand the impact of their misdemeanor, and the mood lightened around the table. By the time the ham and the bowls of carrots, whipped potatoes, and red-eye gravy were passed around the table, a controlled din of contented chatter filled the room. Only Jonathan remained noticeably silent, concentrating on his food. Daniel came to the conclusion that Jonathan Briggs was one very unhappy man.

Lila was seated beside Sam. Presumably to help cut his food, although the youngster had already proved himself adept with cutting tools earlier in the day.

Daniel ladled gravy over a mound of potatoes and took a bite, almost moaning in epicurean pleasure. "What did you do to this gravy?" he asked, looking directly at his hostess.

Lila jumped to a hasty conclusion. "It's no good?" she asked frantically.

"It's wonderful, Lila. What did you do?"

She smiled her relief and poised her fork over her plate. "I just used the ham dippin's, that's all. And I put a little ground coffee in to perk it up."

Daniel graced her with a teasing smile. "Perk?"

It took Lila a moment to understand what he was asking, and then she laughed, thinking that smile of his could put a girl right off her food.

As soon as the meal ended, Jonathan rose from his place at the far end of the table, made an excuse to Daniel, and left the house.

Lila's worried frown was fixed on her father's back until he disappeared from view. And then she turned to face Daniel. "I'm sorry, Daniel," she said quietly as she reached for his empty plate. "He doesn't mean to be rude, it's just . . ." She shrugged then, getting up from the table. "Papa is not a very happy man," she murmured and turned away.

"Can I have cobbler?" Sam piped, breaking the unhappy mood.

Lila smiled secretly as she stacked used plates for washing. "I suppose you've suffered your punishment," she said and turned to smile at the boy. "Yes, you may have cobbler."

There was a whoop of glee as Sammy propped the handle of his spoon on the table. "It's good, Daniel. Want some?"

Daniel would have some, for certain; so far this meal had surpassed anything he'd eaten since he'd had the privilege of enjoying his mother's cooking.

Beth spooned the steaming apple dessert into bowls and delivered them to the table, shyly placing Daniel's portion in front of him. He said, "Thank you," and her complexion immediately turned pink.

Once Lila had returned to her place, Daniel noticed her look around the table as if to check that everything was in order and everyone present was content with his food. He wondered if she ever gave a moment's thought to herself. As the thought occurred, she blessed him with a pretty smile.

"I thought we'd take our coffee outside," she said. "It's such a pretty day."

Daniel looked at the stacked plates and bowls awaiting attention. "I'll help you clean up first," he offered.

But Lila shook her head. "I don't clean up Sundays. I cook, but there are plenty of hands here for the washing up."

Daniel was amazed by the sudden onslaught of activity, but it was soon clear that each small pair of hands had a specific task, and moments later he was following Lila out the door.

Lila had centered a small table between two primitive rocking chairs, and she smiled as Daniel sat and stretched his long legs out before him.

"That was as fine a meal as I've had in a long time, Lila," he said, patting his flat stomach. "Thank you."

Lila nodded, acknowledging his comment as she twisted in her chair and reached for a coffee cup she had placed on the table. "Do you take sugar?" she asked, and when Daniel shook his head, she offered the cup. "I guess bachelors hate to cook for themselves," she commented, settling back in her chair.

"If I'm any example," he said lightly, "you're correct in that."

"There's always a meal here if you get to starvin'," she teased. "But I expect you'll get lots of invitations to suppers. We've got at least a peck of ready-to-marry girls in this town. You won't be a bachelor for long."

Daniel's expression sobered instantly. "I'm not looking for a wife," he said harshly.

Lila frowned as she watched him lift the cup to his lips. "I'm sorry, Daniel. I was only teasing."

He nodded and stared off into the distance.

"Somebody's hurt you pretty bad, I guess."

His attention returned with her softly spoken words. "Now it's my turn to apologize." He sighed, placing his cup on the table. "Marriage is a touchy subject with me," he said, staring directly into her worried eyes. "Let's leave it at that, shall we?"

"Sure."

"I'm sorry I snapped."

"That's all right, Daniel. I understand."

"No," he said softly. "I don't think you possibly could."

That night Lila lay awake in her lonely bed, wondering what could possibly happen to put such a fine man as Daniel Stone off marrying. She also wondered about the woman who had hurt him, as it was a natural conclusion to assume there must have been a woman. A foolish woman, if she could wound a man like Doc Stone.

As a result of all this cerebral activity far into the morning hours, Lila was tired and in fine fettle when she was summoned to the schoolhouse Monday afternoon.

"It's about Edward, Miss Lila," Dermot Clarmont said.

"Is he in some sort of trouble?" she asked.

"You might say that," Dermot drawled, squinting at the papers on his desk.

It always made Lila suspicious when a person couldn't look her in the eye. Dermot had his head bent forward so she could see the balding spot in his yellow hair. She decided that bald spot was likely due to Dermot's habit of scratching his pate when he pondered a problem. Standing in front of his desk at the front of the classroom, Lila frowned at the unclean appearance of the man's hair. "Edward is playful, like most boys," she said. "But he's never been a troublemaker."

Dermot deigned to raise his head at that. "Oh, he's not in that kind of trouble," he said. "The problem is much more serious than pranks or rowdiness."

Before her eyes Dermot's chest puffed out with importance as he placed the palms of his hands wide apart on the desk, locking his elbows. "It is my considered and educated opinion, Miss Lila, that Edward is not intelligent enough to be attending this school."

Lila visibly rocked backward. "What?!" she squealed.

"I believe you heard me, Miss Lila."

"I heard you, but I don't believe you."

"I have considerable experience—"

"Bull chips," she hissed.

"*Miss* Lila," he breathed, aghast.

"And don't you call me up for my language, you little man," she went on, bending over the desk as she spoke slowly and with feeling. "Edward is every bit as intelligent as any child you have in this school."

Dermot tried to back up in his chair as his eyes rounded

at her reaction. "You must be reasonable, Miss Lila. The boy is not learning."

"Then I have to ask myself about the quality of the teaching!"

"Now, see here . . . you cannot fault me for recognizing a slow—"

"Not one more word," she said, shaking a finger under his nose. "If Edward is not doing well in his schoolin', then I have to ask why. Did you bother to ask yourself *why*, Mr. Clarmont?"

"The fact is, he is not doing well—"

"That does not answer my question. If he is not doing well, *why* is he not doing well? And what can be done to help him? Have you pondered *that* question, Mr. Clarmont?"

"Well, no, I—"

"You've just given up?" she asked as her anger jumped to a higher level. "What kind of teacher are you?"

"I think you are being most unreasonable," he said firmly.

"Unreasonable?" she railed. "You've just written my brother off as unteachable with little or no thought or caring, and you expect me to be reasonable? An education is important to a boy, Dermot Clarmont. Or have you forgotten that? I resent the fact that you've not spoken to me about Edward having any problems in school until *you* suddenly decide he's not intelligent. Edward *is* intelligent, Dermot, and entitled to an education. And I'm going to see that he gets it."

Dermot smirked as she removed her threatening presence and turned to leave. "And who will teach him, Lila? *You* can barely read. I'm the only qualified—"

"Qualified nincompoop," she muttered heatedly as she stormed from the building.

At the bottom of the steps leading from the school, Lila's

anger overtook her, however, and she paused there, leaning heavily on the wooden railing as tears flooded to her eyes. "Bumble-pated ass," she cursed as she wiped angrily at her cheeks.

Daniel found her clinging to the railing for support, her head bowed, as he rode toward her. "Lila?" he questioned softly as he dismounted and approached. "What's wrong?"

She raised her head briefly and then turned away in embarrassment. "I'm so mad I could spit," she muttered.

Daniel could see passersby staring curiously as they stood on the public thoroughfare. He tied the bridle's reins to the wooden rail and turned to her. "Let's find some privacy," he said quietly, placing his hand on her elbow. "Come on, Lee," he coaxed and lead her around the side of the building.

Daniel had been of the opinion he would never see the day when this strong young woman would appear wilted and weak, but he was seeing that today. Lila slumped against the building, bracing a shoulder there.

"Now tell me what has you so upset."

"I'm *angry*," she said with force, although scruffing the back of her hand under her reddened nose depleted some of the impact of her words.

"Angry about what?" he asked, crossing his arms over his chest and patiently waiting.

"Not *what*, Daniel. *Who*."

He smiled his understanding and nodded, even though she refused to look up at him. "All right. Who?"

"That bumble-pated teacher! That's who!" she hissed.

"Bumble-pated?" he asked in confusion.

"Well, if you could see his yellow hair . . ."

Nodding again as he dipped his head to try and see her face, Daniel prodded her a bit more. "What's he done, sweetheart?"

The endearment was entirely lost on Lila in her anger, but she did raise eyes that once again flooded with tears. "He said Edward is stupid!" she cried.

Daniel's dark brows arched upward. "What?"

"Well, he said 'not intelligent,' " she explained. "Same thing." Her hands came up to cover her face then.

Daniel reached for her and pulled her against his chest. "Ah, Lila," he whispered, trying to soothe her hurt. "I'm sorry, dear. But let's think about this."

"What's to *think*?" she muttered against his coat front. "He won't teach him."

Daniel did not pause to ask why he so hated to see her hurting like this. He hated to see anyone hurting. But Lila seemed more tender than most. He believed anyone's gentle side would just naturally reach out to this young woman. And he knew that, had her own abilities been attacked, she could not hurt more. "Edward strikes me as a very intelligent boy," he said after a moment.

Lila raised her head, staring up at him. "He is, Daniel," she said, sniffing brokenly. "And boys most of all need educating, don't you think? It's not fair that this is happening."

"Nothing has happened yet," he said reasonably, giving her upper arm a gentle squeeze as he moved her slightly away from his body. "Are you able to talk about this now?" he asked, reaching into a coat pocket for a kerchief. Smiling when she nodded miserably, Daniel wiped the moisture from beneath her eyes with the white linen square. "That's better," he said, tucking the kerchief back into his pocket. "Now, what did this man say about Edward?"

"He said he was *slow* and he wasn't doing well in school. He never said a word about Edward having trouble before today. And now, suddenly, he's decided my brother can't be taught."

"Well . . ."

"He just . . . made me . . . so angry," she choked and then promptly hiccuped.

"I can see that. You're a scrapper, and those children are lucky to have you."

"I'm not very proud of the way I acted," she said as she stared toward the street. "A more sophisticated woman would have handled Dermot differently, I suppose." And then a small smile tilted the corners of her mouth, and she turned to him. "But I think I got my point across."

Daniel laughed easily. "I just bet you did."

"What am I going to do about Edward, Daniel?" she asked, her smile gone in an instant.

Whether he liked it or not, Daniel could see he was being drawn into this family's woes. He liked Lila and respected her for the caring, hardworking young woman she was, but he hadn't intended to become so embroiled in her problems. Still, she was too young to be challenged by so many cares, and he found he couldn't just back away and leave her to flounder. Lila just naturally caught people by their hearts, and Daniel was one of them. He acknowledged that and then set it aside in deference to the problem at hand.

"Is Edward at home now?" he asked.

Lila nodded.

"Let's go and have a talk with him, shall we? Perhaps there has been something bothering the boy. Something that has taken his attention away from his schoolwork."

"He's only six years old, Daniel. He shouldn't have a care in the world. But I hope you're right. I hope it's something as simple as that."

Across the street Mae Belle Willoughby frowned at the unlikely couple as they walked toward the edge of town. Clearly young Lila had been crying and Mrs. Willoughby wondered what that new doctor could have said to the poor girl. She speculated that Jonathan's health was not good. "Probably the drink," she muttered with disdain. But then she saw Dr. Stone dip his head toward Lila, as if the two were whispering some secret, and Mae Belle decided then and there that the problem must be one of the heart. A young girl's heart.

Edward was clearly bemused and more than a little nervous when Lila made him sit up to the table. And in Papa's chair. Lila and Daniel sat on opposite benches, and Edward frowned as he looked from one adult to the other. "Am I sick, Lee?" he asked, startling his sister.

"Do you feel sick, Edward?" she asked with concern.

"No, but why is Doc Stone here?"

Daniel smiled and nodded to Lila, silently asking her to explain to the boy.

"Daniel is our friend. That's why he's here." Lila shifted nervously on the bench and reached out, covering Edward's folded hands on top of the table. "Darlin', is there anything that's been botherin' you?"

Edward thought about that briefly and then shook his head.

"Are you unhappy at school? Do you like the other kids?"

"Well, Lee," he drawled as if she had just asked the most stupid question in the world, "you know I like Freddy and Johnny. They're my best friends. I got other friends, too."

Lila looked at Daniel then, seeking guidance. Now what? her eyes begged.

"Edward?" Daniel said, drawing the boy's attention.

"Sir?" the boy responded, turning his head in Daniel's direction.

"How do you feel about your schoolwork? Are you finding it easy or difficult?"

He thought about that question, too. "Sometimes the reading is hard," he said, frowning in concentration. "Sometimes the letters look all the same."

Daniel straightened on the bench and studied the child thoughtfully for a brief span. "How do they look the same, Edward? Can you explain to me?"

Edward was becoming suspicious of their intent and turned a troubled glance upon his sister. "Did I do wrong, Lee?" he asked in a small voice. "Did Mr. Clarmont tell on me?"

Lila was quick to reassure. "You haven't done anything wrong, darlin'," she said softly, squeezing his hands. "Mr. Clarmont is just concerned about you."

The boy's face began to crumble. "He's always yellin' at me!" he cried. "He says I never get my letters right!" His head fell forward then as he hid his face in shame against his arm.

"Oh, Edward," Lila whispered, moving her hand to the back of his head. "Why didn't you tell me you were having trouble?"

"I thought I could figure it out!" he wailed.

Daniel propped his elbows on the table, his folded hands supporting his chin as he watched this second scene of tears for the day. He sympathized with the child even as he thought about what they might be able to do for the boy. Lila was fussing over Edward, which only made the youth wail the louder, and Daniel could see that her motherlike caring was not going to help in this case. "Do you have a primer?" he asked quietly.

Lila raised unhappy eyes to his. "I think so."

"Get it, would you, please?"

Lila straightened her back, but remained seated as she stared at him in confusion.

"I want Edward to read for us," he explained.

Lila hesitated, concerned about pressuring her brother in this way. But, clearly, Daniel was not going to let this go.

When the child's book was placed on the table in front of Edward, Daniel requested that he read the first sentence. The boy immediately lowered his head close to the book, and Daniel had an inkling as to the problem.

"Do you sit over your books like that in school?" he asked.

Edward nodded.

Daniel reached out and took the book, holding it away a few inches. "Can you see the letters now, Edward?"

Edward shook his head.

Daniel let the book lie on the table. "When Mr. Clarmont writes things on the blackboard at the front of the room, do you see the letters?"

Again, Edward shook his head.

Daniel looked at Lila then. "I think we've found the problem. Let's go to my office. I have a chart there I want Edward to read."

When Daniel got to his feet, Lila did likewise. "He can't see?"

"Not well, apparently." And then he quickly explained that he did not feel the problem serious. "I suspect all he needs is spectacles, Lee, and a little extra practice at reading. Edward has fallen behind in his schoolwork because he hasn't been able to see well." He smiled down at the boy then. "How would you like to ride my horse across town?"

Edward brightened considerably. "Yeah!"

Lila followed Daniel a few steps toward the door and then turned, racing across the room to the jar on a high shelf. She returned to Daniel's side, holding her coins in her palm. "So I can buy him spectacles," she said with a smile.

Lila never knew that Daniel assisted with the financing of the spectacles later that day.

And the following morning Lila marched into the empty schoolroom bright and early, with Edward in toe. She approached Dermot Clarmont with quiet authority as he looked up from behind his desk in dismay. "You almost ruined my brother's life, Dermot, by jumping to conclusions. See that it doesn't happen again."

An hour later Lila could be seen marching barefoot across town, gingerly carrying a large pan. She walked straight to the small house that had once been the home of Edmond and Rachael Fraser. It was the first home Edmond had built for his bride, and it was now the offices of Doctors Fraser and Stone. She invaded Daniel's sanctuary without hesitation, and while he was listening to the irregular thunder of old Mr. Willoughby's ailing heart, too.

"You're a good friend, Daniel," she said, plunking the warm pan down on his desk. "I thank you."

Utterly flabbergasted, Daniel grinned as Lila whirled away from the desk and exited the room.

"What was that about?!" Mr. Willoughby hollered.

Mr. Willoughby was quite deaf and assumed the rest of humanity suffered the same condition.

Daniel walked over to his desk and lifted the white toweling away from the pan. "It's a cobbler!" he said to Willoughby.

"What?!"

"Apple!" Daniel called.

"Apple?" the old man roared.

"Cobbler!"

"Two doors down the street on the left!" he bellowed.

Daniel shook his head and gave up.

CHAPTER
5

  THE FOLLOWING MORNING DANIEL ESCORTED
Virginia Dallard from his office and sat behind his
desk, intent upon updating the notes he had been
keeping concerning Virginia's increasing gastric
problems. His concentration was eventually broken
by the distinct feeling that he was no longer alone
in the room. Looking up, he stared straight into the
smiling eyes of Sammy Briggs.

Surprised, Daniel straightened and returned his
 pen to the ink well. "Sammy?"

"Fix my teeth, Doc," the boy chirped.

Daniel laughed, eyeing the grimy fists that were
 planted deep against the boy's cheeks. Sammy had
to be stretched up on his toes just to have his elbows
reach the desktop. "What's wrong with your teeth?
 Are they hurting you?"

Sammy's head moved back and forth as if guided by

his hands. "They ain't growin'," he said.

Daniel relaxed back in his chair, enjoying this nonworrisome chatter with the child; it was far removed from some of the dire conversations he would have with patients who were very ill. "These teeth you've got now won't *grow*, Sammy."

"I'm growin'. Lee said so. But my teeth ain't."

This seemed to be a serious concern to Sammy, so Daniel turned his chair to the side and motioned the boy around the desk. "Come here, son," he said. Sammy scampered around and Daniel lifted him onto his lap. "I noticed Edward is missing some of his front teeth."

Sammy nodded, staring up at the man, granting Daniel his complete attention. "They falled out."

"Well, Edward will get new teeth," Daniel said, smiling. "Bigger teeth, to replace his smaller ones. You'll get bigger teeth, as well. When you are six or so."

Sammy gave that a breath's worth of thought. " 'Kay," he said and took to smoothing the fine hair on the back of Daniel's hand. A moment later Sammy turned his head and grinned up at his new friend. "I got a birthday!" he chirped.

Daniel played along and reared back in his chair. "You do?" he asked in feigned wonder.

Sammy's head nodded fiercely.

"When?"

"Tomorrow."

"Really?" Daniel asked fondly.

"I'll be this many," Sammy said proudly as he held up five fingers.

"Five, huh? And what are you going to do to celebrate this birthday?"

"Nothin'," the boy said miserably.

Daniel did not like to see a child this unhappy. "I'll bet your sister will make you a cake," he offered.

Sammy seemed to perk up a bit, but not much. "What I really need is to go fishin'," he said seriously. "You could take me."

Here he was, *involved* again. And Daniel did not like usurping Jonathan Briggs's territory. "I'm certain your father—"

"Can't," Sammy mumbled. "He's gotta work."

"Well, Lila—"

"She hates worms!" the boy cried in disappointment.

Daniel would rather spend a day reading a book than struggling with worms himself, and he hadn't been fishing since *he* was a boy. But he found he couldn't say no to this tyke. "All right, boy. You win."

The concentrated look of despondency vanished, and a quick smile lit the child's face. "Wow!" he crowed and made to leave his perch.

"Hold on!" Daniel laughed, holding the boy in place by gripping the back of his shirt. "What are you doing here?"

"I came with Lee," Sammy answered, as if Daniel should have already known the answer. "Annie's here, too."

Daniel's smile melted into a look of concentrated concern. "Is Annie sick?"

Sammy shook his head.

"Lee?"

Again the small, shaggy head was shaking. "Lee's fixin' things."

"Fixing?" he asked, perplexed.

"Lee says ya got a real mess out there, Doc."

With a sudden sense of foreboding, Daniel lowered Sammy to his feet. "Let's go see," he muttered and led the way to the large reception room.

He found Lila conducting traffic.

"You here to see Doc Fraser or Doc Stone, Ned?" she was asking a man with a sickly, gray complexion.

Daniel studied her back for a moment, noticing the hand resting on her hip was holding a rag.

"Doc Fraser," Ned answered.

"Right. You're next," she said decisively. She turned then and saw Daniel staring at her in confusion.

"Mornin'," she said brightly.

"Good morning," he replied uneasily.

"Is there somethin' you wanted, Daniel?"

Daniel blinked stupidly, feeling as if he were a guest in his own place of business, as if he had lost control at some point during the morning. He turned his head briefly and noticed Annie buffing the finish off a small corner of a table. "I suppose I'm curious about your reason for being here," he said at last.

"Oh, that," Lila said happily before moving past him. "We're tidying up. That's all."

Daniel watched her walk down to the end of the hallway and enter the small room that had been converted from a pantry to a supply room. He followed. Quickly. "Lila, did Edmond ask you—?"

"Who washes these cottons for you, Daniel? They're not very white lookin'."

When her hand reached out toward the stack of sheets, Daniel lightly gripped her wrist. "Lee. What are you doing?"

She turned her head then and smiled up at him. "You mean, what am I doin' here?"

"Precisely."

"Well, I owe you something, Daniel. For helping Edward, I mean. And cleaning up this place is the only way I could think of payin' you back."

Daniel understood then and released her wrist, crossing his arms over his chest. "The cobbler was fine payment," he said kindly. "You don't need to—"

"I've already straightened all those papers you and Doc Fraser had lying around."

Attempting not to signal his instant alarm, Daniel asked calmly, "What papers?"

"The ones on the table in the old kitchen. I put them in two tidy piles, Daniel. One for the womenfolk and one for the men," she said proudly. She was fairly certain, at least, that she had made out the names properly.

Wearily Daniel covered his eyes with the palm of his hand.

"Could you try to keep them neat?" she pleaded sweetly when his hand dropped away.

Daniel found he just had to laugh. "I'll speak with Edmond about it," he said wryly.

Lila was satisfied and turned to study the shelves.

But Daniel was not about to let her loose in *this* room. He and Edmond knew exactly where everything could be located. "Lila," he said, quickly grasping her shoulders and turning her toward the door, "this room is fine."

"I don't think so, Daniel," she said over her shoulder as he gently pushed her out of the room.

"Really," he said firmly. "You've done enough already."

Once in the hall Lila turned and faced him. He had such beautiful blue eyes, such a kind face. "I can't ever repay you for what you did for Edward," she said softly.

"You already have, dear," he said in a fatherly tone before he attempted to hastily usher her farther along the corridor.

Edmond stepped out of his office then and sauntered toward them. "Lila," he said in greeting. "You haven't got sick young ones again, have you?"

Lila's cheerful smile returned, and she turned her back on Daniel, facing the older man. "Everyone is fine," she said. "Thanks to Daniel."

Edmond nodded sagely.

"Lila feels she has to return a favor," Daniel informed his colleague. "She's been . . . ah . . . *rearranging* our filing," he added pointedly.

Edmond frowned in confusion over Lila's head, staring at the younger man. When Daniel emphatically shook his head, Edmond shrugged. "That's fine, Lila," he said hesitantly. "Thank you."

"Oh, I haven't finished yet," she said.

Daniel placed a hand on her shoulder and spoke before Edmond could have an opportunity to respond. "Lila, you've paid me back a hundredfold," he said uneasily. "And I'm grateful. But surely you have enough to do in a day. You don't need to tire yourself here," he added sincerely.

Lila was touched by his concern and turned to face him. "Thank you, Daniel."

He nodded.

Lila sighed and looked from one man to the other. "Well, if there's nothing else I can do, Annie and I will just finish sweeping up."

Edmond thought that sounded safe enough. He realized Daniel had not known the town's folk long enough to realize how deeply gratitude could run. But *he* understood the girl's sense of commitment. "That's fine, Lila," he said expansively. "That's fine."

Daniel wondered if it would be *fine*, but he let her go.

It had been a very long day. A hectic day. Edmond had been called away to attend a difficult birthing, and Daniel had been left to see to the steady flow of patients.

Late in the afternoon Daniel wandered out to the reception area and noticed a woman sitting in a corner of the room. Lila was there, intently chattering away. It occurred to him that he had seen the woman before. But where? And then it dawned on him; he had seen her enter the house much earlier in the afternoon.

His brows arching over the bridge of his nose, he called, "Miss Briggs?"

Lila's head popped up and she smiled at him before placing her hand upon the elderly woman's and whispering a word or two. She then moved quickly toward him. "You need something, Daniel?"

Daniel nodded once. "It seems to me that woman has been waiting for quite some time."

"Oh, well," she said, before taking his elbow and propelling him down the hallway and out of earshot. "That's Mizz Harper."

"Miss Harper?" he parroted.

She nodded, grinning. "Alice."

Bone-tired and quickly becoming exasperated, Daniel sighed. "Lila, is she, or is she not, waiting to see a doctor?"

"Oh, yes!"

"But I remember that woman coming in here hours ago."

Lila leaned toward him and whispered conspiratorially, "She's not sick."

"She's not?" he whispered in return.

Shaking her head vigorously, Lila attempted to explain. "Everyone knows Alice isn't sick, Daniel. She just comes to see Doc Fraser all the time 'cause she's lonely. I thought you should see the *sick* people first."

Straightening abruptly, he scowled. "What?" Daniel was accustomed to the professionalism of trained, experienced nurses who were familiar with the diagnosis of illness and the orderly routine of a city hospital. Somehow he doubted Lila's expertise in determining whether or not a body might be ill.

Lila interpreted his concern as being directed to the treatment of Alice Harper. "All you have to do is talk to her for a bit. If you give her a sugar pill or somethin', she'll be even happier."

"Lila, supposing Miss Harper *is* sick? You've made that poor woman wait all afternoon."

"Oh, I've been keeping her busy visitin'. She doesn't know how long she's been sittin' there." She took a step toward the hall entrance, but Daniel's hand shot out and gripped her upper arm. "I'm just goin' to send her down here, Daniel."

"Where are Sammy and Alice?" he asked, fearing the answer.

Lila didn't understand why he was frowning so. "They're all right, Daniel. They're just playin' outside."

Daniel breathed a sigh of relief for that small mercy, at least. He liked the children a great deal, but after the day he had put in, their big sister alone was becoming more than he could handle. God help him if *three* of them had been continually *fixin'* things. One thing he knew for a certainty, he had to convince Lila Briggs not to be quite so *helpful* around his office. "Could you stay here a few moments more?" he asked reasonably. "I would like to speak with you after I see Miss Harper."

"Of course, Daniel," she said agreeably.

Daniel sat behind his desk, thirty minutes later, as Lila entered his inner office, followed by Sammy and Annie. They put him very much in mind of a mother duck and her ducklings as the two children walked close behind her and then stood on either side of her chair.

"Do you want the little ones to wait in the other room, Daniel?" Lila asked as soon as she was seated.

Daniel's gaze promptly met hers. "No. No. They're fine where they are," he said absently. He still did not know what the devil he was going to say to her. He had to admit he had grown fond of this young woman and was fearful of bruising her good intentions.

When he failed to speak after several moments had gone by, Lila became uncomfortable. "You wanted to talk to me?" she prompted.

"Yes." He cleared his throat. "Lila, I appreciate all you've done here today, but—"

"Oh, we didn't do much."

"Yes, well . . . I appreciate all you've done," he said again, ruefully. "But Edmond pays a woman to clean this place and—"

"Yes, I know. Hilda Jenkins," she said, nodding her head in agreement. "But, from what I found here today, Daniel, she should be ashamed to take Doc Fraser's money."

Daniel stared directly into her earnest brown eyes. "But Doctor Fraser is apparently happy with the arrangement he has with Mrs. Jenkins," he said gently.

Lila understood almost immediately. "Oh!" she said, pressing her fingertips briefly to her forehead. "Of course. You're afraid Hilda will get upset," she added, genuinely concerned. "How stupid of me."

"Not *stupid*, Lee," he responded.

"I should have thought."

Daniel smiled with ease now, fully convinced this was going nicely. "Well, you've certainly repaid whatever debt you felt you owed me on Edward's account."

Lila leaned forward and placed a determined fist on top of his desk. "Daniel, there will never be enough I can do to repay you for that boy's education."

"I hardly did all that," he protested.

But Lila was nodding her head, and Daniel began to experience a sinking feeling, knowing the tide had turned against him once more.

And then, out of nowhere, inspiration struck; Lila's strengths may not be evident in a medical office, but he had seen for himself exactly where her talents lay. "There is an agreement *we* might reach, however," he said.

Eager to please this man, Lila gave him her full attention and settled back in her chair again. "I'm listenin', Daniel."

"I know you have very little time to spare with the children to care for and a home to keep."

"School will be out for the summer in a few weeks, and Beth will be able to help out. She's a good little helper."

"I'm certain that she is," he said. "I want you to understand, however, that I realize exactly how hard you work, and you must feel free to say no to my proposal if it will be too much for you."

Lila was anxious to hear about this *agreement* he had in mind and failed to understand why he was so busy trying to persuade her to turn him down. "Just say it flat out, Daniel. I'll tell you yes if it's a good idea, or no if it's not."

So, she could be impatient, he realized as he relaxed, leaning his elbows on the arms of his chair. "I've been thinking of looking for a woman to come into my home," he said.

Lila blinked in surprise, not certain what he needed. "Your home?"

"Once a week, I should think. It's not often that I'm there."

Lila's heart thumped once, hard. "Once a week?"

"Yes."

Lila looked at Sammy and then turned her head toward her sister; they were both listening intently, leaning heavily on the arms of her chair. Her brown eyes were not looking quite so soft and doelike when she returned her attention to him. "To do what, Daniel? And remember there are small ears listenin'," she added hurriedly.

Confused, Daniel's hand fell to his lap. "To clean," he said slowly.

"Oh!" She laughed, her palms slapping her thighs. "Why didn't you just say so?"

Daniel's eyelashes lowered suspiciously. "What did you think I meant?"

Now Lila felt foolish, and the warming of her face told her she would not be able to fool him. "I wasn't certain," she muttered. "I'll come to your home Friday," she said as she jumped to her feet and reached for Sammy's hand. "Let's go, Annie," she said, refusing to look at Daniel again as she ushered the children toward the door.

"Wait!" Daniel called, rounding his desk and stepping to her side. "We haven't talked about your wage."

Lila had managed to embarrass herself a moment ago. Now he was adding to her shame. "I won't clean your house for money, Daniel," she said without looking at him.

"Then we don't have an agreement," he returned firmly as his arms crossed over his chest.

She managed to raise her head just enough to allow him to see that she would not be swayed. "I'm not for hire," she said softly.

He realized instantly that something had gone wrong. "I did not mean to insult you, Lee," he said, placing his hand on her shoulder. "I need help and it's only fair that I find some way to reimburse you for your time."

Lila could feel the heat of his hand burning right through the thin material of her dress, reminding her of the heat of his arm around her the night they had danced. Her heartbeat quickened as she stared up at him, and her distress was increasing at the same rate. He did not understand the depth of the feelings she had for him; the admiration, the gratitude. This man had touched her life in a way no other person had touched it. It went far beyond his caring for two sick children and his discovery of Edward's problems. It went far, far beyond these things. She considered their relationship to be that of very good friends. And friends did not take pay for favors. Friends *did* for each other. "Maybe we can trade off," she suggested.

"Trade off?"

"I'll tidy your house once a week, and if some bodies give you too much of somethin' for doctorin', I'll take what's left over."

"Excess food?" he questioned. "If I have more potatoes or meat than I can eat, you'll take the extra? Is that correct?"

Lila nodded.

"Agreed!" he said happily.

Lila smiled happily, too. "You see, Daniel, friends can usually work things out."

"So they can," he said softly.

"I'll be at your house Friday, then."

Lila turned to go, but Daniel stopped her once again.

"One more thing," he said thoughtfully. "I'll leave a key for you above the window near the back door."

"A key? You lock your house?" she asked in surprise.

He was equally surprised that she would even bother to pose the question. "Of course," he replied.

"Why?"

"Why? Why do people usually lock their doors?"

"I guess you must have somethin' worth stealin', then," she said frankly.

"Lila." Daniel's gaze darted to the children briefly. "I'll be certain to leave early Friday. I think it would be wise if I'm not there when you arrive."

Lila thought his suggestion was a good one. They were friends. Certainly, she did not want to give the townsfolk the impression there might be anything more; she was of the opinion that gossip never did a girl much good.

If she had tapped into the feelings she had successfully suppressed, however, Lila would have admitted there was more. Much more. And it had happened one night in a schoolyard.

When Lila had danced her first dance.

CHAPTER
6

 MAE BELLE WILLOUGHBY THOUGHT DR. STONE looked a little ridiculous marching through town carrying a freshly cut pole and a wooden box late the following morning.

Mae Belle's young companion of the moment, Beatrice Stern Bundy, thought he looked rather fetching, however. Daniel was wearing tan hide trousers that fit his long legs and lower torso rather well, from Bea's point of view. And his brown cambric shirt set off the lightness of his hair, making him altogether too attractive. Beatrice knew there was hardly a woman in town, married or otherwise, who did not give Daniel Stone a second look when he perchance passed them by. "He's going fishing," she muttered.

 "I can see that, child!" Mae Belle returned in incensed, hushed tones. Mae Belle was nobody's fool. "It didn't take him long to give in to the easy life, did it?" she speculated. "It's the middle of the week, and instead of tending the sick, our new doctor is goin' off fishin'."

Daniel passed closely by on the boardwalk then, smiled, nodded, and offered a polite good day to the two women.

Bea continued to look after him, her entire body turning to follow his progress. "He's certainly entitled to his leisure time," she said quietly. "I understand the medical offices are *very* busy lately. Why, half the women we know have come down with one malady or another since Daniel Stone has come to town."

Mae Belle sucked in a large breath. "Beatrice Bundy," she scolded with disgust. "What kind of a suggestion is that?"

Well, it was true from what Bea had heard. She had even found she had not been feeling all that well herself of late. "He *is* very good-looking," she told the older woman.

"*You* are a married woman," Mae Belle reminded her.

Yes, Bea thought as she watched Daniel disappear around a corner of a building, but I'm not dead.

Daniel walked to the front door of the Briggs house and tucked his wooden box under his arm before knocking.

Lila threw the door wide open and stood, stunned, as she inspected this strangely dressed version of the medical man. His clothes, the box under his arm and the pole in his hand, just did not fit. To her way of thinking anyway. "Hello, Daniel," she said slowly. "This is a surprise."

Daniel's brows arched in surprise of his own. "Didn't he tell you?" he asked.

"Who?"

"Sammy. Is he ready to go?"

Lila thought the change in climate, or perhaps overwork, had tipped the doctor off mental balance. Frowning in confusion, she inspected his eyes for signs of madness. "Go where?"

Daniel thought she was being deliberately dense and wondered if he had wakened her from a nap perhaps. "Fishing," he said. "It's his birthday, if you'll recall."

It took several seconds before Lila questioned, "What?" and then a slow dawning of the meaning behind his words caused her eyes to grow large and round with dismay. "Ohhh, no," she whispered, briefly ducking her head. When she again looked up at him, Daniel was surprised to see a heated blush darkening her cheeks. "You'd best come in, Daniel," she said. She stepped back to allow him entrance. Once she had closed the door, Lila marched to the rear door across the room and disappeared outside.

Daniel was perplexed, to say the least. He set the wooden box on the floor and propped his newly cut fishing pole against the wall near the door before he ambled over and took a seat at the long, narrow table. The back door opened then, and Sammy charged inside, his face lighting up with delight when he saw his friend sitting there.

"Hi, Doc!" he chirped. His hands were stuck under his suspenders and into the waistband of his pants as he sauntered close.

He was all boy and very cute, and he never failed to make Daniel smile. "Hi, yourself."

Lila followed her young brother inside and sat on the end of one of the benches, close to Daniel's knees. Once seated, she reached for Sammy's hand, squeezing lightly until he turned his attention toward her. "Sammy, do you remember why Daniel is here?"

Sammy looked from his sister to Daniel and then around the room, frowning until he spied Daniel's belongings beside the door. With a brilliant smile he turned back to Lila. "We're goin' fishin'!"

"And why are you goin' fishin'?" she asked softly.

Sammy couldn't believe that Lila hadn't figured it out. "To catch fish, Lee," he groaned.

Lila shook her head in growing exasperation. "What did you tell Daniel to get him to take you fishin'?"

Daniel propped his elbow on the table and braced his chin on a closed fist as he patiently watched this scene being played out.

Sammy did not hesitate in answering his sister's question; he remembered what day it was. He caught a handful of her skirt and pressed his fist into Lila's knee as he reminded her, "It's my birthday."

Painfully embarrassed, Lila flashed Daniel a worried look and his expression said, quite clearly, "All right, I've been duped by a four-year-old." He understood and he continued to watch.

Lila cupped Sammy's small face between her hands and concentrated on making herself understood. "Darlin', I've told you before, you can't have a birthday just because you want one. You've already had your birthday, remember?"

Sammy's eyes dimmed, but he had little choice but to look up at her. "That was before," he muttered. "Now I'm this many." He held his hand in the air, fingers splayed.

"You won't be *that many* for a long time, Sammy. I've told you, you only get one birthday a year. Now, Daniel's supposed to be workin', and instead he's here because you made up a story," she said patiently but firmly as her hands dropped to his shoulders. "You can't keep makin' up stories to get people to do what you want."

Sammy's face began to crumble. "I didn't," he insisted as tears flooded his eyes. "It's my birthday."

When the child buried his face in her lap and wept, Lila shot Daniel a beseeching glance, which disintegrated the moment their glances met; he was laughing!

Daniel tried to dispel the silent laughter, hiding his grin behind his hand momentarily. He shook his head, still smiling at her as Lila tried to fathom what was going through his mind.

"He doesn't understand that he wasn't telling the truth," she said apologetically.

"I can see that."

"Sometimes he just gets an idea in his mind and he thinks it's so."

Daniel nodded his head. "I understand." He reached for Sammy, pulling him away from Lila's skirts. "Come here, son," he coaxed and lifted the boy onto his lap.

Sammy immediately turned his tear-stained face into Daniel's chest.

"It's not so bad as that."

"It's my birthday," he wailed.

Lila leaned to the side and rested her arm on the table as she watched, hoping Daniel could make the child understand. Certainly she had failed.

Daniel dipped his head, attempting to coax Sammy into looking at him. "What month is your birthday?"

"March," he whispered.

"What month is it now?"

There was a drawn-out hesitation before Sam admitted, "I don't know."

"It's not March, is it?" Daniel asked.

Again a hesitation. "No," he drawled slowly.

"So it can't be your birthday."

The small face twisted again in genuine anguish as Sammy's eyes flooded with tears once more. "I thought it was!" he cried.

Daniel folded strong arms around the small body and held the child close against his chest. "All right, Sammy. There's no harm done. But I don't want you telling any more stories, do you understand? You don't have to make up birthdays just to get me to go fishing with you."

Sammy rotated his head against Daniel's chest.

Lila bent her elbow and rested her chin in the palm of her hand as she smiled ruefully. "I'm sorry, Daniel."

"Don't be," he said kindly. "There is really no harm done."

Quick to understand when he had the advantage, Sammy raised his head and tipped a tear-stained face upward. "Can we still go fishin'?"

"Sammy!" Lila groaned.

Daniel ignored her dismay. "You had better ask your sister about that," he told the boy. "I think you're in a bit of a fix with her."

Sammy's head turned slowly toward Lila; he obviously wasn't quite so confident about *her* reaction. "Can we, Lee?"

With a dramatic sigh, Lila crossed her arms under her breasts and frowned. "I don't think we should be keepin' Daniel away from his patients," she said.

"It would be a shame to waste all those good worms I dug up," Daniel teased quietly.

"Pleeease, Lee," Sammy begged.

Lila looked from boy to man and back to boy. "No more stories? No more inventin' birthdays?" she asked. "You promise?"

Sammy hesitated on that one. "But how will I know when it's my for-real birthday?"

"I'll tell you," she said. Lila could see the wheels of thought were turning, but he did promise. And to Daniel, she said, "I'll fix you a lunch."

Before she had moved across the room, Daniel suggested, "Come with us."

Lila hesitated for a moment, considering the matter as he

watched her. "I've got all this ironin'," she said, pointing to a large basket, filled to overflowing with clean clothes. It was a chore she loathed and one left over from yesterday because she had disrupted her schedule by going to his offices and *tidying* things.

"It will wait," Daniel said persuasively. "It's a chore better left to the cool of the evening, isn't it?" And he doubted she often had an afternoon of just relaxing in the sun. Besides, conversations with Sammy could be limited, and a little adult dialogue would be welcome.

Lila knew how much Sammy would enjoy an afternoon of fishing with Daniel and gave his request serious thought. "Annie will have to come."

"That's fine," Daniel agreed. "We'll have a fine afternoon. All of us."

Sammy sensed that all was right in the adult world and squirmed down from Daniel's lap. "I'll tell Papa we're goin' fishin'," he announced happily and sprinted out the back door.

Lila poured Daniel a cup of coffee and then prepared a substantial lunch for four. By the time the basket was packed, both Sammy and Annie were standing on the porch with their fishing poles in hand.

Daniel took the laden food basket and nodded toward the small box he had left on the floor beside the door. "That one is lighter," he said.

But Lila suspected what was in the box and balked. "I would rather carry the food."

He laughed and conceded, scooping the box up with his free hand before they joined the children. "Could you carry the pole?" he teased.

She would. And she laughed as she followed him through the door. "Have you asked yourself how you got into this?" She knew she had failed to make herself clear when he looked over his shoulder at her. "I mean, have you asked yourself how you became so involved with us?"

Daniel's smile was gentle and warm as he hedged. "There are a number of reasons, I suppose." He stared off after the children, who were skipping ahead as Lila fell into step at his side. "It's very different here from Boston. In the city the patients come and go, and most doctors never have an opportunity to get to know the *person* behind the illness."

Lila grinned. "You mean you never treated a small boy for the bellyache and then ended up havin' to take him fishin' because of a trick?"

Daniel laughed. "Well, it won't do me any harm to spend an afternoon sitting on a riverbank. In fact, I'm rather looking forward to it. I haven't been fishing since I was a boy."

"I hope you remember how to hook your worms," she said ruefully. "You'll get no help from me."

"Yes, I heard about your aversion from Sammy."

Lila detected the note of fondness in his voice and realized that Daniel thought Sammy was quite a fellow. "Sammy does love to talk," she admitted.

Daniel nodded, staring ahead at the bend in the road. "We had a very serious chat," he said, flashing her a suggestive grin. "Man to man, of course."

Lila could barely prevent her curiosity from showing. "Of course," she drawled casually. Truth be told, she was dying to know what a doctor and a four-year-old boy could discuss, *man to man*.

She never did learn that Daniel and Sammy had talked about teeth.

Daniel did more baiting of hooks than he did actual fishing, but he realized halfway through the afternoon that he was genuinely enjoying himself. Sammy and Annie became bored with just sitting still waiting for something to happen, so they wandered downstream in search of adventure. Daniel remained sitting on the embankment with his boots removed and his trouser legs rolled up to mid-calf.

Lila sat off to the side and a bit behind him, silently watching him study the lazy flow of the river. "What's so fascinatin' down there?" she asked.

Daniel shot her a quick grin over his shoulder. "This is wonderful, you know? I'm just sitting here like a mindless, inanimate object."

"Whatever that means," she muttered.

"It means I'm without a thought to call my own."

Lila laughed, the sweet sound echoing across the narrow river. "I doubt that," she said with conviction. "A smart man like you must be thinkin' all the time."

Daniel wondered about that. If he was *smart*, why did he find himself thinking about a woman who was totally devoted to her father and her six siblings? If he was *smart*, he would find a woman who was free of obligations and responsibilities; a woman who could dedicate copious amounts of time to getting to know him and developing a relationship. Instead, he found himself drawn to a woman with whom he could not even spend a private moment because she was continuously surrounded by family.

He had given considerable thought to his frequent bouts of needing to seek her out and had decided it was due to his curiosity; she was different from other women he had known. Lila Briggs was totally lacking in sophistication, and she was too open and honest to ever be coquettish. She was pretty and sweet and more *pure* than anyone he had ever known. There was something totally new and refreshing about her, and he felt more and more cleansed of his previous life's falsehoods each and every time he met her.

Lila eventually broke into their lengthy silence. "There you go again," she teased. "You're thinkin'."

Daniel laughed guiltily, laid his fishing pole aside, and allowed himself to fall backward so that he was lying half on the blanket upon which she sat with his head very close to her bent knees. "I confess, I was thinking how enjoyable this afternoon has been and that I would like to do it again."

Lila looked down and smiled at the picture of a man who was so relaxed he looked as if he could drift to sleep in the warmth of the afternoon sun. "You can always count on Sammy to go fishin' with you," she said.

Daniel stared up at her, silently examining her face for several moments. "The enjoyment is due only in part to Sammy," he said softly.

Lila felt nervous suddenly, not totally understanding. She looked around the pretty place where she and the children spent many a summer afternoon. "It's nice here," she said, failing to look at him. "It's relaxin'. That's why you like it."

"The *place* is only another small part of it," he said.

Lila did look at him again, confused by his tone. "What are you sayin', Daniel?"

He shrugged and stared up at the overhanging tree limbs in an attempt at maintaining a casual air. "I'm saying I enjoy your company," he said. "It's quite simple, really."

But it wasn't simple, Lila knew in a moment of panic.

In fact, it could become very, *very* complicated.

CHAPTER
7

 THE ARRANGEMENT BETWEEN LILA AND DANIEL
worked well over the following weeks, and once
Beth was out of school for the summer and able to
 lend more of a hand, Lila found the added burden
of tending Daniel's home much less troublesome.
In fact, Lila definitely felt she had the better end of
the agreement.

Daniel was seldom home, making the chores
around his house very light in comparison to a house
filled with children. Based on the few wrinkles she
found in his sheets, she felt he did not even spend
many nights in his bed. Either that or his head hit his
pillow and he did not move again until morning.

 Additionally, the foodstuffs patients would press
upon the doctor for his services were varied and
plentiful. Lila supplied many a fine meal for her
 family from Daniel's ample stores. It seemed to

Lila that she received much more than she gave. Once again, she found herself feeling indebted to Daniel.

Still, every Friday morning, with Sammy and Annie as her constant companions, Lila Briggs marched across town and did her best to make Daniel Stone's house a home. It was clean and bright, and she would leave fresh flowers in a jar on his table, but it was very empty.

Sammy adequately voiced his sister's sentiments as Lila opened the back door and permitted the children to enter the house ahead of her. "It's like nobody lives here, Lee," he said, wandering into the kitchen. "I don't know why we come. Nothin' ever gets mussed up."

Lila smiled and set her key on the table. "Dust does settle, my boy," she said before turning away. "I'll fetch the linens, and you two get me some water."

"Ahh," Annie groaned.

"And don't be spillin' more on the floor than you leave in the bucket," she warned.

Lila lifted her skirts and darted up the stairs, turning right at the top. She was well into the master bedroom, however, before she realized that the room was inhabited. As Sammy had said, normally the house felt as if no one lived there and to find Daniel in his bed brought her to a surprised halt, to say the least. It actually took a moment for her mind to assimilate the fact that there was a man's naked body stretched out before her very eyes. A man's very *beautiful* naked body! "Oh, Lordy," she breathed but could not manage to tear her eyes away.

Daniel lay flat on his back with his head turned away from her, toward the open window. His arms were outstretched and one leg was bent at the knee. He had managed to rid himself of the bedclothes, with the exception of a corner of white cotton covering his right foot. His chest rose and fell slowly, the only movement she could detect.

Lila gave his anatomy enough scrutiny to determine that the hair on his chest appeared darker than the dark blond hair on his head. Once that thought penetrated her haze, Lila decided *now* was the time to make her exit. "He looks like a fallen angel, and I'm standin' here gawkin' like a fallen *woman*," she muttered before she turned, swept up Daniel's discarded clothing from a chair, and silently fled the room.

When she returned to the kitchen, Annie was feeding wood into the stove. "You didn't try lightin' it, did you, Annie?" Lila asked.

"No."

Lila automatically dropped her hand onto the top of the child's head as she peered into the black hole. "We've got too much here," she said quietly and removed a few of Annie's offerings.

"Lee!" Sammy called as he raced through the back door. "Can I take off my shirt!"

"Shhh!" Lila warned.

"It's *hot*," he whined.

"Yes, take off your shirt, then. And speak quietly. Daniel's still sleepin'."

Sammy's eyes sparked with light, like sun reflected off a mirror. "Doc's here?" he asked in wonder.

"Yes," she said as she bent over the boy and pulled the shirt up and over his head. "We have to be quiet. Maybe we'll make some biscuits for him before we start the wash."

But Sammy didn't care much about biscuits. Once he was free of his shirt, he bolted for the door.

Lila reached out and grabbed the seat of his pants. "Where do you think you're going?"

"I gotta see Doc."

"Oh, no, you don't," she said, reaching for his hand. "Come and help me mix biscuit batter."

"Ahh, Lee."

"Don't you 'Ahh, Lee' me," she teased. "Daniel has probably been up all night tendin' sick people. You just let him sleep."

It was hard for Sammy at times, being around women and helping with women's chores. Cooking things was fun only when the ingredients were sweet or gooey or both. He just naturally craved a man's attention sometimes, and Daniel was a man he enjoyed being with. So, at the first opportunity, he was up the stairs and leaning over the side of Daniel's bed.

Sammy did not break Lila's command to be quiet, however. He just propped his chin on his fists and stared silently at the sleeping man.

That was Daniel's first vision when he awoke; he rolled over and stared directly into a pair of smiling brown eyes.

"Hi, Doc."

Daniel could not help but smile at the warmth of the greeting that was becoming so very familiar. "Hi, Sammy."

"Are you goin' to get up now?"

"Soon." Daniel groaned as he raised his arms above his head and stretched his entire body. He then rolled onto his back, rubbing his chest with the palm of his hand as he fought against the sleep he still needed. It did not take long, however, before the demands for food outweighed the demands for sleep, as he caught the scent of something wonderful happening in the kitchen. He turned his head and grinned at the boy. "Your sister is downstairs?"

"Uh-huh."

"What's she cooking, Sammy?"

Sammy's elbows pressed more deeply into the mattress as he leaned forward, closer to Daniel. "Biscuits and bacon and fried 'tatoes."

" 'tatoes, huh?" Just then Daniel's stomach contracted and growled.

Sammy laughed. "You sound like an aminal."

Daniel ruffled Sammy's hair and swung his legs over the side of the bed. "I need some pants, Sam," he said in a businesslike tone.

Sammy was eager to please and ran to the wardrobe. "Which ones?"

He watched Sammy balance on his toes on the wooden base. "The light-colored ones."

Sammy pulled the garment out and raced back to the bed. "Here, Doc."

"Thank you, my friend." Daniel took the doeskin trousers and shook them out before plunging one foot into a pantleg.

"Lee says you was probably out all night," Sammy said as he threw one knee up on the bed and attempted to climb up.

Daniel placed his hand under the small bottom and gave Sammy a boost.

"Thanks," he puffed.

"You're welcome." Daniel plunged the other foot into the trouser leg and stood, turning as he began to button his pants.

"Was ya?"

"Was I what?" he asked, finger-combing his hair as he ambled over to a chest of drawers.

"Out all night," Sammy said with noted exasperation.

Daniel was awake enough and *thinking* well enough now to remember that he had, indeed, been out all night. And he remembered why. "Lila was right," he said simply.

"Was ya sittin' up with a sick person?"

Daniel grinned at the boy's tone of wonder. "I was." He pulled a white cambric shirt over his head. He supposed doctoring appeared fascinating to a boy of Sammy's age. And it was. Doctoring, to Daniel, was challenging, fascinating, wonderful. At other times it was just plain shit. Like today. And last night. Daniel tried to put last night's case out of his mind. Just for now. Just for a time. Later, he would have to ponder the dilemma again. Perhaps Edmond would have some clue.

Forcing a smile for his young companion, Daniel held out his hand. "Let's go get some food."

Sammy jumped down from the bed and reached up for his idol's hand. "I'm goin' to be a doc," he announced.

"We'll talk about that," Daniel told him as the face of a very sick little girl swam before his tired eyes and whispering shadows of frustration and doubt crept into his mind once more.

They entered the sunlit kitchen and found it completely devoid of human presence. But Daniel felt a comforting warmth wrap around him as certain as if a woman had been there and greeted him with a morning smile. And all because a petite gutsy lady had cooked his breakfast and put flowers on his table.

"I'll get Lee," Sammy offered as he broke away from Daniel's handhold and raced for the back door.

The temperature in the kitchen had risen by several degrees with the fire in the cookstove, and Daniel had just made up his mind he would fix a plate of food and sit outside to eat when Lila rushed into the room.

"He woke you, didn't he? The little devil."

Daniel dropped the cloth covering the warm biscuits and smiled, ignoring her comment. "Good morning."

Lila stopped a few steps away from him. "Good morning. I told Sammy to leave you be," she added unhappily.

Daniel shook his head and turned, reaching for the coffee-pot. "He didn't wake me, Lee."

"I'll fix you a plate," she said when he stepped away from the stove, cup in hand. "That boy is just like bees buzzin' honey when he's around you," she muttered.

"Do you have an obsession with bees?" he teased.

Lila stared at him in confusion.

"You talk about bees a lot. The 'bumble-patted' teacher?" he pressed.

Lila thought he must be addled from lack of sleep. "Are you a little bit hungry or a whole lot hungry?" she asked.

Daniel laughed at her failure to fall for his bait. "A whole lot hungry."

Lila buttered a second biscuit and added it to the plate. A mound of fried potatoes and several strips of bacon followed.

Daniel scooped up the plate, thanking her. "I think I'll eat out back where it's cooler," he said.

Lila blushingly remembered that he must have also been warm in his bed, since he had kicked the bedclothes away. The heat in the kitchen would certainly be too much for him.

Daniel watched a flattering blush steal across her cheek and wondered what had caused her discomfort. She looked like a breath of summer morning in a yellow dress that, in spite of its faded condition, complemented the red highlights in the single braid of her chestnut hair. The capped sleeves of the garment left her arms exposed to the harshness of the sun, and as usual, Lila was barefoot. Barefoot and appealing, he realized. *Softly* appealing. "Will you join me?" he asked.

"We've eaten," she said and failed to make eye contact with him because she had mentally pictured him lying naked. "I'll have coffee, though," she said on second thought; pouring the coffee gave her an opportunity to turn away from him.

Daniel wandered out to the porch and sat on the top step, setting his coffee beside his hip.

"Hi, Daniel!" Annie called as she ran across the yard.

"Hello, sweetheart," he returned warmly.

"We can wash your sheets now."

Daniel grimaced, realizing his thoughtlessness would cause more work. "I should have stripped the bed."

"Sammy and me can get them," the girl offered. "Come and help me, Sammy!" she called.

But Sammy was squatting in the dirt nearby. He'd found a caterpillar.

"Sammy!" Annie bellowed.

"What?!" he shrieked.

Lila stepped out of the door then, and the boy paid better mind. Without her having to say a word, Sammy turned his back on the fascinating creature and shuffled off in Annie's wake.

Daniel laughed, shaking his head as he bit into a biscuit.

"They're somethin', huh?" Lila commented as she joined him on the step.

"They are something," he agreed.

Lila watched him attack the food on his plate during a moment of silence. "You were good and hungry."

"Starved," he muttered around a mouthful.

"Were you out all night?"

Daniel nodded his head and reached for another strip of bacon.

"The rope for the laundry broke," she offered conversationally.

Daniel turned his head, obviously surprised; he'd strung that rope, and it had been sturdy. He did not have to wait for an explanation.

"Annie and Sammy were swingin' on it, Daniel. I'm sorry. I was cookin' breakfast and . . ."

Daniel held up a hand, set his plate aside, and reached for his cup as he wondered what the children had against clotheslines. "Not to worry. I've another length of rope in the shed. I'll have it fixed before the wash is finished."

"So, who's sick?" she asked.

Daniel wondered if she ever missed a beat; just change the topic . . . wham! Unfortunately, *this* topic did not revive happy memories. "Do you know the Rutledge family?"

Lila nodded her head. "East of town. They've got a big family."

"June is sick," he said.

Lila could easily detect the unease in his voice, and she frowned in concern. "The littlest one?"

"She's only four," he said miserably as he studied a spot on the boards between his feet.

"Same as Sammy," she whispered slowly. "Not bad sick, Daniel, is she?"

Daniel turned his head and stared off toward the woods at the rear of his property. "I don't know," he admitted. "That is . . . I'm not certain, but I think she's very sick."

Lila's breath whooshed into her lungs, and she was a long time in letting it out. "Lordy."

"I hope He's listening." He stood up without another word and walked to the shed.

Lila watched him go through the motions of repairing the broken line; removing the old rope and coiling it under his bent elbow and up across the palm of one hand. He was masculine in every movement and methodical in a distracted sort of way. His thoughts were heavy and sad, and Lila did not know how to help him.

The new clothesline was ready by the time Lila had the first small articles of laundry finished. The fire, over which the large kettle was suspended, was well away from the spot where the clothes would hang and dry. Lila dropped a hand-wrung towel into the basket at her feet.

"I'll carry this, if you're ready," Daniel said.

"It's not heavy."

"I'll carry it just the same."

Her hand reached down and captured his forearm as he straightened with the basket suspended between two hands. "She'll be all right, Daniel."

His blue eyes dropped downward, and he stared at her. Hard. "What makes you so certain?"

Lila's smile was confident. "Because you're a very good doctor."

"I'm not so good that I bloody well know what's wrong with her," he snapped.

Confidence turned to compassion, instantly, as her smile disappeared.

"I'm sorry," he said hurriedly and bent quickly, returning the basket to the ground. When he straightened again, he came up reaching for her hand. "Forgive me, Lee. I'm not angry with you."

"I know that. You're angry with whatever's made June sick."

Daniel just stood there, his arms hanging between them, gripping her fingers. Eventually his gaze drifted away from the understanding in her eyes, and he stared off into the distance again. "I've seen one case such as this before," he said softly. "If my suspicions are correct, June Rutledge is a very sick little girl. If I'm right, that child will probably die." He looked at her then, and his troubled gaze reached right to her heart.

Lila's fingers twisted until she was holding *his* hand. "There's little use in saying I hope you're wrong this once, Daniel. I can see you know. You know what's wrong with that little girl."

She waited, watching as his face became expressionless. "I know," he said.

"And you don't want to say it. You don't want to think about it," she whispered. "Because you have a kind heart and it's hurtin' you that you can't help her."

"Wouldn't you hurt?"

"Oh, yes. I would. I do hurt. I hurt for that little girl, and I hurt for her folks. But, Daniel, you, at least, have the learnin' to ease her way."

"That isn't enough," he said gruffly, but then he lightly touched her cheek and erased the harshness that she knew had not been directed toward her. "I think I'll go and talk with Edmond. Perhaps he has other ideas. Perhaps he can convince me I'm wrong."

Lila watched him disappear into the small barn to get his horse, her heart aching for him. Every step he took bespoke of a weariness that went far beyond a lack of sleep. Daniel Stone carried a very large burden.

They both knew he wasn't wrong.

Beatrice Bundy thought Daniel Stone was extremely rude in not acknowledging her ladylike wave of greeting as he raced past her and along the street. But the sound of children laughing nearby drew her attention before she could give Daniel's lack of tact too much consideration. She stopped in front of his house and frowned in surprise at seeing two children playing alongside the small white home. "The Briggs brats?" she muttered.

That is exactly who they were, she realized as she continued to stare. "What on earth . . . ?" She turned her head toward the street, but Daniel had made a hasty departure.

Staring at Sammy and Annie again, she began to speculate why Daniel had been in such a hurry. She squinted briefly toward the sky, noting the sun was high. "A little late starting his day." She pondered that only briefly before verbalizing her next thought concerning the presence of the Briggs children at the home of Dr. Stone. "And where those two brats are found, Lila most certainly can be found." The fact that Lila was nowhere to be seen provided Beatrice with the reason for Daniel's mad dash toward his office and his tardiness in starting his working day. "Why, he's just jumped up from bein' in bed with *her*," she gasped. With the small black feather in the brim of her hat all aquiver, Beatrice looked up and down the quiet street. "My Lord," she breathed, "Lila will surely ruin that man." About fit to burst her stays, she started toward the shops at a pace that would chagrin any creditable hare. Beatrice was now on a mission; Mae Belle Willoughby would confide in Rachael Fraser, who would confide in Edmond Fraser, who would enlighten Daniel Stone right smartly about the danger he was courting. "*Courting*?" Beatrice laughed gaily at her own pun as she rushed onward.

CHAPTER
8

 IT WASN'T A FULL TWO DAYS LATER THAT MAE Belle Willoughby ran into Dolly Patrick in Cuthbert's store. Mae Belle acknowledged that Dolly was a terrible gossip, but the woman's family was one of the founding families of the town, and Mae Belle could hardly ignore her.

 Dolly was tucking a small brown-paper-wrapped parcel under her arm when Mae Belle approached. "Mrs. Cuthbert. Dolly," Mae Belle said politely.

 Dolly smiled; she had a smile for just everyone. "Why, Mae Belle Willoughby. How is that poor, sick husband of yours?"

 "Oh, my Mr. Willoughby is survivin'," she said, gripping Dolly's elbow and steering the woman toward the rear of the store. "I know your good friend Mrs. Wilder must be positively devastated over the news," Mae Belle whispered. "But I want you to assure her that everything will be looked after."

The crease over the bridge of Dolly's nose deepened considerably. "What on earth are you talkin' about? What news?"

"Why, about our own Dr. Stone and that Lila Briggs. They're . . . well . . ." She stalled as she looked around, ensuring that no one was eavesdropping. "They're *involved*."

"Involved?" Dolly questioned. She stared at Mae Belle's fluttering eyelashes and ventured into the possible meaning behind *involved*. "Do you mean they're cohabitatin' or just fornicatin' now and then?"

Mae Belle turned absolutely porcelain white. "Shhh!"

"Don't you *shhh!* me," Dolly said firmly.

Flustered now, Mae Belle tried to redeem herself. "I have it on absolute best authority that Lila Briggs spends time alone with Daniel Stone in his own home."

"Perhaps Lila's makin' him a pie," Dolly said tartly.

Mae Belle missed the point and shook her head. "My *source* knows very well what they're doin'."

Dolly gave the matter a moment's thought. "Victoria Wilder will be disappointed if there is somethin' between Daniel and Lila," she said quietly. "She was counting on Daniel for her young Jenny."

Mae Belle blinked at that. "You said Daniel Stone was escortin' Jenny Wilder to the Summer Frolic?" she countered worriedly. She had already informed Beatrice Bundy of that, and Mae Belle did not want to ruin her own credibility.

Dolly attempted to recall Victoria Wilder's exact words concerning Jenny and Daniel and could not. Unwilling to risk her own position of command, Dolly was forced to go along with Mae Belle's supposition. "Of course, of course," she said hastily. "Now explain to me just how this . . . *matter* will be looked after."

Mae Belle warmed to the woman again, now that she was no longer the challengee. "Well," she said, leaning toward Dolly's ear, "I known that Edmond Fraser . . ."

Dolly continued to listen intently.

On the street Lila, Annie, and Sammy were making their way toward the Cuthbert's store.

"Let's go see if Daniel wants to go fishin'," Sammy suggested.

Lila reached for his hand to keep him from dashing off toward the medical offices. "Daniel is very busy, Sammy," she explained as she helped him up the high steps toward the shop.

Sammy thought about what his sister said for a moment. "Maybe if we got sick, he would come and see us."

Lila could barely believe the capacity this child had for plotting. But she laughed and squeezed his hand. "Don't even *think* it," she ordered. And while she spoke, Lila watched Beatrice Bundy bearing down on them.

The smartly dressed young woman gave Lila's worn dress a disdainful glance and then smiled insolently. "Why, Lila Briggs. I haven't seen you in just ages."

"Just *ages*," Lila returned. "How are you, Bea?" Sammy, already bored, jumped down from the boardwalk and began hunting for good stones. Annie was clinging to Lila's skirts.

"I'm dashing madly," Beatrice said breathlessly. "The Summer Frolic is just next week, you know. I'm in charge of the refreshment committee. It's so difficult to organize all the ladies involved and ensure, of course, that we have enough of everything."

Lila silently agreed that Beatrice might find those chores difficult. "It must be positively overwhelmin', Bea."

"Well, one has to be civic-minded when one has a *position*."

Lila wondered what that "position" might be; she could think of several, but none of them were flattering.

"Well, I must be about my business," Beatrice said, skirting around the shy little Annie. "Oh!" she gushed, turning back to face her old schoolmate. "I almost forgot. Have you heard the latest, Lila?"

Lila's grin reflected her thoughts about this silly woman, but Beatrice was too wrapped up in herself to interpret anything but approval. "Depends what 'the latest' is."

Beatrice blessed them with a tinkling, sly little laugh. "Of course! Silly me. Why, it's about Daniel Stone."

Lila's stomach dropped and her heart jumped to her throat, but she did not permit her smile to falter. "Daniel Stone? What about him?" she asked.

Beatrice leaned forward in the stance of a conspirator. "Why, it's said about town that he's courtin' Jenny Wilder."

Lila almost swallowed her tongue. "What?!"

"I know." Beatrice giggled. "Isn't that just too wonderful? Well, I know Jenny isn't very pretty, but she is of *quality* and one of my best friends. I'm just that *thrilled*," she added.

"I just bet you are," Lila said easily. Now that she was over her initial fear that something had happened to Daniel, Lila thought this was hilariously funny. "Ah, Beatrice," she drawled casually. "Wherever did you hear this *wonderful* news?"

"Dolly Patrick told me."

"Oh, well, then . . . it must be true."

"Absolutely," Beatrice agreed. "Dolly is *very* reliable. And she is very close to Jenny's mother, you know."

Tongue in cheek, Lila replied, "Yes, I know."

"Jenny is bein' a sly old thing, however," Bea murmured with obvious disappointment. "She just refuses to talk about this affair."

"Tsk," said Lila.

Beatrice was decidedly disappointed that she had not been included among Jenny Wilder's confidantes, but as of this moment, she was positively frustrated by Lila's lack of reaction. Never one to give up hope, however, Beatrice brightened her smile. "That's why everyone is just buzzin' about the Spring Frolic. We all fully expect that Dr. Stone will escort Jenny to the party."

"Really?" Lila glanced quickly to the side to be certain Sammy was not getting into any mischief.

"It is just bound to be a wonderful evenin'."

"Bound to be," Lila murmured and then remembered to smile. "Why, with all your plannin' and hard work, it's just *bound* to be." She reached for Annie's hand then and called Sammy to her. "You'll forgive me? I have to get on with my shopping."

They traded places, Beatrice carefully protecting her skirts as Lila and the children squeezed by on the narrow walk.

"It's a pity you can't make it to the dance," Beatrice called as Lila walked away.

"A pity!" Lila returned over her shoulder and continued on her way.

"Pooh!" It was the closest thing to profanity that Beatrice would permit.

Lila's reflections of that conversation did anything but keep her laughing during the tedium of morning shopping. She hated the thought of Daniel with Jenny Wilder. Why, Jenny was a bigger snob than Beatrice Bundy would ever be. Daniel was too fine a man to be hooked by a scheming, spoiled woman such as Jenny. No, she did not like the thought of Daniel and Jenny together one bit. Lila simply failed to realize just how much the *thought* distressed, and why.

She put the last of her packages on the counter and looked around. Annie was close at hand, as usual, but Sammy was nowhere to be seen. "Where's your brother?" she asked the child.

"I think he went outside," Annie whispered.

Lila smiled at the elderly woman behind the counter. "Sorry, Mrs. Cuthbert, I'm missin' one. Be right back," she promised as she moved quickly toward the shop door.

Sammy almost collided with her as Lila stepped into the summer sunlight. "Hey, Lee! Somebody's horse got loose! See?" he asked, pointing up the street.

Lila followed his direction and saw a sturdy Appaloosa prancing in their direction.

"I ain't never seen a horse with spots," Sammy said excitedly. "I'm gonna catch him!"

He took a running jump and was in the middle of the street before Lila could move.

"Sammy, no!" she called, picking up her skirts and running. "We don't know that horse!" And an unknown horse could have any kind of temperament.

Lila could see that the animal was shocked by the small person running in his direction, and she increased her pace. "Sammy, no!" she called frantically. "That's a stallion! Sammy!" She reached her brother and pushed him behind her. Lila was now facing an animal poised to fight; ears back, eyes wild. "Easy," she said softly. "Easy, boy." Slowly, slowly, she reached for the loose-fitting halter. But her fingers failed to hold on when the stallion jerked his head back and whirled around.

Lila felt a jolt to her body and watched the stallion run off with his tail held high before her right leg seemed no longer capable of supporting her. She folded slowly to the ground.

"Lee!" Sammy cried, dropping to his knees beside her. "Lee!"

Lila stared up at the summer sky that no longer seemed quite so sunny and reached for Sammy's hand. "You're all right, darlin'?"

"He got ya, Lee," Sammy said miserably.

Lila attempted a smile as she moved her head to face her brother's tearing eyes. "Don't cry, darlin'," she said. "Can you run and fetch Daniel, Sammy?"

Sammy needed no other urging and ran as fast as his short legs would carry him.

By now a crowd was gathering, and Lila became aware of the murmurs going on around her in addition to Annie's frantic wails.

"I'll be all right, Annie," she said, squeezing the girl's hand.

"Is there something I can do, dear?"

Lila turned her head and found Mrs. Cuthbert kneeling beside her. "I'm feelin' a little silly lyin' here in the street," she said.

Mrs. Cuthbert looked up at some of the faces she knew well. "Would you men carry her to the back of my shop?"

Teddy Shoemaker suggested they should not move the injured woman. "Young Sammy's run for one of the doctors," he said. "Best let her lie still."

Beatrice Bundy was returning home and was attracted by curiosity toward the crowd. "What's happened?" she asked anyone who cared to respond.

"Lila Briggs has been hurt."

"Really?" she said, stretching her neck to see over the people standing in front. She had little success.

"Kicked by a stallion," the man volunteered.

"Really?" Beatrice murmured again. Not so much fun as sleepin' with one, she pondered silently. She then began the arduous task of pushing her way toward the front of the crowd.

Sammy ran so hard he developed a stitch in his side, but he would not stop. He had to get Daniel. He had to get Daniel, fast!

Several startled people raised a brow or two as the small boy charged through the waiting area of the small house and ran down the hall toward the doctors' private offices. It seemed a shame that Lila Briggs could not keep that boy under control!

Sammy remembered exactly which door would lead to Daniel, but he did not have to run quite that far. Daniel was escorting a female patient from his office when Sammy ran into them.

Literally.

"Whoa!" Daniel laughed, casting an apologetic glance at the woman as he reached for the small boy.

"Lee's been hurt!" Sammy cried before Daniel could say another word. "Ya gotta come, Daniel! She's hurt!"

Daniel forgot everything else and dropped to his knees, gripping Sammy's bony shoulders. "What happened? Where is she?" he asked as Sammy's tears fueled instant fear in his gut. "Where, Sammy?"

"Down . . . down"—he hiccuped—"the street. Cuthbert's store," he managed.

Daniel darted into his office and snatched up his black bag. He had retraced his steps and run past Sammy before he'd had another thought.

Edmond was in the hall by now, confused by all the commotion.

"Help Sammy, Edmond," Daniel ordered as he ran past

the man. He continued his headlong dash out of the building and down the street.

"Lila's hurt bad!" Sammy wailed as the kind face of Edmond Fraser turned in his direction.

Edmond picked the boy up from the floor and balanced him on the slight protrusion of his stomach. "Daniel will take good care of her," he soothed as he walked quickly toward the waiting room. "Sorry, folks," he said as he rushed past. "We've got a bit of an emergency."

Daniel could see the gathered crowd a few blocks ahead of him and closed the distance at record speed. "Move back!" he called. "Let me through."

Just as Moses had parted the sea, an opening in the crowd appeared.

Daniel raced through the opening and found Lila lying on the ground, holding tightly to the hand of Abigail Cuthbert. "Move back!" he ordered to the crowd at large. "Give us room."

He dropped to his knees as he softly called her name. "What happened, love?" he asked hastily. "Where are you hurt?"

Lila smiled with acute embarrassment, more aware than Daniel of what he had just done. "I'm all right, Daniel," she assured him. "It's my own stupid—"

"Where?" he pressed.

"A horse kicked me," she said and placed her hand over her right thigh.

Daniel reached for the hem of her skirt, and several women in the crowd shared a mutual gasp, which he ignored.

"Perhaps you would like to move her to my store," Mrs. Cuthbert offered hurriedly. "There is a cot in the back room."

Daniel looked toward the kind woman and nodded briefly before slipping his hand beneath Lila's skirt and toward her thigh. He did his best to protect her from view of the others, but it wasn't good enough. The sight of a shapely ankle and a good portion of calf were enough to set nearby tongues to wagging.

"Really! In the middle of the street!"

"In front of all these men!"

And so it went.

Daniel ignored them and pressed gently upward along the length of Lila's thigh.

She closed her eyes, listening to the murmuring voices that surrounded her in a vain attempt to remove her mind from the pain he was causing. "I didn't feel anything for the longest time," Lee said softly, and in spite of all her efforts she moaned with pain.

"That's not unusual with an injury such as this," he said. And then his gaze turned from her thigh to her eyes. "I'm sorry, sweetheart, I know it's paining you now."

That endearment did not escape Beatrice Bundy, and she sucked in a shocked breath that turned instantly sour. How on earth, she wondered, could they be so flagrant about their relationship? How could Daniel Stone be so unfeeling? The cad. Poor Jenny. Still, as she continued to watch Daniel with Lila, Beatrice was not unmoved by his "bedside manner" and determined that she definitely was coming down with something dire.

Daniel did not believe the leg was broken, and after requesting that someone carry his bag, he eased Lila into his arms.

Before he could take even one step, Lila allowed her head to fall to his shoulder.

"You're going to be all right, Lee," he said softly.

Lila managed a smile and nodded her head. "I know. I have a very good doctor." She felt very tired suddenly, drained of all energies, but even through her exhaustion, it seemed to Lila that there was a great deal of chaos over the next few moments. Daniel settled her on a cot in the back room of the store and tried to make her comfortable while people pressed around them. Edmond had arrived with Sammy, who continued to cry, and Annie stood in a corner wailing, fit to wake the dead.

"Let Sammy and Annie come to me," she said to Daniel as he set his medical bag on a chair beside the bed. "Let them see that I'm all right."

Daniel agreed and gathered the two children close to his knees as he sat on the cot beside Lila's left hip.

"You must stop cryin' now," Lila said as she squeezed their small hands. "I just have a bruise on my leg, and Daniel is goin' to fix that right up." When they continued, she pulled lightly on their hands to gain their attention. "Listen to me now. Cryin' can be catchin', you know. Do you want me cryin', too?"

Two small, bowed heads wavered a bit, and Lila managed a laugh for their benefit. "You're a fine pair, you are."

Daniel watched her thoughtfully, admiring the way she could be with these little ones who were scared half to death. He had seen her this way with them often; all softness and love. And yet, she was nobody's fool. If the children got into mischief, Lila would set them back on the right path. And she disciplined with love, not anger or cruelty. Sammy and Annie were fortunate to have her. The *entire* Briggs family was fortunate to have her. It occurred to Daniel then and there that Lila should soon be having babies of her own. Very soon.

Lila noticed the intensity of Daniel's blue eyes as they remained on her and was puzzled by his expression. But then Mrs. Cuthbert stepped forward and smiled as she turned Sammy and Annie away. "I'll look out for them," she said. "We'll pick some candy, shall we?" she asked the little ones.

"I don't got a penny," Sammy sniffled.

"Oh, I don't think you'll need a penny today, dear," the woman said as they made their way into the store.

Edmond literally herded the remainder of the curious from the room and closed the door firmly. When he reached the side of the cot, Daniel had raised Lila's skirt and was examining Lila's thigh. "Badly bruised?" Edmond asked, catching a glimpse of the hoof-size injury.

Daniel nodded and smiled at his friend. "Bruised but not broken. I'll see to it, Edmond."

Edmond chuckled knowingly as he began to retreat. "I just bet you will, my boy," he said jovially.

"And, Edmond," Daniel hastened to add. "Thank you."

Edmond nodded and waved a hand before he, too, disappeared from the room.

Lila sighed. "Lordy!"

Daniel turned back to her and frowned. "What?"

"I hate all that attention."

She was a beautiful woman; she should *bask* in attention. But not this kind, he supposed. "Well, you are now reduced to receiving attention only from me."

He leaned across her lap, raising her skirt and petticoats higher and out of his way. "I've never understood why you women insist on wearing numerous petticoats under your skirts during the heat of summer. But all these layers of cloth have saved you from a greater injury, I suspect."

"You see, there is method to our madness," she quipped.

He raised his head and smiled, ceasing his gentle probing of the flesh of her thigh. "You've got a nasty one here, Lee," he said. "You won't be walking for a few days."

"I have to, Daniel, I—"

"No argument," he said as he pulled a brown bottle from

his bag. "This is a serious bruise and you'll have to keep off your feet." He stood, removed the cork from the bottle, and poured a generous amount of odious liquid into his cupped hand. "I'm going to massage this liniment into the bruise."

He leaned over her and began to kneed deeply into her thigh with both hands, using the added strength his standing position afforded him.

The ache was like nothing she had experienced before, and Lila closed her eyes against it. Still, she could not keep her nose from twitching within a few moments. "Lordy, Daniel. That stuff must be meant for horses."

"Horses love it," he teased, but there was no smile; he hated hurting her.

She groaned. "Are you sure? I bet if I'd uncorked that bottle out on the street, I wouldn't have been kicked. The smell would have"—she groaned again—"had that stallion racing for the hills."

"I'll give you a bottle to carry around," he returned seriously.

Lila opened her eyes then and watched him as he concentrated on his task. He was frowning and intent, and small beads of moisture had popped out on his brow. "You're not hurting me," she said quietly.

Daniel's gaze met hers then, if only briefly. "Liar," he whispered fondly.

His tone was intimate, and Lila felt a rush of pleasure as if he had touched her more as a lover than a doctor. It was confusing just to be near him lately, and Lila knew that the safest place for her to be was away from him. She hardly had that choice at the moment and chose conversation to ease her feelings of awkwardness. "I hope you'll enjoy the Summer Frolic," she said.

Daniel was lost in his own thoughts as he watched his

hands try to ease the deep bruise. "What?" he asked absent-ly.

"I understand you'll be escortin' one of Frankfort's finest young ladies."

That got his attention, and he looked at her. "I am?"

Lila nodded although she found she could barely speak around her sudden envy as she realized it would not be *she* dancing with him. "I'm certain Jenny will enjoy it."

Confused, Daniel lowered his buttocks to the cot while he reached for more liniment. "Who?"

"Jenny," she said pointedly.

Daniel's hands came to an abrupt halt above her thigh. "What the devil are you talking about?"

"I have it on the highest authority," she said, warming to the game of teasing him. "Beatrice Bundy was told by Dolly Patrick, and if Dolly says it's so, then it must be so."

"Are you sure you didn't hit your head when you fell?" he asked, feeling the first little knot of anger rise in his chest.

Lila shook her head. "Dolly told Beatrice that you were courtin' Jenny Wilder and—"

"What?!" he snapped.

Lila was relentless about this and did not stop to ask herself why. "And everyone, absolutely everyone is holdin' their breath just anticipatin' the moment when you escort Jenny to the Summer Frolic."

"For the love of God!" Daniel growled.

"Daniel, my leg feels better when you're rubbin' it." She studied his expression as he returned to massaging her leg, secretly enjoying the fact that he was angry about the news she had just provided. "Don't you have gossips in Boston?" she asked.

"Not that I'd personally ever run into," he growled. "Gossip always seemed to revolve around other people."

"Are you tellin' me you're not courtin' Jenny Wilder?"

"I don't even know who Jenny Wilder is," he snapped.

"Don't take it seriously, Daniel."

Daniel appeared to concentrate his complete attention where it was most needed but failed when his mind refused to give up the subject. "How do these damned rumors get started?" he asked shortly.

"It's probably wishful thinkin' on Jenny's part. Maybe it's wishful thinkin' on her mama's part, too," she added as she thought about it. Half the mothers of available daughters would probably die for a chance at making a match between their darling girls and Dr. Daniel Stone.

Daniel watched her eyelashes flutter and knew she had been fighting exhaustion for the past several moments. It was a post-shock symptom, and it didn't surprise him. "I won't be taking Jenny Wilder to any Summer Frolic," he said softly. He would have enjoyed escorting Lila Briggs to the dance, and he wondered how many were speculating about the possibility of that? Edmond had told him of the gossip and what was being said about them. And Daniel knew he should be sharing that information with Lila, but now was certainly not the time. She had enough to worry about, although he suspected she would scoff at wagging tongues just as she had told him to do.

Daniel recorked the liniment bottle and returned it to his bag. And as he looked again at the dark bruise that was as wide as his hand, he knew that escorting Lila Briggs to the Summer Frolic would be out of the question.

CHAPTER
9

THE LONG DAYS OF SUMMER PROVED TEDIOUS after a while, and Lila found it increasingly difficult to entertain the four children and keep them out of mischief. Particularly since her mobility had been drastically hampered by someone's frightened horse. Annie and Sammy were accustomed to playing together, and as long as Lila could hear them, they seldom got into any serious trouble. But Edward, once free of school, could influence the younger ones, and their playful pranks eventually grated on the nerves. Even the ten-year-old Beth could run wild when she set her mind to it, although the girl tended to be more subdued than the others.

 Lila often left chores waiting until evening during the summer months, finding it cooler to work after the sun had gone down. This change in her schedule also gave her an opportunity to occupy the children with picnics, adventures in the coolness of the forest beyond the town, and long, lazy swims in a gentle creek. They could do these things when her father was in a generous frame of mind and would allow Jon to hitch one of the horses to a rig, thereby allowing Lila to avoid long walks on her injured leg.

Late in the evening, when the youngest were all in their beds, when Jon and Tommy had wandered off somewhere and Jonathan was warming a chair at the saloon, Lila would find quiet time to sit on the porch and mindlessly watch the stars chase the moon.

Occasionally a horse and rider would pass by on the road heading into town, but these occurrences were few as the hours marched on. If she happened to recognize someone beyond the light of the lantern swinging gently from a hook in the porch roof, Lila would call out a greeting. Otherwise she remained silent and content with only the sound of the creaking runners of her rocker and the rasping of the crickets breaking the silence.

Lila became alert when the gentle *clip-clop* of a horse's hooves on the hard-packed earth stopped beyond the yard, intruding upon the peacefulness she cherished.

"It's a beautiful evening," the man said as he tied the reins to the fence.

It was Daniel.

"It's a good night for sittin' and rockin'," she said, searching his face as he moved into the circle of light.

"May I join you?" he asked, lowering himself to the other rocking chair before she could respond.

She could see the lines of weariness that outlined his eyes. "Would you like a cool drink?" she offered.

Daniel nodded his head. But when she would have stood, Daniel motioned her back into her chair. "I'll get it," he said.

"The pitcher is on the table."

While he was gone, Lila wondered at the shadows of weariness she had seen beneath his eyes; she supposed little June Rutledge was not better.

Daniel emerged from the house moments later with a cup in each hand.

"Thank you," she said, taking one of the drinks.

Daniel sank into the vacant rocker and smiled wearily in her direction. She was wearing the same faded yellow dress he had often seen, and her feet were bare. But the single braid was gone, and she had caught her hair loosely on top of her head, leaving her neck bared to the slightest breeze that could, perchance, pass her way. She looked cool, clean, comfortable, and entirely beautiful. Her complexion reminded him of rich cream, and he had an impulsive urge to direct his hand across the small distance between them and run his fingertips along her cheek. But he didn't.

"You've been out to the Rutledge place?" she asked.

He nodded tiredly.

"June is no better, Daniel?" she asked softly.

"I doubt she'll live to the end of the month," he said in a steely tone. He seemed to look around then, his gaze wandering over his shoulder to the darkened house. "I suppose the little ones are in bed?"

"Yes."

He had known they would be, but somehow he was disappointed that Sammy was not about to run out of the house hollering, "Hi, Doc!" "You know, I remember my third or fourth visit here. I walked into this house and found it full of noise and laughter. That was after Annie and Sammy had recovered from their illness." He grinned, sipping his lemonade before continuing. He sighed and allowed his head to drop back. "A house full of chatter," he said, recalling the scene. "And such chaos. It was all very startling. Almost overwhelming."

Lila interpreted his comments to mean he did not care for that kind of commotion. "I suppose if you're not used to the noise of children—"

"I'm an only child," he said, raising his head and smiling at her. "I always envied friends who had brothers and sisters."

"I guess an only child would think that way. I love my brothers and sisters, but sometimes it is difficult to find a moment's peace."

"And I've interrupted your private time."

"I'm glad for your company," she said with a soft smile.

"Are you?" He stared at her then, until, obviously uncomfortable, Lila hid behind the motions of drinking. "I suppose you rarely have time for yourself. You're always doing for them, aren't you?" he asked with a softness that echoed his admiration of her.

Something about his tone set her to feeling that he had wrongly placed his thoughts about her. "Children need caring for, Daniel," she said simply. "That's all I do."

"But they are not your children," he said. "You devote your entire life to this family when you should be out having fun. You should have beaux lined up at your door by now, Lila Briggs."

Lila had never had a beau, had never been courted. And she had certainly never had a frank, serious discussion with a member of the opposite sex. At least not in this fashion. She did not exactly know how to deal with these comments made by a man she respected as deeply as she respected Daniel. "There will be plenty of time for beaux," she said awkwardly.

"When? When Annie and Sammy have grown and are the last to establish families of their own? That could be twenty years, Lila. A good part of your life will have passed you by in that time."

Lila had not cared to think that far ahead and took exception to Daniel bringing these facts to her attention. "They are my family to care for and love," she said firmly.

"To the exclusion of all else?"

"That's *my* business, Daniel Stone."

Daniel paused a moment, realizing his intrusion into her life had placed her on the defensive. "I'm sorry," he said, scrubbing his face with both hands. "I have no right to judge."

"I do the best I can," she said unhappily as she tore her gaze away from him.

"And you do it well," he returned kindly. "I'm sorry if I've made you angry."

Lila felt the warmth of a large hand cover her own, and she looked down to where their two hands lay on the arm of her chair. "The little ones need me."

They also needed their father, but Daniel was under the impression that Jonathan Briggs had little time for his family. "Well," he said, backing off the topic. "I didn't come here just to invade upon your quiet time." He'd come here for several reasons, the primary one being he just needed to be with her. A small girl was going to die, and Daniel felt helpless and frustrated. And only Lila's own brand of wisdom and softness made him feel better when he was troubled. He set his drink on the table between them and rose, fetching the lantern from the hook above their heads. He turned to Lila and held the thing out to her. "Hold this, please," he said, and when she took it, he dropped to his heels, reaching for the hem of her dress.

"Daniel!" she scolded softly as she attempted to push the hem back into place.

He looked up at her then. "I want to look at that bruise," he said in a firm tone.

"Well, not here, for heaven's sake." She peered beyond the lantern light, into the darkness.

"There's no one out there," he said and laughed softly. "Women are so damned anxious about a little honest flesh."

"I don't like bein' on display," she said hotly.

Daniel won the tug of war and raised her skirt. "If there were someone out there, Lee, they couldn't see a thing," he assured.

"They'd see you kneelin' at my feet," she pointed out.

He chuckled and probed her thigh with his fingertips. "Perhaps they'll think I'm proposing."

Lila scoffed at the likeliness of that. "That's a farfetched thought."

Daniel smoothed her skirt and stood. "Is it?" he asked softly before moving away to return the lantern to its place.

Lila's mind shut down and her mouth opened; she could find no retort.

Daniel noticed a tall, slender box on the table and, seeking a diversion, reached for it. "What's this?"

Lila watched him look inside and sighed, trying to rid herself of the weightiness of his previous comment. "Pickup sticks," she said simply.

"Really?" Daniel turned the box, and a handful of thin sticks fell into his palm.

"Jon made them for Annie."

Daniel raised his eyes to hers and grinned before dropping to his knees.

Startled by this abrupt change, in addition to the fact that he would want to partake of a child's game, Lila could only stare at him.

"I haven't seen these in years." He tipped the box and

allowed the sticks to fall in a heap on the porch floor-boards.

Lila frowned down at him. "You've been drinking, haven't you?"

Daniel shook his head and picked up the sticks that were unencumbered by others, on the outer edge of the pile. "Not a drop," he said quietly.

"It's been a long time since I've seen a grown man play children's games." And in her mind's eye she could not dispel the very *adult* manner in which he had looked at her when he questioned, "Is it?"

Daniel grinned up at her briefly, his hand suspended over a delicately balanced stick. "It has occurred to me that children's games are refreshing."

"Refreshing," she muttered, worried that he had been working too hard. But she watched his progress and marveled at the steadiness of his hand as he removed one stick after another without nudging the sticks below or to the sides. "You think you're very clever, don't you?" she said lightly as she felt herself regain control over the anxiety he had caused.

"I'm not so old that my hands shake," he returned, concentrating on the task at hand.

"I think you have wonderful hands," she blurted.

Daniel's head popped up, and he ruined his record as several sticks turned.

"You're out," she said cheerfully.

"What?"

Lila's laughing brown eyes moved downward. "You moved a lot of sticks, Daniel."

He looked downward, frowning when he looked at her again.

"That was a trick," he accused.

"What was a trick?" she asked innocently.

"The comment about my hands."

"No, it wasn't. I've watched you with sick people, with Annie and Sammy. And I've felt your touch. You have very gentle hands."

She had become uncomfortable with the topic as she was speaking and had turned away from the probing look in his eyes. Now Daniel sat back on his heels, watching her carefully. She had been watching his hands, had she? He wondered what else she had been watching. *If* she had been watching. He had thought about her a lot lately; ever since she had "tidied" his filing system, ever since he had talked with her about June, ever since Edmond had told him of the gossip that linked them, possibly, ever since he had *met* her. He just found himself wanting to be with her. Like so many others who depended on her, Daniel needed the gentleness of her. He gave in to his need and raised up on his knees, reaching out to gently cup her cheek within the palm of his hand. "My hands can be gentle with you in other ways," he whispered.

Lila's gaze collided with his. "For what purpose, Daniel?" she asked unsteadily. She was startled and afraid again.

"Just to touch," he said, searching her eyes for some indication of what she might be feeling. "To please." And, he thought, to awaken the woman in you.

Lila forced herself to look at the box of sticks. "You're tired and overworked," she said hastily, wanting nothing more than to have him remove his hand.

Daniel let his hand fall away. "I've made you uncomfortable."

"Not at all," she lied. He was too close. Too close! And not only in a physical sense.

Daniel took note that she refused to look at him. "Why would a simple touch bother you so?"

"We were playin' a game," she said lamely, "and then . . . and then, suddenly . . ."

Daniel was literally at her feet, smiling up at her with understanding. "Suddenly something changed?" he asked, not really expecting an answer. "Did you like it? My touching you like that?"

Lila concentrated on pressing an imaginary pleat in her skirt between her fingers. "It was just a friendly touch," she said.

"*That* good," he said ruefully, getting to his feet. "I had better go and let you get to bed." But he turned back briefly before stepping from the porch. "You just weren't ready, Lee. Think about it, will you?"

Frowning, perplexed, Lila stared after him until he had ridden out of sight. *Think about what*?

A few days later, long after the Briggs family had gone to bed, Lila heard a strange noise coming from outside the house.

She walked cautiously through the darkness to the front door and paused, listening. When she identified the squeak and groan of one of the ancient rocking chairs, she dared to open the door a crack.

"Who's there?" she asked quietly.

There was a long silence in which the dark shadow seated in the chair refused to speak.

She dared to go a single step beyond the door, straining to see in the darkness. "Daniel?" she whispered in disbelief.

"Before the end of the month, I'd said. And I was right," he explained in a strangled whisper. "Damn!" he thumped his thigh with a fist. "I wish I had not been *right*!"

June! She realized instantly what had happened.

Without a second thought Lila rushed across the wooden porch and wrapped her arms around him, pulling his head against her waist. "Oh, Daniel."

"I lost her," he agonized, tightening his arms around her.

"I'm so sorry."

He clung to her, feeling as close to tears as he had ever felt in his adult lifetime. He had come to Lila because he needed her; needed her special kind of warmth and the caring affection she so liberally granted to all within her small world. It was always at the times of his greatest failures that Daniel felt the most lonely, the most lost, and he had known that only Lila could ease his pain.

Penelope had never been able to do that. Despite the love he had felt for her, he had known all along that she had little to share with others; her concern had always been reserved for herself. He had understood that back then; that she had been pampered and spoiled by older, doting parents of wealth and influence. He had understood and thought that he could perhaps pamper her, too, and that they could be happy if he did. And Pen had been the type of delicate little creature that men would just naturally want to pamper. Daniel had been no exception.

But he had not seen the cold side of Penelope until he had gone to her one evening in despair. An evening much like this one. *That* evening he had watched his own mother die and had been powerless to help her. *That* evening Penelope had coldly informed him that he had best get used to death because death went hand-in-hand with his profession. Directly after his mother's funeral, he told Penelope goodbye. Within one month he had responded to Edmond's advertisement for an associate. Within two he was packed and leaving Boston.

Daniel turned his face into the warm spot between Lila's breasts, drawing from her. "I will never, ever accept death," he said harshly.

Lila's long, slender fingers combed through his wavy hair. "You wouldn't be the fine doctor you are, Daniel, if you felt differently. But, Daniel, you have to remember that June was never really yours to lose. God had already planned for her long before you ever came here. You can't expect to change Fate, no matter how fine a doctor you are. You must grieve, but you must not blame yourself."

She was so strong in her beliefs, so gentle in her caring, that he found himself almost overwhelmed by her. She was soft and warm and *alive*. And he needed to know that life existed in this, its purest form.

He moved from her, pulling her down onto his lap and staring into her startled eyes as he tipped her back against his arm. He said not one word to her as he continued to stare, and then his head slowly descended, his face moving ever more closely to hers.

Lila understood what he was about to do and would not deny him. She wanted this, too. And yet, she did not want it. She had wanted him to kiss her for a very long time now. And yet, she had been afraid that he would. Afraid that a kiss, just one simple kiss, would lead to complications she could not deal with in her life.

"I'm going to kiss you," he announced softly.

"Yes. I know," she whispered.

"You won't be afraid?"

"Not of a *kiss*," she said truthfully.

He seemed to take note then that her hair was free and flowing, and he buried his fingers in the strands of silk as he continued to look at her. "And you won't be afraid of me, will you?"

"I've never been afraid of you, Daniel." But all that could change, she realized, if he wound himself too securely around her heart.

He lowered his head then, and she felt a pleasurable

warmth and shock so unexpected that she abruptly drew her head back.

"Why did you pull away?" he whispered, lightly caressing her cheek.

"I didn't think your mouth would be so warm and soft."

He smiled and traced her lips with a fingertip. "Isn't your mouth warm and soft?"

"But I'm a girl," she returned bluntly.

He laughed briefly, continuing to caress her. "You're a *woman*, Lee, whether you want to think that way about yourself or not." His head lowered then, and his lips slanted across hers.

The kiss that was meant to be a gentle exploration quickly became more likened to demanding need. Daniel's tongue urged her lips apart and, as he explored her, his hand moved to cup her ample breast. He gently kneaded the firm flesh that was protected from him only by her thin cotton nightdress.

Lila detected the growing harshness of his breathing, and while his touch was pleasurable, the pleasure was also very frightening. And it was wrong, what they were doing. She admitted that even as his caresses became more bold and the sense of urgency in his movements made her fear that he would not control this thing that was happening between them. She was disappointed to realize that he expected from her what she could not give; not here, not now, probably not ever.

"Daniel," she said as she tore her lips from his and pushed at his shoulder.

Daniel's lips found the soft spot beneath her ear and lingered.

"Daniel. No," she said quietly but firmly.

He breathed in the night air, aware that he had frightened

her when he had promised himself he would not; when she had promised that she would not be. "Lila, don't be frightened," he whispered, resting his cheek alongside of hers. "Don't move for a moment, darling, please," he begged on a ragged breath. "I . . . won't. I promise. I won't frighten you anymore . . . please."

"I thought you were only going to kiss me," she said, as if she were accusing him of stealing her virtue.

Daniel smiled ruefully. "I thought so, too," he said.

"You wouldn't have stopped."

He heard her hurt and disappointment and moved his head back until he could look into her eyes. "I would have stopped, Lee, I swear. I might have touched you . . . I needed you, you see. But I would not dishonor you. You have to understand."

"I don't understand, Daniel. That's the point."

He straightened in the chair then, raising her to a sitting position. "I think you'd best move to the other chair," he said, sighing as he combed unsteady fingers through his hair.

Lila moved to the other rocking chair and gripped the wooden arms tightly. "You didn't want me honestly."

Daniel closed his eyes briefly and laughed. "Oh, didn't I?"

And what if he had? What would she do about that? Lordy! What could she be thinking to ever say such a thing to him? "Well, you came here for other reasons," she ventured, hoping for a change of topics.

"I came here for a number of reasons, Lila. The fact that I wanted you just now had a lot to do with some of them."

To actually hear him put into words what had just happened caused her to swallow heavily.

"I'm sorry if I've hurt you," he said sincerely. "Some-

times a man's need . . . well, it just gets the better of him.
It can override his good sense at times."

"I always credited you with havin' better than average
good sense, Daniel," she said tightly. She now realized that
he had bounded out of control because of her; she could no
longer deny it. And, on the heels of her acknowledgment,
Lila realized she had a problem.

But Daniel was completely oblivious to the pattern of her
thoughts. He smiled at her comment, but he was chagrined
by his own foolishness. "My libido got the better of me."

"Pardon?"

"Never mind."

"Maybe you should go and visit Miss Flora," she muttered, hoping he would agree, thereby giving her cause to
see the situation differently.

"What?"

"You heard me."

"I heard but I don't believe it," he said with a short
laugh. "Lila, what happened here between us tonight was
about—"

"You needin' a woman," she said flatly. "I'm not stupid,
Daniel."

"Of course you're not," he hurried to say. "Lee, I care
about you—"

"Course you do," she interrupted again because she did
not want to hear any more. "We're friends, aren't we? I
think you should go now, Daniel."

"Not like this," he said, reaching for her hand. "Let's talk
about this. Please."

Lila eased her hand out of his grip and stood to go. "I've
about done all the talkin' I can manage today, Daniel," she
said miserably. "I'm sorry."

After entering the quiet house, Lila heard the solid thud
of a fist connecting with some portion of the wooden porch.

"Daniel," she whispered to the night. One thing was certain, she could not allow this to go on. It would not be fair to either of them, because a happy ending was just not possible. Obviously Daniel's blood was running hot, but *she* was not about to be the one to cool it. And it was becoming increasingly difficult to turn away from him.

She entered the room where her two sisters slept and listened to their soft deep breathing for a moment before moving toward her own bed.

There could be no future in continuing to enjoy his company when she knew she was falling deeply in love. She was hurting already, and yet, it would be suicide to continue. Suicide, because it would be unfair to expect anything of Daniel for any of a number of reasons.

She had only to count the number of heads that resided under her father's roof.

In the dead of night, in a town where all slept but a few, Jonathan Briggs stumbled drunkenly from the smithy and watched Daniel Stone ride away from his house.

CHAPTER
10

 THE FOLLOWING MORNING LILA SLAMMED HER way around the kitchen. It was fair warning to everyone that all was not right with the world and they should remove themselves from *hers*. At least for a time.

Life was not fun anymore, she had decided. Daniel Stone had complicated her life, just as she had feared. And with one single kiss! Well, perhaps it had taken more than a kiss. She had known him for quite some time now, and she was angry that she had allowed herself to fall into this quagmire of confusion. She was attracted to a man a cut above. That should be problem enough. But Lila knew she had the forti- tude to overcome the insignificant differences of their educations and their rearing; she had a few talents of her own. The one thing she could not over- come was responsibility. Plural. A family of large number who had no one else except for her. How in the world could she ever expect a man to share the responsibilities of five children? Six, if Jon did not soon strike out on his own; he could demand a lot of caring for in his moments.

She had silently talked to herself half the night and most of the morning. It was impossible. She could never impose her family on a man. And because she had to reluctantly admit she harbored some very deep feelings for Daniel, she had decided the safest thing to do would be to distance herself from him. The more she saw of him, the more her fondness would grow. She knew that instinctively. And in view of that scene on the porch last night, she would never again risk being alone with him. Having come to that conclusion, she had decided she would no longer go to his home. She would not risk having only Annie and Sammy as chaperones. She would return his key to him this very morning.

"What in God's name is all the racket out here?" Jonathan rumbled as he slumped against his bedroom door. He was a big man, almost filling the doorframe. And he looked particularly bad this morning. His dark brown hair had been left in precisely the way his pillows had arranged it, and his beard was dark and heavy with several days' stubble. His shirt had been buttoned but hadn't made it inside the waist of his trousers as yet.

Lila had the grace to be embarrassed by her behavior and gently set a pot on the stove before she turned to face him. "Sorry, Papa."

"Get me some coffee," he ordered and made his way to his place at the table.

Lila reluctantly poured coffee into a mug; in spite of being saddened by her father's unhappiness, she disliked being ordered about in that manner. Walking to his side, she thumped the mug down, sloshing some of the hot brew over the table.

"Dammit!" Jonathan spit. "What's got into you?" And then he remembered a dark shadow moving off his porch and a man riding away in the dead of night. He remembered, too, that he had planned to talk to this girl about a few facts of life. "Sit!"

Lila *stood*, crossing her arms under her bosom.

"I told you to do something, girl."

"You should *ask* me, Papa," she said quietly.

"Don't play games with me this mornin', Lila," he said wearily.

She could see it was not a morning to teach him his manners.

Lila sat.

Jonathan cautiously raised the cup of black coffee with a hand that shook because of years of drink. His eyelids fluttered as the steam rose at him, but he sipped and sipped again before lowering the mug to the table.

Meanwhile, Lila waited patiently, wondering what could be on his mind this morning. It was unusual for her father to have a clear thought so early in the day.

"I want to know what that man was doin' on my front porch last night."

Of all the subjects he could have raised, this was not one she would have guessed at. "What man, Papa?"

"Don't talk to me as if I'm a half-wit, daughter. Daniel Stone!"

Lila started, her spine stiffening as her eyes grew large and round in surprise. "Papa, I—"

"Tell me you didn't have him in this house in the wee hours of the morning?" he asked.

His tone caused Lila's heart to leap to somewhere within the region of her throat. "He was not in the house," she returned cautiously. "He was out on the porch."

"Why would a man come callin' in the middle of the night, Lila?"

"Well, he didn't exactly come callin'," she answered, growing more uneasy with the conversation.

"Then why was he here? Was somebody sick?"

"No."

"Then he came to see you? What would you call that?"

Lila dared to look at the bloodshot eyes that had narrowed and were accusing. "We're friends, Papa. Nothing more. He needed to talk."

"Talk!" Jonathan thundered, rolling back in his chair with a caustic laugh. "My God, Lila. I thought we'd raised you to be wise to the ways of men."

We? She had hardly been old enough to learn that kind of thing before her mother had died, and Jonathan was not much of a talker.

"Lila," he said unhappily as he gripped his cup, "you're goin' to find yourself in a whole heap of trouble if you two don't leave off."

"Papa! He's a doctor!" she cried stupidly.

"And what's that got to do with anything?" he asked, his dark eyes staring directly into hers. "Don't you understand he's got the same thing in his trousers as any other man and he's sure to know how to use it?"

Angered now by this unfair attack, Lila jumped to her feet. "We haven't done anything! *He* hasn't done any-thing!"

"The more time you spend with him, girl, the harder it's goin' to be *not* to do something. You're not stupid, Lila. You must see that. And if you keep on, without thinkin' about how things appear, you'll have the whole town talkin'."

Lila returned to the bench and placed her hand over his.

"You raised me right, Papa," she said quietly. "I'm a good girl, I swear. I haven't done anything wrong, and I've already decided I won't be seein' Daniel anymore, friend or not. I know nothin' can come of it."

Yes, Jonathan thought, but did Daniel Stone have the same understanding?

Mae Belle Willoughby and her husband were seated in the small waiting room in the offices of Doctors Fraser and Stone when Jonathan Briggs raced past, acknowledging none of his friends or acquaintances.

"Well!" Mae Belle gasped. "Not so much as a how'do."

Mr. Willoughby bellowed, "*Do* what?!"

Jonathan wasn't familiar with the layout of the doctors' offices and invaded Dr. Fraser's sanctuary in error, startling Miss Geraldine Gordon who was caught in a near compromising position.

Edmond had been listening to Geraldine's wheezy chest but straightened away from the woman, glaring at the intruder. "Jonathan Briggs!"

Miss Geraldine fainted in her chair as Jonathan backed from the room.

Edmond cursed as he grasped the woman under the arms to prevent her from sliding to the floor.

Jonathan turned to the only remaining door in the small corridor and sidestepped a small woman who inched by him, staring up at him warily. In the next instant he stood face to face with Daniel Stone.

Daniel had heard Edmond's bellow of rage and had risen from behind his desk to investigate just as his patient was leaving. "Mr. Briggs?" he questioned, frowning at the older man. "Could I help you?"

Jonathan knew he could trust his daughter, but this man was more worldly, and Jonathan's concern, and his hangover, overrode his good sense. "I want to know what you thought you were doin' on my front porch in the middle of the night?"

Daniel blinked, his eyes darting to the waiting patients who were clearly within earshot. Jonathan Briggs had just provided the gossips with enough tidbits to keep them busy for a week. Now Daniel knew he and Lila had some serious problems to overcome. "For God's sake, man," he said quietly, reaching out for Jonathan's elbow. "Come in here."

Jonathan needed no second invitation.

Daniel closed the door, shutting out unwanted ears, and turned to face the man who was possibly only ten years his senior and looked a hundred more.

"I came here because of my Lila," Jonathan said.

"Yes, sir, I assumed that."

"Doctor or no," Jonathan said firmly, "I want to know your intentions toward her. I won't have you ruinin' Lila's good name."

Daniel thought Jonathan might have achieved *that* all on his own. He stood tall, facing the man squarely and proudly as he said, "I assure you, Mr. Briggs, my intentions toward Lila are honorable."

Jonathan was too intent on speaking his mind to catch Daniel's point. "She's a simple girl, my Lila. Not likely to know how to handle a man like yourself and . . ." Some outside influence seemed to pull Jonathan up short then. "What did you say?" he asked quietly.

Daniel smiled and motioned Jonathan to a chair, while he rested his buttocks on the edge of his desk. "Mr. Briggs, my intentions are honorable, I promise you. I've had it in mind to request your permission to court Lila."

"You have?" Jonathan muttered, looking frantically around the room; he thought he *really* might need a drink to get through this conversation. "But you haven't," he noted.

Daniel crossed his arms over his chest, and his smile turned rueful. "Lila doesn't seem to understand the depth of my affection for her. And I'm not certain, at this point, just what she feels for me."

A *doctor!* In love with his Lila? Jonathan could hardly credit it. "Why don't you just come right out and ask her?" he suggested.

Bad idea, Daniel thought. "I don't know that she's ready, Mr. Briggs. And there's a matter that Lee has yet to learn about," he said, not quite as confident as he appeared. "I'm not certain how she's going to react and . . . well . . ."

Jonathan's eyes narrowed suspiciously; when a man hesitates like the Doc just did, it's a sure sign of trouble. "What's this *matter* you're talkin' about?"

Daniel looked directly into the older man's eyes. "You're aware that Lila has been helping me care for my home?"

Jonathan nodded.

"I've always made it a practice not to be there on the days that she comes," he said frankly. "Several days ago, however, I had been tending a sick child all night, and I was still sleeping when Lila arrived. The gossips have gotten hold of the fact that we were there together."

Jonathan failed to react, and Daniel began to seriously wonder about the man's intentions to protect his daughter's good name.

But Jonathan had reached another conclusion. "Well, Sammy and Annie were with her, weren't they?"

Daniel nodded. "The children were seen playing outside, and much is being made of the fact that Lila was nowhere to be seen at that particular moment."

"Judas!" Jonathan hissed and got to his feet. He paced away and then rounded on the doctor. "Was this *before* Lila's accident?"

"Yes."

"That's why they're goin' on about you havin' your hand up her skirts," he muttered.

Daniel shook his head, dismayed by this news of additional chatter and amazed that he, after all these years of tending the sick, could actually be flustered over a frank comment made by the father of one of his patients. Things like this had never happened to him in Boston, and he'd had affairs with a few fathers' daughters over the years. The irony of *this* situation was that he had barely touched Lila, and they were both apparently being verbally crucified.

"I thought *that* was just the talk of a bunch of prudish old hens," Jonathan continued. He returned to his chair then as a moment of doubt overtook him. With narrowed eyes he looked up at Daniel. "Lila tells me she's been a good girl, and I'm apt to believe her," Jonathan said quietly. "Can you look me straight in the eye and tell me the same thing?"

What? That he had been a good *boy*? "I can," Daniel replied without hesitation. "I will not dishonor her, Mr. Briggs."

Jonathan scrubbed at his beard thoughtfully. "Looks like that's been taken out of your hands, Doc."

Daniel nodded unhappily and rounded his desk, knowing that, thoughtlessly, Jonathan had complicated the issue the moment he had entered this building. Once he was seated, he presented his thoughts on *that* matter. "If I were to have your permission to court Lila openly, I would hope we could do away with most of this talk."

Jonathan could honestly say he had no problem with one of his girls catching herself a doctor. "You have it," he said frankly. "Sounds as if you might have a bit of a problem convincin' my offspring, though."

Daniel did not think so. Not really. He sensed that Lila had feelings for him but had been unprepared, until now, to consider a serious relationship with anyone. Not surprising, he'd told himself a dozen times in the past few weeks; she was far too wrapped up in her family to give much thought to herself. "I have hopes of convincing her, Mr. Briggs," he said simply.

Jonathan seemed on the verge of wanting to say more, but hesitated.

"Is there something else?" Daniel asked.

The older man shifted uneasily in his chair and scrubbed at his beard uneasily. "It's known hereabouts that I ain't been much of a father these past years," he said. "And I ain't denyin' that. Lila just naturally took things over after my Sarah died, and . . . well . . . I guess I just let her. But I'm warnin' you, Doc, she's fierce about those kids. You'll not be takin' her away from them, so don't even think about it or you'll not convince Lila of anythin'."

Daniel could see that it had taken courage for Jonathan to admit his failure as a father, and he was forced to admire him for having done so. He also felt great sorrow over the man who appeared determined to drink himself to death. "I know how much Lila loves her family, Mr. Briggs, and I have never given a thought to taking her away. You see," he added with a smile, "I've also become quite fond of the children."

That was that and Jonathan felt his job was done. "I'll leave you to it, then," he said as he stood to leave. "I'll not be sayin' a word to my girl, and I'm trustin' you to do right by her, Doc. If you cause her any grief, I'll be back for a different sort of a talk with you."

Daniel met the man at the door and shook his hand. "Is there something I can do for you, Mr. Briggs?" he asked sincerely.

He was referring to Jonathan's drinking, and they both understood that, but Jonathan merely shook his head. "Trust me, Doc. There's nothin'."

Sadly Daniel let him go.

Edmond had managed to revive Miss Geraldine and allowed her time to rest in his office while he went to investigate the meaning behind Jonathan's intrusion. As he stepped into the hall, however, he encountered Mae Belle Willoughby pressing herself against the wall as Jonathan Briggs walked past her in order to exit the building.

Edmond frowned, knowing damned well why she had been standing in that corridor.

Mae Belle knew that Edmond knew.

But eavesdropping was not a trait she acknowledged as wicked in herself, and therefore having been caught caused her little grief. "I think my Mr. Willoughby might be next," she told Edmond.

"Your Mr. Willoughby will have to wait a moment more, Mae Belle," he said firmly and turned to enter Daniel's office as soon as the woman walked toward the other room.

Edmond found Daniel standing behind his desk, staring thoughtfully out the window.

"I hope Jonathan's visit wasn't about what I'm thinking it was about," Edmond said quietly.

Daniel looked over his shoulder and smiled ruefully. "I have his permission to court his daughter," he said. "Is that what you were thinking about?"

"Frankly, no," he admitted. Edmond was clearly amazed by this bit of news.

"Well, there was some discussion about my talking with Lila on her front porch last night. And further discussion about the less than appropriate hour. And a few other things."

"Daniel," Edmond groaned as he lowered himself into a chair. "With Mae Belle Willoughby in this office, the whole town will be jumping to conclusions before the afternoon is out."

"It's just something more for people to talk about," he said quietly, turning his back to the window. "I have to tell Lee about what's going on. And soon. Before she hears it from someone else."

"Daniel, have you compromised the girl?" Edmond asked, staring severely at the younger man.

Daniel was very disappointed in his friend for having felt the need to ask, but he replied reasonably. "Only in the minds of the gossips, Edmond."

Edmond sighed, whether with relief or concern, Daniel was not certain.

"Jonathan hasn't helped matters today, that's for certain," Edmond said.

"His intentions were honorable," Daniel said ruefully. "That's why he was here . . . to see if *mine* were."

"Why on earth would you be sitting on the Briggses' front porch at a 'less than appropriate' hour?"

"I'd lost the little Rutledge girl, and . . . I needed to talk."

"Why didn't you come and talk to *me*?" Edmond asked harshly.

Daniel grinned. "You're not as pretty as Lila," he said lightly.

Exasperated, Edmond took a deep breath. "Daniel, I am genuinely concerned about this mess. This isn't Boston, and people here have very long memories."

Daniel shrugged, although he silently admitted he was concerned for Lila's sake; he didn't want her hurt. "Now that I have Jonathan's permission to court her openly, people will come to understand that this is merely a case of two people getting to know each other. There is nothing dishonorable in that."

Perhaps not in Boston, Edmond thought.

But this was not Boston.

CHAPTER
11

 AT THE SAME TIME JONATHAN BRIGGS was talking with Daniel Stone, fourteen-year-old Tommy Briggs walked across town to buy his sister some sugar for baking. He came home with a swollen eye that turned as black as strong-brewed coffee in less than an hour.

 He would not say with whom he had fought nor why.

Only Lila was not aware that her brother had tried to defend her honor.

She figured it out, though.

And all it took was a walk to the store the fol- lowing day; the day *after* the Summer Frolic. It was the first day Lila had felt her leg would support her without difficulty during the long walk across town.

She was not aware, however, that Daniel's failure to escort Jenny Wilder to the Summer Frolic was about to complicate life. When the partygoers had not been dancing, they had been talking, and most people ended the evening thoroughly convinced that the link between Lila's and Daniel's names must be warranted.

"Why is everybody starin' at us, Lee?" Annie whispered as they made their way along the boardwalk.

"I don't know, darlin'." But she did not like the looks they were getting. The people in this town knew them; spoke with Lila and the children on a regular basis. It took a bit of time, but Lila realized the stares were of disapproval.

When they entered the store, she could hear the tittering of female voices as two women she knew pretended to be examining bolts of cloth. She was confused about *how* she could have earned this apparent condemnation, but it was obvious that she had.

Lila suddenly wanted to groan aloud as she saw Beatrice Bundy bearing down on her from the back of the store. She was a woman on a mission, that much was clear. Why, the silly black feather in her hat was all a-quiver. "Probably because Bea is all a-quiver," Lila muttered softly and with more than a little trepidation. "She must really have her teeth into a good morsel." But, determined to put on a brave front, Lila smiled and said, "Hello, Bea."

Beatrice wasted little time on preliminaries. Frowning dramatically, she whispered loudly, "Oh, Lila, I am absolutely devastated for you. How embarrassed you must be over this utter nonsense."

Lila's smile melted into a frown of confusion. "My leg is much better, Beatrice, thank you," she said wryly. Lila did not know why she had said that, she'd just *said* it. Now she waited, knowing whatever Bea had to say would come gushing out; Beatrice loved to *gush*.

"I mean, your father must have been beside himself yesterday"—with drink, Beatrice suspected—"to have publicly
come to your defense and seemingly *accuse* Daniel Stone
of impropriety the way he did."

Her father?

"Mae Belle Willoughby said she couldn't help but hear
your Papa demandin' to know why Dr. Stone had been
visitin' you in the night."

Lila turned stone-faced rather than give away her dismay
as one horror after another flooded her thoughts.

"Well, of course, I know it's all nonsense," Beatrice went
on. "Whatever would a man like Daniel Stone have to do
with you? He's not going to land on your front porch in the
middle of the night. Unless one of those numerous siblings
of yours was sick? And that's how I explained the matter
to Mae Belle," she added cheerily.

Lila thought that was bloody *good* of Bea. She also
thought she might be the one to be sick. And soon.

Beatrice laughed lightly and brushed at a stray curl that
had peeked out from beneath the rim of her bonnet. "It's
absolutely ludicrous for anyone to think that a man like
Dr. Stone would . . . with you . . . well . . ." She hesitated
meaningfully. There was only one reason why any man
would visit a girl like Lila, as far as Beatrice was concerned.
"We've been friends for just ages, Lila, and I know you
have a good head. You would never dare to set your sights
as high as Daniel."

Daniel? Not "Dr. Stone"? But the woman's last remark
forced an unwilling break in Lila's silence. "You'd be
amazed at how high my *sights* might go, Bea," she said
softly.

Startled by this revelation, Beatrice blinked. "Oh! You
mean you did?"

Sighing wearily, Lila glared at her. "Did what?"

"Go after Daniel?"

A slow smile graced Lila's lips as she half turned, retrieving her parcels from the counter. "Has it occurred to you, Bea, that I don't have to *go* after any man?" Leaving Beatrice Bundy staring in stunned, confused silence, Lila turned, hurrying the children before her, and left the shop.

Once they were out of sight, Lila chastised herself and muttered, "Well, you just thickened the soup, Lila my girl."

"Can we have a penny, Lee?" Sammy asked.

"No," she said shortly as she took his hand and all but dragged the boy toward home.

"But you said we could have a candy," he whined.

"Not today, Sammy."

Lila left the younger children outside to play while she went in search of Tommy. She found him on the back porch, pitching stones to pass the time.

Sitting beside him on the top step, Lila hugged her knees to her chest and said quietly, "I thought you were going to help Papa today."

"I got tired of workin'," he said miserably.

"Oh, you did?" she returned with a short laugh. After a moment of silence, Lila had her thoughts in order. "Tommy, how did you get that shiner?"

Tommy choked on something she supposed should have been a laugh. "Dumb question, Lee," he said scornfully. "I walked into a mule."

"The two-legged kind, Tommy?" she asked quietly.

"Yeah," he said unwillingly. He didn't want to talk about this. Not with Lila.

"What was that mule sayin' to make you fight?"

Tommy looked off toward the smithy, once again toying with the idea of taking a round-fisted swing at his own father. The whole town knew of Jonathan's visit to Daniel

Stone. And it seemed there were other things that were causing people to point fingers.

"Tell me, Tommy. Please," she pleaded.

"I think you know. You should."

"Should I?" she asked miserably. "Does that mean you believe whatever they're sayin'?"

Tommy's head snapped around. "God, no, Lee! Why do you think I took this shiner? And you should see . . . the mule," he added earnestly.

Lila smiled sadly and placed her hand on his forearm. "I'm sorry you had to fight for me. But I thank you."

"Welcome."

"I need to know," she said, gently squeezing his arm.

With a deep sigh Tommy hung his head. "They say you're fornicatin' with Doc Stone."

The silence that followed those softly spoken words was painful for them both.

Lila fought back the tears that threatened to overwhelm her and slowly got to her feet. "Thank you, Tommy," she whispered.

Lila knew that people would think what they liked, regardless of guilt or innocence, and she, therefore, became determined to hold her head high and live her life as she had always done. She was a good Christian woman. She worked hard and had a care for others. If the folks in Frankfort chose to think otherwise, then hang them. She wasn't about to hibernate.

Lila had one dilemma, however. She had yet to return the key to Daniel's house as she had decided days ago. Now, if she returned it and stopped going to his home, she thought she might look all the more guilty. After all, she had never made secret of the fact that she had been cleaning Dr. Stone's residence once a week. It had seemed so very innocent at the time. Why, with one exception, Daniel had never been in the house when she was there. And yet, prudence dictated that she should never set foot in that house again.

Later that day Sammy was on his knees on a high stool, committed to the weighty decisions that went into selecting a penny's worth of candy from the wide selection facing him in glass jars. Lila was intent upon her own selection and was sorting through a bin of potatoes.

When Daniel entered the general store, it was Sammy who caught his eye first. Walking to the boy's side, he rested his elbows on the countertop and studied the row of jars. "Tough decision, huh?" he asked.

Sammy's head turned and his eyes lit up. "Hi, Doc!"

At the far end of the counter Lila heard, closed her eyes, and moaned silently before resuming her search for flawless potatoes. Not here! she moaned silently. She had planned to go to his house that evening, under cover of darkness, to talk with him. But she was not prepared to talk here in a public shop.

When Daniel turned his head to smile at Sammy, he noticed Lila bent over a bin. "I'm going to go talk with your sister," he told the boy.

Lila knew he was walking her way, and her heart began to pound so strongly she could feel the painful pulses all the way to her temples.

"Hello, Lila," Daniel said quietly.

She looked up with a smile that, from all outward appearances, was as genuine as the sun in a blue sky. "Daniel." Lordy, he was standing there, hat in hand!

"I've been wondering if I might invite myself to supper one evening soon," he asked boldly.

That brought her to an upright position. "Supper!" she croaked. There was talk about them all over town, and he wanted to come to supper? Her father would just as likely greet Daniel at the door with a scatter gun.

Daniel leaned against the counter and, in a low voice, informed her, "We need to talk."

Lila turned her attention back to the potatoes. "Talkin' has already got us into a pretty nice fix," she returned.

Daniel reached down and briefly touched her forearm. "We need to talk about making it right."

Lila straightened then and, with a weary sigh, faced him squarely. "We *need* to talk, Daniel, that's true. But not here."

"Meet me, then," he whispered. "Where?"

Lila had already thought about where, and she knew she would have to ask Tommy to mind the little ones. But she could trust Tommy to keep her secret; after all, he'd already taken a black eye on her account. "Tomorrow morning at the fishin' hole," she said softly.

Daniel nodded his head, greatly relieved that he would finally be alone with her. He was already wondering just how much he should tell her; he did not want to frighten her with the intensity of his feelings. "What time?"

"At dawn," she replied miserably and returned her attention to the potatoes. It would not be easy separating her life from his. But, as time went on, it would only become more difficult if she did not. In the long run it was the only fair thing she could do for him.

Daniel had lain awake most of the night, rehearsing a number of things he wanted to say to Lila. He was of the opinion that she still did not understand what had happened between them that night on her father's front porch. Yes, he had gone to her for comfort. But she must understand *why* he had chosen to go to her. She had not given him an opportunity to explain anything, and he was looking upon this meeting as their opportunity to mutually discover each other's feelings.

Daniel was a happy man as he rode out of town that morning on his way to the bend in the creek that he remembered fondly. He felt a little foolish, sneaking off to a clandestine tryst as he was, however. In Boston, most people were too busy to worry about others' behavior. If the President were to come to town and steal the mayor's wife, that might cause some attention. Otherwise, no one cared to concern themselves about everyday people and their affairs. Many things were different in a small town, however.

He arrived at the clearing near the bend in the creek and dismounted even as he looked around for her. And then he saw her, stepping out from behind a stand of trees and walking toward him. She looked so small and vulnerable as she walked with her hands behind her back, and he felt a momentary failing of his resolve. He was about to ask her to stand beside him and face a sizable number of the townfolk who, at this moment, would not approve of their courtship. But he was going to ask just that and pray that he could somehow protect her. But he also wanted Lila to have an opportunity to examine whatever she might feel for him, without outside factors influencing her decision.

"Hi, Daniel," she said softly as she stepped before him.

Daniel looked down into the doe-brown eyes and smiled. "Hello, Lee."

"Thank you for comin'," she said, inwardly cursing the hesitation in her voice.

"I wanted to come. I asked that you meet me, remember?"

"So you did," she said and turned away. When she arrived at the edge of the creek, Lila turned and faced him again. "I haven't much time, Daniel," she lied, but she did not want to drag out this meeting. Now that she was here, facing him was suddenly painful.

"That's too bad," he said. "I have a lot of things I want to say to you."

Lila wasn't about to give him that opportunity. She seemed to be weak where he was concerned and she could not let him distract her from her purpose in coming. She reached into her pocket and then held her hand out to him. "I wanted to explain that I had planned to return this to you many days ago. *Before* my father came to talk with you."

Daniel stepped forward and looked at her outstretched palm. A key. His key! His heart fell to somewhere within the region of his stomach and turned over. He refused to take the key, and after a moment his intense, questioning eyes stared at her.

"You've heard about the other, then?" he questioned softly.

Lila's brows arched upward and her frown altered distinctly. "What other?"

Daniel realized, in that moment, that she had heard very little. And now, as he had intended, they would have to discuss it all. "Of course you haven't heard," he muttered, angry at his own stupidity. "You've barely been out of the house." Still, he had guessed that *someone* would have spoken, if only her own brothers. He reached for her hand, but Lila moved nervously away.

"Just tell me, Daniel."

He folded his arms across his chest, feet apart. "All right. There is talk about you coming to my home. About us being there alone together."

Lila was completely dumbfounded. "What? That happened only once."

"Once is apparently enough around here," he muttered. "Look, Lee, it doesn't matter. I've talked with—"

"Doesn't matter?" she cried.

"Well, it won't matter in time. If you'll just let me—"

Lila looked down at the key in her hand. "I should have given this back long ago," she said, more to herself than to him. And then she shook her head and extended her hand to him again. "You'd better take it," she said, knowing that the gossip did not matter. Staying away from Daniel for the sake of them both was what mattered.

Daniel frowned at the key. "I'm not taking it. Lila, please, I . . ."

She dropped the key into the grass at her feet and turned away.

Daniel reached for her and caught hold of her arm. "Why won't you let me speak?" he snapped. He was becoming angry because he was losing her before he'd even had an opportunity to tell her he loved her.

Lila's head dropped forward wearily. She would not look at him, because looking at him was painful. She would miss him and she did not want to remember him this way, when he was angry. "There's nothin' to say, Daniel. Just let me go," she pleaded.

"I've spoken with your father," he said quickly. "I have his permission to court you."

Lila thought someone must have pulled the axis out of the center of the earth just then, because it sure had stopped spinning. "What?" she breathed.

He was able to turn her to face him then, his hands gently gripping her shoulders. "It's true, Lee."

"You mean Papa wouldn't have greeted you with a scatter gun?" she muttered, trying to grasp at the concept.

"I care for you very deeply. I thought you must understand by now," he said as a slow, appealing grin twitched at the corners of his mouth. "I asked you to think about it, remember?"

Oh, she remembered. It was one of the reasons she had made the decision to stay away from him before they both got hurt. "It's impossible," she whispered.

His smile vanished instantly. "What are you saying?"

"I thought I was very clear, Daniel."

"Is it the gossip, Lila?"

She shook her head without hesitation. "Words can't hurt me, Daniel. Neither can people's dirty minds."

"Does 'impossible' mean you don't care for me?" he urged. "That you have no feelings for me?"

"*Impossible* means just the opposite and more," she said before swallowing painfully. "I have family who depend on me, Daniel. I can't leave them."

So that was it! Jonathan had been right. "I'm not asking you to leave them, sweetheart," he said tenderly. "I would never ask that."

She knew he would never ask her to leave. That was the point, and he was missing it. Fighting tears that threatened to drown her on the spot, Lila turned and took a step away. There were just too many things against them; even though Daniel cared for Sammy, he could never adjust to the responsibilities of a large family, and it was unthinkable to ask a bridegroom to try. And how on earth would she ever care for two households? Impossible. "Impossible," she whispered and continued to walk away.

"No!" he said, reaching for her again.

But this time Lila snatched her arm away; one of them had to be strong.

"Don't go, Lee," he said, darting to her side. "Talk with me."

She continued to walk, and Daniel eventually stopped in his tracks, angered and confounded by her determination. Now he understood the vague symptom his patients often tried in vain to describe to him; it was pain. "Where the devil did I go wrong?" he questioned softly. "She cares for me," he said in a stronger voice. "I know she does." And then he cried out to her retreating back, "You care for me, Lila Briggs! I know you do!" He watched her enter the thickness of trees that would lead her to the road. "Think about this, Lila!" he called. "*Think!*"

Think? She could not *think*. Not now.

Truth be told, Lila could not even *see*. She was crying violently, her vision badly impaired.

She was glad that she was far away from Daniel when she tripped and fell.

CHAPTER
12

 IT TOOK CONSIDERABLE CONCENTRATION ON Lila's part to appear normal and content after her meeting with Daniel. Her days ran to sameness after that. She had lost the spark of anticipation that had once smoldered within her when she thought it possible that she could turn some corner and find Daniel there, smiling. He had brought variety and sweetness into her life, and she missed him desperately. Now, if they did chance to meet, her eyes would instantly dart away, as if to belie the fact that they had ever even met. Which was preposterous. The entire town knew they had met and more.

 And the entire town watched.

Lila refused to appear shamed. She had no reason to feel shame, after all. She had done nothing wrong. And eventually the good citizens of Frankfort lost interest in the pair, and the long, curious stares were replaced once again by neighborly smiles on the faces of most. There were those who were, no doubt, disappointed that the scandal had fizzled, and those who would never forget, but Lila thought, hang 'em!

July passed quickly, as did August, and before she could believe it, the children were back in school. Tommy would finish this, his last year, and then he would be bound for work in the smithy alongside his father and his brother.

. Lila was happy that Annie had one more year before she started school; no matter how much work there was to do, it was Sammy and Annie who filled the empty hours.

The heat of August extended into early September, and Lila received a note penned by Rachael Fraser. It was curious, indeed, that Rachael should invite Lila for tea— and on a Saturday afternoon at that. "Leave the children in the care of those men," the note said. "And come have a quiet visit with me."

But Rachael's husband was Daniel's partner, and Lila was instantly suspicious. Since she could not write, Lila had Tommy pen a brief note back to Rachael: "Is this a trick?"

The following day, a boy delivered Rachael's reply: "Your smiling face would ease the loneliness."

Well, it was true that Edmond worked long hours, and Rachael had never been blessed with children, so Lila thought being *lonely* was a good enough reason to invite a body to tea.

She arose particularly early that day to see that the Saturday wash was completed before she spent a bit of time on her appearance. Tea with Rachael Fraser deserved her best dress, she figured. *And* her shoes, as sturdy and worn as they were.

The eyes of the townsfolk perked up that day as Lila walked through their midst in her Sunday best; she appeared to be a lady with a purpose. But then, Lila had little time to waste, they knew. There were too many things and persons demanding her attention.

She marched up the stone path to Doc Fraser's fine house on Wilkinson Street as if she had been to tea a hundred times before. It wasn't until she had raised the iron door knocker that she hesitated. "Lordy!" she breathed. It just did not seem real, this summons to visit, although the Frasers had always been kind and generous to a fault. It was simply too out of the ordinary for Lila to comprehend, and she began, once again, to doubt the sincerity behind Rachael's note.

"Well, if it does prove to be a trick," she muttered to herself, "you'll just have to get yourself out of here."

Taking a deep breath and holding it, she let the door knocker fall back into place.

Rachael Fraser was plump and rosy-complexioned with a decidedly motherly air. She smiled warmly as she opened the door and gestured for her guest to enter. "Come in, dear!" she said in a voice that cracked unexpectedly. Blushing, Rachael added, "I'm so glad you came."

Lila stepped into the expansive foyer and turned. "Thank you for inviting me," she said quietly.

"Come right this way. Tea will be but a moment."

Rachael seemed to corral the younger woman with her arms, while directing her toward the parlor.

Doc Fraser was standing across the room with an elbow supported by the fireplace mantel. He smiled before his eyes darted away from her.

Lila smiled in return. "Hell . . ." Her eyes followed the old doctor's fleeting glance, and the breath caught somewhere in her throat. "Ooo," she finished, expelling a whoosh of air.

Daniel Stone was standing in a corner of the room, looking decidedly sheepish.

"Now, dear," Rachael cajoled when Lila turned suspicious eyes upon her. "There's a very good reason for this."

"I hope so, Mrs. Fraser," Lila said quietly.

"Yes . . . well." Rachael's worried gaze sought her husband's, pleading for assistance. "Oh, Edmond," she breathed.

Doc Fraser came forward then, reaching out a hand. Lila's fingers were cold in his, and he smiled with reassurance. "He's been fretting for weeks, Lila. We had to help him meet with you. Just talk with him, will you?"

"I don't—"

"You're perfectly safe here. And if you're particularly uneasy, Mrs. Fraser and I will be in the very next room the entire time you are here." He motioned to sliding doors that were partially opened. They would be waiting in his study. "Are you willing to talk with him?"

"I've always been willing to talk with Daniel, Doc Fraser," she said. "That's the problem."

He smiled kindly and touched her cheek with his fingertips. "I somehow don't believe *that* is the problem, my dear."

Rachael had hastily placed a tray laden with teapot, cups, saucers, and small cakes on the round table between two settees that were situated before the fireplace. The wily woman had thought to add a decanter of brandy and two snifters at the last minute.

At her husband's nod Rachael followed him from the room and closed the sliding doors.

"Hello, Lila," Daniel said, finally moving out from the corner.

"Well," she said uneasily. "You've resorted to tricks?"

He smiled and motioned her toward one of the settees. "I've had to," he said. "Please don't blame Rachael; she is only trying to help and I can be *very* persuasive when I have something of importance to achieve. This was the only way I could think of getting you alone so I could talk with you."

"You must have had a powerful urge to talk," she returned as lightly as her jangled nerves would permit. She sat, smoothing her skirts. "You've gone to a lot of trouble."

He sat opposite her and smiled. "I happen to think talking with you is worth any amount of trouble."

Lila's head cocked to one side. "Do you?"

"Of course," he said, leaning forward and pouring tea for her.

"I do believe you mean that, Daniel." But that is all she would allow herself to believe. They couldn't start up again, that was for certain. There were too many obstacles and too many worries behind them for that. And she didn't think her heart could stand a repeat of the past few months.

"How have you been, Lee?" he asked quietly, placing a pretty floral cup and saucer on the table in front of her.

"Fine," she said, lying easily. "And you?"

"Miserable," he said bluntly.

"Oh!" she returned, her eyes growing round in genuine dismay. "Why?"

Daniel's blue-eyed stare affixed itself on her pretty face. "I think you know *why*," he said softly.

Lila leaned forward, resting her elbows on her knees. "Leave it be, Daniel." She was begging again, and she hated that, but she was only one faint-hearted woman against a man of enormous fortitude. She was afraid she could not hold out against another one of his determined onslaughts.

Daniel's smile was a bit lopsided and not understood by her as he poured a generous quantity of brandy into a glass.

"No. I know I can't leave it," he said tightly. "I've learned that over the past weeks." He motioned to the brandy, silently offering to pour her a glass.

She watched him raise the glass to his lips and take a long pull on the amber liquid. "Daniel, have you taken up the drink?" she asked with concern.

"Not really," he said, shaking his head. "Sometimes it warms a cold spot I've got in my belly."

Exasperated, Lila sat back. "You're not makin' a whole lot of sense."

"I should be," he said. "I don't think you're listening, Lee." He got to his feet then and paced away. When he returned to lean against the carved wooden mantel, he was not smiling.

A frown instantly marred her pretty face, her head lowered, her eyes apparently examining the fine woven carpet.

"I want to talk about us," he said calmly.

Lila started back against the cushioned upholstery of the settee. "Us?"

Daniel smiled crookedly. "I don't think the word *us* should be such a surprise, Lee. I've practically opened my chest and exposed my heart to you. And I'm convinced that this is not a one-sided affair. You know there's an *us*."

Frowning, she looked at him askance. "There was a time when I thought we were friends, Daniel."

"You don't feel that way anymore?" he asked quietly.

Lila raised slim fingers and lightly stroked her brow. "I don't know what we are," she muttered.

"Has it been terrible for you, Lee?" he asked. He'd been wondering all these weeks.

She did not answer. She could not, or the miserable tears might reappear.

"Frankly, it's been terrible for me," he said in a tone that appeared cold on the surface. He returned to the settee across from her, closely examining the contents of his glass. "You'll have to be patient with me, Lila. I'm not certain how to act around the woman I love, knowing she does not love me in return," he said softly.

"That's not—"

"Yes?" he prodded.

It wasn't true; if she had ever loved anyone in her lifetime, it was this man. "I'm sorry," was all she could say.

Daniel was already cursing under his breath, and he had promised himself he would be patient. He was determined to uncover her reasons for casting him aside, and he would not achieve that by becoming angry. Either she had no feelings toward him, or there was something else frightening her that caused her to break all ties to him. He had missed her; missed the possibility of seeing her, laughing with her. Anticipation had disappeared from his life, and Daniel felt empty and alone. He missed her sweet, smiling ways and her soft-spoken drawl. He even missed the ruckus caused by the children, who were constantly around her.

In an attempt to stem the flow of agitation that was threatening to overwhelm him, Daniel rose again and paced back to his spot near the fireplace.

"Have you been eatin' sweets, Daniel?" she asked softly as her eyes followed him.

He flashed her a puzzled frown.

"You're havin' trouble sittin' still. Sammy gets like that when he eats sweets."

Daniel laughed at the analogy; it wasn't sugar that was causing his turmoil. "You're eighteen years old, Lila," he said, shoving his hands into the pockets of his trousers. "It's time you stopped running in fear of men. What is your heart telling you about me?"

"You're a bold one," she muttered. "My *heart* isn't tellin' me anythin'," she insisted.

She was lying. He just knew she was lying. "Tell me something," he continued conversationally. "Do you find my appearance unpleasant?"

Startled by the question, Lila could not think fast enough to wonder about his tactics. "No. You're easy enough to look at."

He had heard more flattering descriptions in relation to his appearance, but he accepted her comment without flinching. "Are my manners lacking?" he asked.

Still confused, Lila could only answer honestly. "Your manners are just fine, Daniel."

"Does my personality offend you?" he asked, walking slowly toward her now.

His *personality* made her heart race, that's what his personality did. "Why are you askin' these silly questions?"

"Do you dislike me, Lee?" he asked quietly as he stood very close. "Do you despise me?"

He was too close. She could feel the material of his trouser leg against her skirt. Lila jumped to her feet, gripping her hands together as she moved away. "Why are you pressin' me?" she asked, having finally gained some insight into what he was trying to do.

"Why aren't you responding?" he countered.

Because it would be dangerous.

"What are you thinking?" he demanded softly. "What are you feeling?"

Nothing! Nothing!

"I've admitted that I've missed you, Lee. Have you not missed me at all?"

He was not going to give it up, she could see that, and one of them had to have a lick of sense about this. Stiffening her back, she faced him squarely. "I'm using my *head*," she said. "I've got a family of six to care for, and—"

"Family?" he returned, his arched brows accentuating his confusion. "Lila, we've already talked about your family. I understand about them."

Shifting uneasily, Lila started to speak and suddenly raised her hands, dropping them abruptly again immediately. "No, you don't . . . you can't . . . understand!" she blurted.

"What don't I understand, love?" he prodded as he took a step around the table.

Aggravated by her obvious failure to take charge of this situation, Lila stamped a small foot as her hands fisted at her sides. "You're confusin' me!" she hissed.

"I know," he said, smiling in sympathy as he advanced beyond the end of the settee. "I can see that." He could tell by the nervous way she twisted her fingers that his instincts had been correct; she *was* attracted to him. Now he had to uncover the reasons behind her denial of her feelings. "It's like that when you meet someone who makes you feel things no one else has ever made you feel. And other things get in the way, too, don't they, Lee? Like loyalty to others? Responsibilities can weigh very heavily."

"Please stop," she whispered, but they both knew she was not referring to the fact that he was moving ever closer to where she stood.

"You deserve a life of your own," he said. "In fact, you're more deserving than any other person I've ever met."

She shook her head, and he wondered just what she was denying.

He stopped, directly in front of her, a hairsbreadth away. "Let's be honest with each other, shall we?"

Knowing she would be totally defenseless against him if he continued much longer, Lila reached deep within herself and turned to anger. "I have to leave now," she said firmly, racing across the room.

"Running away again?" he accused. "I thought you had more courage."

Lila stopped, facing the door that would take her away from him, the source of her anguish. "I have to run away," she said in a tortured whisper. "Don't you see that?"

"Because the minute we take up, the gossips will have a field day all over again?" he asked. "Because your family needs you? What are the *real* reasons for your wanting to escape this, Lee?"

Lila turned abruptly and faced him with the truth. "Because it wouldn't be fair to you!"

Whatever he had been expecting, it certainly had not been *that*. Particularly in view of all she would have to bear if they were to begin seeing each other again. "Why on earth would you think that?" he asked.

Clearly exasperated, Lila said, "For heaven's sake, Daniel. What about my brothers and sisters?"

"As I said before, I care about them, too."

"I can't . . . how can I ask you to share in the responsibility for six children?" she cried.

"So that's it," he whispered and reached for her hands, holding them tightly against his chest. "I like being in your home when the children are racing about. You know that."

"That's a *visit*," she scoffed.

"And financially, well, we'll make do."

"You get paid in potatoes," she said brokenly.

He grinned at her and squeezed her hand. "What's your point? At least we won't starve."

"I wash and cook and clean for them."

"I know that," he said easily. "I know just how hard you work."

"It isn't the work," she argued. "The little ones need me."

"I need you, too, Lee. And I know I will have to share you."

"I'm gettin' nowhere," she muttered and tore her hands away.

But Daniel followed her back toward the fireplace, gaining confidence now that she had moved away from the door and *that* avenue for escape. "You're getting nowhere because you haven't got an argument. You know I'm deeply fond of those children. You must have been able to see that. If I'm prepared to share you and the responsibilities I know you will never shirk, then you have to accept that."

Lila turned and stared at him. "You don't know what you're doin', Daniel. You don't know what it's really like to live in a house *full* of people. You'll never have any peace."

"Well, we'll have two houses," he teased. "Maybe we can spread everybody out."

"I'm bein' serious," she said, not able to tap into his good humor. "I just can't ask you to . . ."

Daniel reached out, gripping her shoulder and preventing her from moving away. "Look," he said, teasing aside, "you cannot make this kind of decision for me. And I've already made the decision at any rate. I know what I want. If I wanted *peace*, I would climb a mountain and live in a cave. Be honest," he demanded. "Forget the children and everything else and just be honest with yourself and with me. Tell me how you feel, Lila."

"Why are you doin' this to me?" she pleaded weakly.

He could see he had worn her down and took a last step forward, pulling her against his chest. "Because I *know* how you feel," he whispered. "I *think* I know. And I know how I feel. Don't deny all the good that could be between us, Lee."

Lila sagged against him then. "Ahh, Daniel," she cried softly.

"Forget the rest, my love," he whispered as he wrapped his arms securely around her. "We'll work it all out."

"Six children," she muttered against his neck.

"Four," he countered. "Jon and Tommy are practically grown. They won't need us as much."

Us? He said *us* so easily. So, her arguments were deflated. He had, indeed, worn her down. Weary to the point of exhaustion, Lila allowed herself to rest against him, comforted by the strength and warmth in the strong arms that surrounded her. She had never had anyone to share her worries and her woes in the past. And she wasn't certain if Daniel truly understood the magnitude of the obligations he so easily said he would share. But Lila could not fight him anymore. Truth be told, she had never wanted to fight Daniel. Now she would draw what strength she could from him and prepare to do battle on at least one other front: the town of Frankfort.

CHAPTER
13

 THEY TALKED SO LONG THAT AFTERNOON THAT Lila was reduced to racing back across town in order to get supper on the table by the time her father finished working for the day.

Leaving the potatoes and beans to boil, she set Beth to frying ham steaks while she ran into the bedroom and hastily brushed her hair. She knew Daniel would get good and sick of seeing her in the dress, but it was the only good one she owned. As she tied her long apron in place, she wondered if her father might be willing to spare a few extra coins for a length of cloth. It was doubtful, as most of any extra went to buying rum, but she had to do something. And all of her small hoard of coins had gone to buy Edward's spectacles. She had not been able to save much since.

 Once everyone was seated at the table, Lila

spooned whipped potatoes onto Sammy's plate as she agonized over how much she should explain to her family.
Introducing the subject was near impossible, and they were
halfway through the meal before she spoke.

Jonathan and Jon sat at opposite ends of the table, and
Lila sat with Annie and Sammy on either side of her.
She glanced briefly at her father before concentrating on
a major excavation of her small mound of potato. "I had
tea at Rachael Fraser's today," she said.

That wasn't news and no one interrupted their eating
over it.

"Daniel Stone was there," she said nervously.

That brought the attention of every pair of eyes in the room.

She looked at her father then, setting her fork on the side
of her plate. "Daniel will be payin' a call this evenin'," she
said quietly. "He's comin' here for coffee and cake."

"Boy! Doc's comin'!" Sammy chirped.

Jonathan nodded and returned his attention to his meal.
He had wondered when they were going to get around to
this, but now that the moment was upon them, he had mixed
feelings. He still could not argue that a doctor was a good
match for his girl; she would never want for anything. The
problem was, he had somehow missed Lila's growing up
and she was still his little girl. He had not taken the time
to think about giving her over to a man, a husband. And he
found, in that moment, that he was entirely unprepared.

"You didn't tell me you'd talked with Daniel, Papa," Lila
said quietly.

Jonathan nodded his head again, wiped his mouth with
the back of his hand, and got to his feet. "His business," he
said gruffly and turned toward the door. "I have business
across town."

And then he was gone, leaving Lila staring in stunned
silence at the closed door.

"Business," Tommy said scornfully. "With a bottle."

"Leave it, Tommy," Jon ordered. And then he grinned at his sister. "So, you're steppin' out with the doc. Good for you, Lee."

Tommy agreed. He was happy for his sister. Having Daniel Stone court Lila made taking that shiner worthwhile.

Beth understood that things were about to change around the Briggs house, and she wasn't so certain she was going to like it.

Daniel hurriedly scoured the town and bought the best boxed candy he could find. He earned himself a knowing smile of encouragement from Abigail Cuthbert for his efforts. He then returned to the Frasers' home with the intent of raiding a single rose from Rachael's gardens; he came away with a dozen pink roses tied with lace and ribbon. Rachael's efforts.

"This is so wonderful," the woman said happily before he mounted his horse to ride across town.

Daniel felt a bit foolish; the last time he had paraded anywhere with flowers and candy, he had been all of fourteen and madly in love with Mary Pardee. And she had been a scandalizing sixteen at the time!

Edmond chuckled as he waved the younger man off. "You show 'em, my boy!" he called.

People actually stopped on the street to watch Daniel and his roses ride by.

"Lordy," he muttered and then, when he realized what he had said and just how much of an influence Lila must have on him, he tipped his head back and laughed.

"I say he's been drinkin'," Harmon Fielding challenged his brother.

Homer wouldn't take the bet.

Sammy steadfastly refused to eat dessert until he could share with Daniel and removed himself from the table to "stand watch" on the front porch. Tommy had stationed himself there, too, rocking slowly and grinning widely when Daniel rode into sight.

"Hi, Doc!" Sammy called and ran to duck his head inside the front door. "Doc's comin', Lee!" he bellowed.

Lila turned anxiously toward the door. "Sammy, keep it down to a roar, please," she said firmly.

Sammy was undaunted and ran back outside to stand on the porch steps.

Tommy had already walked the length of the yard to greet Daniel. "I'll take your horse, Doc," he said, reaching for the reins. "Nice posies," he teased.

Daniel cast the boy a pained expression as he pulled the boxed candy from a saddlebag. "You and half the town think so," he said ruefully.

Tommy laughed and led Daniel's horse toward the smithy.

Sammy wrapped his arms around a porch post. "Hi, Doc! I saved some cake for you."

Daniel stepped up onto the porch and tousled Sammy's soft hair. "Thank you, my friend."

And then he turned and Lila was standing there; she looked as nervous as he felt, and he found himself suddenly laughing.

Lila was forced to smile in the face of his laughter. "What?" she asked.

Daniel shook his head and cast a brief glance at Sammy and then toward Annie, who, as usual, was clinging to Lila's skirt. "I'll explain later," he said lightly. He extended the flowers then, and in spite of his previous embarrassment, he was instantly gratified that he had brought them.

Lila's expression was one of awe as her hands reached out and took his offering. "For me?" she breathed. Her eyes were mysteriously moist when she looked up at him for acknowledgment.

"Of course they're for you," he said quietly, staring intently at her for the sheer joy of seeing delight take over her amazement. It was clear she had never received a gift of flowers before, and while the thought saddened him, it also made him very happy; he would see to it that she experienced a world full of *firsts*.

"Thank you, Daniel," Lila said before raising the roses in order to catch their scent.

"Oh, and these," he said, remembering the candy.

Sammy was bored by this quiet exchange and said, "I'm gonna get cake," before he squeezed between Lila and the doorframe.

"You're goin' to spoil me," Lee said as she took the ribboned box.

"I'm certainly going to do my best," he proclaimed.

His tone of voice reached out and touched her just as if he had caressed her with his hands. Flustered, she stepped back and ducked her head in the pretense of seeing that Annie was out of his way. "Come in," she said. "Coffee is ready."

Daniel stepped past her, and Lila became aware of the appealing scent of him; as if she had never been near him before. She wondered at this awakening of her senses and nervously sidestepped away. "I'll put these in water," she said.

Daniel reached out and captured her wrist, bringing her attention back to him. "It's going to be all right, Lee," he said softly. "We're still the same people."

Lila stared up into his beautiful blue eyes for an extended moment before she said, "It doesn't *feel* the same."

He smiled his understanding. "No, it doesn't. And that's good. Trust me," he added.

She did. Suddenly she did.

She nodded her agreement, and he grinned at her.

"I understand Sammy saved me a piece of cake."

"*Sammy* did, huh?" she said lightly. She looked toward the table and the one under discussion; Sammy was hovering over the cake dish. "Maybe," she said ruefully.

Daniel went to join the boy at the table, greeting Beth warmly as he sat down. He noticed the girl's caution in returning the greeting and sensed this child, of all the children, just might face the most painful adjustment of all. He made a mental note to speak to Lila.

Sammy's feet were swinging freely under the bench as he concentrated on his cake. "Me and Tommy went fishin' today," he said between mouthfuls. "I caught this many."

Daniel smiled at the small hand with the extended fingers; five, always five. "You did, huh?"

Lila turned from the stove in time to see the count. "Sammy Briggs, you did not," she scolded.

Daniel laughed as she set a cup of black coffee and a plate of cake in front of him. "Fishermen always exaggerate their catch," he told her.

"Yes, but this little *fisherman* is always tellin' tall tales," she muttered as she fetched her own cup.

Beth had finished the supper cleanup and walked toward the door. "I'm goin' over to Sue Ellen's," she said miserably.

"You be back before dark," Lila called, but the girl was gone. Lila was clearly mystified, but Daniel thought he understood the girl's unusual behavior. "I think Beth might be feeling a bit threatened, Lee," he said quietly as he picked up his fork. "She's just old enough to understand and might be afraid that she could lose you."

"I should have thought," Lila said, but there had been little time for thinking, it seemed, beyond Daniel and herself. "I'll talk to her tonight."

"We'll both talk with her, if you like," he said, smiling as he dropped his hand over hers on the tabletop. "I'll reassure her that I will not be taking you away."

Sammy jumped on that remark. "Lee's not goin' away?"

"No, I'm *not*," Lila assured him. "And don't talk with your mouth full."

They took seconds of coffee out to the front porch to enjoy the warm summer-like evening, in addition to each other's company.

Sammy was right there, leaning on Daniel's knee.

Lila laughed when she spied a flash of frustration that Daniel failed to hide. "I warned you!"

"Can we go fishin' tomorrow?" Sammy asked, grinning as he tipped his face upward.

"Tomorrow is Sunday," Daniel explained. "We're goin' to church tomorrow."

Sammy nodded thoughtfully. "Are you goin' with us?"

"I am."

Sammy thought that was grand, but "After church?"

Lila smiled and wondered if Daniel was going to get himself free of a commitment.

"Maybe the fish will be in church," he teased.

"Ahhh, Daniel." Sammy laughed and dropped his forehead to the man's knee.

Daniel laughed, too, and ruffled the boy's hair affectionately. "Go play with your sister," he said easily.

Annie had been hanging on to the arm of Lila's chair but was just as happy to run off with Sammy.

Daniel smiled at Lila and placed his cup on the small table between them. "Is everyone occupied?" he said lightly.

Lila's eyes flashed toward Annie and Sammy in the small front yard. "Not for long, most likely."

"I'll take what I can get," he said, getting to his feet.

Lila watched him move the small table forward and then turn to face his chair. "What are you doin'?"

"Rearranging the furniture," he said quietly. When his rocking chair was close to hers, he sat down and reached for her hand. "Better," he announced contentedly as he gave her hand a gentle squeeze.

Lila looked down at her hand surrounded by his, felt his warmth, and gave a playful tug. "It's still daylight," she pointed out.

"Yup," he drawled as he watched the two children run sticks along the picket fence.

"Someone is sure to ride by."

"Uh-huh."

She laughed. "You don't care!"

He turned his head toward her and smiled. "I don't. All I care about is that this feels *right*. It feels good. How do you feel about it?"

Lila thought about it briefly. Only briefly. "I'm warmin' up to it, Daniel," she said lightly.

He was pleased with that; hurdle one was behind them. But as he looked off toward town, he knew there was more that they must accomplish. "I don't want them hurting you," he said. And when he turned back to look at her, Lila was shaking her head.

"They can't hurt me, Daniel," she said adamantly. "I've got you."

"Thank you for my penny, Lee," Sammy said as he clung to her with one hand and clutched a penny's worth of candy in a small paper bag against his chest.

"You're welcome, darlin'," she said. Lila's spirits were high this Monday morning.

As they turned the corner onto High Street, Lila recalled the shocked expressions on a number of faces when Daniel Stone had escorted the Briggs family into the church the previous day. They had set a few good Christians on their ears when he'd sat down beside her. It was going to be bothersome, she suspected, convincing the townfolk that she and Daniel were a legitimate, courting couple, but it would come with time. She would simply have to be patient. The difficulty was, of course, that men usually came out smelling all the sweeter for scandals; the women were always labeled the shameful hens and the men were always the much celebrated roosters. Well, she had decided she was not about to waste much energy over the problem.

They had already spoken of marriage, mutually agreeing that an interval of time was required; enough time to be *proper*. Daniel was insisting on a courtship and that their banns be read in church in a few weeks. *That*, she thought, should be *that*. The second difficulty was the waiting. Lila now suspected the waiting would be agonizing; now that she had made her commitment, she was finding she wanted to spend all of her time with Daniel.

As they made their way along the street, Lila was the first to see Mrs. Willoughby, accompanied by her friend Addie Grant, walking toward them. "Oh, Lordy," she whispered and contemplated crossing the street. But that would be cowardly, and Lila was *not* a coward.

Mae Belle Willoughby sighted Lila and stopped in her tracks.

Lila stopped, pulling Sammy to an abrupt halt.

"Ow! Lee . . ." he complained.

"Shhh . . ."

Sammy looked at the two women facing them, at Mae Belle in particular, and then frowned up at his sister. "Has she been suckin' lemons?"

"Sammy . . . " Lila warned.

"Well . . ."

Lila gave his hand a squeeze, begging for silence, and then she beamed a smile at the two older women. "Mizzuz Willoughby. Mizzuz Grant."

Mae Belle sucked in an astonished breath, causing her massive bosom to rise vulgarly. "Bold as brass," she muttered.

Addie's head bobbed in concert with her friend's words. "Shouldn't be allowed on the streets."

Righteous and Christian as she was, Mae Belle decided that someone in town should let this girl know that besmudging the good name of Frankfort's upstanding citizens would just not be tolerated. She stepped forward until she could be heard without raising her voice. "I've been informed that you have subjected Dr. Stone to a compromising situation."

Lila's head tipped saucily to one side. "You've been *informed*, Mizzuz Willoughby?" The old witch was the one to spread the rumors, as Lila heard it. And it was old news; the woman was several days behind time.

Mae Belle could simply not believe the girl's defiance. "Don't you have any shame?"

"We missed you in church yesterday, Mizzuz Willoughby," Lila said easily.

Mae Belle drew in an affronted gasp. "My Mr. Willoughby was poorly yesterday," she said. "And all that aside, you enticed Dr. Stone into your home in the middle of the night, and there's no gettin' away from your actions," Mae Belle informed her angrily.

"No, ma'am. I didn't." Lila marveled at the purple hue of the woman's complexion; Mae Belle really was angry.

"Are you saying your own father lied?" Addie joined the fray.

Lila turned an expressionless face toward the other woman. "I'm saying my father wasn't there."

"Ah-hah!" Mae Belle jumped on the remark. "So Dr. Stone *was* in your house that night."

"No, ma'am. He was on my front porch for all the world to see."

"But no one would see in the middle of the night!" Mae Belle pointed out.

"Supposin' there was nothin' to see?"

Mae Belle was becoming a little flustered that Lila was not backing down. Nor did the girl seem to feel any remorse. "I think you should stay away from Daniel Stone, Lila."

A hint of a smile caused Lila's lips to twitch. "I think that's goin' to be nigh impossible, ma'am."

"I think you are being deliberately antagonistic!"

"Oh, no, ma'am."

"You truly have no shame," Addie Grant offered. "Don't you care what you might be doing to Dr. Stone's reputation?"

"I care," Lila agreed. "I also care about my own."

"You're not acting as if you care," Mae Belle threw in.

Lila's eyes turned stormy as she turned again to the older woman. "How am I supposed to act, Mizzuz Willoughby? You've got me tried and hung, and I've done nothin' to earn it."

"You've been going to his home for weeks," Mae Belle said scathingly. "Dr. Stone's own neighbors have seen you there."

She was quickly growing tired of this game and the bickering that was not about to end unless she ended it.

"I'm not defendin' myself any further, ladies, because I need no defendin'."

"You, of all people, shouldn't be chasing after a man like Daniel Stone," Mae Belle said firmly.

So, they didn't think she was good enough for their town doctor. That didn't surprise Lila. She also felt these women were in the minority, for many people seemed to think highly of her. That did not make this assault any less painful, however. With a weary sigh Lila said only, "Daniel's a doctor. Other than that he's like a lot of men."

"He's considerably higher in the scheme of things!" Addie gasped.

Lila's head tipped to one side, and her eyes sparkled with sudden mischief as she turned her head once again. "I wonder if Daniel knows that?" She reached for Sammy's hand then and led him around and away from the two indignant women.

"The good Lord will put that girl in her place. I just know He will," Mae Belle could be heard to say.

"Does she know God?" Sammy breathed.

Lila's lips twitched. "I doubt that very much, darlin'."

CHAPTER
14

 THE MOST DIFFICULT THING, OF COURSE, WAS AR-
ranging their meetings times. And when they managed times and places, they were always well chap-
 eroned; Sammy and Annie could not be left at home
to fend for themselves.

Their favorite corner of the world became the
creek where the children loved to play. Late September continued to bless them with Indian summer
days that remained warm enough for Sammy and
Annie to paddle about near the edge of the water,
leaving Lila and Daniel to sit on the green, grass-
cushioned bank to watch and talk.

 Daniel laughed as the children splashed and
shrieked, scaring off any frogs that were within
reach. "They are remarkably good company for
 each other," he said.

Lila turned her head against the bark of the tree

at her back and smiled a bit sadly. "I don't know what poor Sammy will do with himself a year from now," she said. When Daniel shot her a questioning glance, she explained. "Annie will start school next year."

He nodded his understanding. He reached for her hand and pulled it up against his lips. When he released her, he pivoted, stretching out on the grass and resting his head on her lap. He laughed softly when he looked up and saw a blush steal across her cheeks. "I seem to make you nervous, Miss Briggs," he teased.

"You're a bold one," Lila muttered but belied her concerns when her fingers began to stroke through his hair.

Daniel was soothed by her touch and, totally relaxed, he closed his eyes. "The smartest thing I ever did was to move here from Boston," he said quietly.

"Don't you ever get a little homesick for the city?"

His head rotated against her thigh, warming her flesh. "There's nothing there for me to miss," he said.

"Not even a woman?" she asked, knowing there had to have been.

Daniel's eyes popped open. "What makes you ask that?"

She shrugged casually, watching her own fingers reach out and cover the hand he had resting on his chest. "I just feel there must have been," she said softly.

Daniel stared up into her inquiring brown eyes for several moments before he responded. "There was. But no one near as fine as you."

Lila smiled, continuing to stroke his soft, silky hair. "Why, thank you, Daniel." They were silent for a moment, continuing to caress each other with looks that told no lies. "Was she pretty?" Lila asked eventually.

Daniel laughed. "Why don't you simply say you want me to tell you about her?"

"Was she?" she persisted.

"Not as pretty as you."

"That's a lie, Daniel Stone."

"No, it isn't."

"I'm not pretty."

Daniel grew serious for a moment. "Oh, yes, you are, my love," he whispered.

Lila loved that special tone he used that made her feel as if they were already lovers. "I bet she was rich, too," she said.

"Filthy," he agreed.

"And from a good family," she said with conviction.

"With all the right connections," he added.

Lila felt a sense of doom as the vision of the perfect mate for him unfolded. "And you gave up all of that?" she asked nervously.

"What I gave up was a selfish, nasty-spirited witch," he informed her. "And a life that suited me not at all." He sat up abruptly, turning to face her and resting there, hip to hip. He propped a hand on the grass on the other side of her lap and stared intently into her eyes. "What I gained is a quiet, unpretentious life where I can work with honest folk who have honest ills. But I gained something much more precious, Lee," he said as his right hand moved down the length of her arm to capture her hand. "I gained the affections of a soft, loving, and beautiful young woman who is sweet beyond my wildest imaginings. A woman who makes me fall in love all the more every time she smiles at me."

This adoration was something totally foreign to Lila, but it was something she was learning to accept from him.

Daniel reached out and pressed the palm of his hand against her cheek. "Don't you ever, for a moment, doubt again that I am not *exactly* where I want to be."

Lila heard the conviction in his tone and saw it reflected in the blue of his eyes, and she loved him for it. "Yes, Daniel," she said meekly.

He was so surprised by this uncharacteristic display of submission that he laughed. "You were playing with me, weren't you? You were testing the depth of my feelings for you."

She hadn't been; at least not consciously. Now that he forced her to think about it, why had she asked all those stupid questions? And why had she been afraid of the answers? "I don't know," she said honestly. "Maybe I was."

Honesty and sincerity were two additional reasons why he loved her. "I love you," he murmured as he tipped slowly forward.

Lila knew he was about to kiss her and remained perfectly still. "The children," she whispered.

"They've seen me kiss you before," he said before his lips touched hers. Her lips were sweet, her kiss innocent and unschooled, and it drove Daniel to want to teach her. He scooped her up against his chest and deepened their kiss as he felt her arms go around him. He turned his head, slanting his lips across hers, feeling his breath catch in his throat. He pulled away from her just enough to whisper, "Open."

She did. But it was to speak. "Daniel . . ."

"There is only one other place I would like to be, love," he murmured, "and that is closer to you. I need you, Lila."

That husky whisper of his caused her to tease. "I guess you didn't go visit Miss—"

"Lila, don't you dare," he said firmly.

"Well, you've been very high-strung lately, Daniel."

The mood broken, Daniel arched a questioning brow. "High-strung?"

Lila nodded her head adamantly. "I saw a stallion that

way once," she said. "After he'd mounted the mare, he was much calmer."

Daniel stared at her, dumbfounded, and then he threw back his head and laughed.

Lila's cheeks grew hot and deep red as she poked him firmly in the shoulder. "Don't you laugh at me!"

"High-strung?" he teased.

"You know what I mean."

"My dearest love," he said patiently, pulling her against his chest again and pressing her head to his shoulder. "I agree. I know I'm 'high-strung,' because of you. And I think it's time we did something about it."

"Daniel . . . !" she breathed, shocked by the suggestion.

"I mean it's time we moved on and got this marriage arranged," he said as he gently cupped her breast. "My poor body is sending out distress signals," he murmured. When she would have pulled away, he tightened his arm and kept her there. "No. Just let me touch you."

"Sammy and—"

"They can't see a thing," he assured her and glanced over his shoulder toward the creek; the children were downstream, creeping up on some unsuspecting creature. "Let's talk with your father today and ask that the banns be read this Sunday." He pushed her back just a bit as he bent one knee, supporting her back with his leg. "Will you agree, darling, that the time is right?" he asked as he began to unbutton her cotton dress. As the fifth button slid free, Daniel eased his hand inside her bodice, unerringly capturing the soft flesh beneath her chemise.

Lila drew in a long slow breath and closed her eyes. "I think we're *past* time, Daniel," she whispered.

He laughed. "Now you understand a little of what I feel when I'm near you." He laughed again. "Or when I'm not near you, for that matter."

Lila was beginning to experience that breathless state that she had previously detected in him. Still, she managed to question him. "You get . . . all . . . high-strung?" she breathed. "When you're only *thinkin'* about me?"

Daniel spread the material of her bodice wider and leaned forward, cupping her other breast as his lips hovered over hers. Her fingertips were digging into his forearms and gave him some indication of what she was experiencing. "Don't you?" he countered her question. "When you're thinking about me? Tell me what you feel when you're thinking about me, Lee."

Lila failed to respond; she couldn't manage the words just then.

"Do you feel the way you're feeling now?" he probed before he kissed her. He kissed her long and sweetly, toying with her, nibbling her lips between his kisses. "Does it feel good, love?" he murmured, foresaking her mouth and lightly stroking her chin with his tongue.

"I feel hot," she gasped.

He chuckled briefly and moved his lips close to her ear. "Me, too."

Lila became very aware of the hard bud of her nipple pressed against his palm and moved her shoulder forward, pressing more firmly against his hand. "Daniel, I think I'm goin' to die," she whispered.

"You won't, darling, I promise." His lips inched back toward hers again as he lightly squeezed her tortured nipple between his fingers.

Lila moaned, turning her head to meet his lips; this had to be the most *bold* he had ever dared. She pressed frantically against him now, her chest feeling as if someone were trying to suffocate her. "I'm hurting," she breathed as her hand covered his and pressed his palm downward to ease the aching in her breast.

Daniel raised his head, easing away from her. He dropped one brief kiss upon the high swell of her breast before moving his hand away. "I think we'd best stop," he said huskily.

Confused by his abrupt departure, Lila frowned. "I didn't mean for you to stop," she said. "I just thought you could do something about the hurting."

Daniel took a deep breath and smiled regretfully as he pulled the material of her bodice together in order to refasten the tiny buttons. "There are only two ways that I know of to give you ease, my love. One would be to continue and see our love play through to its natural conclusion. Under the circumstances," he teased, glancing quickly over his shoulder toward the children, "I don't believe that would be advisable."

"And the other?" she asked with obvious disappointment.

"The other is to stop." He fastened the last button at her throat and smiled in the face of her scowl. "Not what you wanted to hear?"

"Am I permitted to admit that I would choose the 'natural conclusion'?"

Daniel laughed. "You are."

"I don't think I'm supposed to get all feverish like that, Daniel," she muttered as she sat up and checked to be certain her clothing was back in order.

Daniel grinned and watched her, resting a forearm on his bent knee. "You are, if I'm doing my job."

Puzzled, Lila frowned at him. "Your job?"

"Mmm-hmm," he drawled thoughtfully as he ran his thumb along her jawline. "My part is to make certain you're relaxed and *feverish*."

"What's my part?" she asked recklessly.

"To enjoy," he informed her quietly. "Do you know about the ultimate in enjoyment?"

"Is that when we make babies?" she asked bluntly. She

thought that must be what he meant, and she would have to talk with him about that. Lila had made a decision about babies already.

Daniel searched her expression for a long moment, loving the soft way her eyes gazed back at him. "It isn't reserved for making babies, love."

"It isn't?"

"No."

Lila became impatient, wondering about this "ultimate enjoyment." "Aren't you going to tell me, Daniel?"

"No," he whispered, leaning forward to tease her lips. "I'm waiting, breathlessly, to show you, Lee." This was still another indication that she knew very little, and just thinking about introducing her to love's magic made his erection even more painful. He smiled and touched her cheek with his fingertips. "Soon, my love. Soon," he said softly before getting to his feet.

He did not turn away from her but extended a hand. Lila had seen him in this condition before, and he supposed modesty had prevented her from commenting or questioning. He suspected that would change once they approached their first night of lovemaking. "We'd best get those two little ones home." He had suddenly realized the afternoon sun was losing its strength.

Lila stretched upward, and he pulled her to her feet. "I love you," she murmured. "And I think you're a *poop* for not tellin' me."

And then she turned to call Sammy and Annie back to her as Daniel enjoyed a good laugh.

Sammy was the first to reach them, and he ran straight to Daniel and was immediately enfolded in strong arms. "Are you goin' to come live with us?" the boy asked.

Daniel was surprised by the question. "Why would you think that, Sam?"

Sammy grinned at the man for whom he had developed a great fondness. "You was sparkin' with Lee. I saw ya."

Daniel looked quickly at Lila, who was carefully giving her full attention to drying Annie's feet. Daniel thought she just might be holding her breath, however. He returned his attention to the boy, reaching for a towel as he dropped onto his heels. "Lila and I were just talking," he said foolishly.

Sammy held on to Daniel's shoulders as he raised one foot for drying. "You kissed her," he crowed. "I saw ya."

"How would you feel if I had kissed your sister?" Daniel asked Sammy as he reached for the boy's shoes.

Sammy shrugged, not really caring one way or the other. There was only one thing on his mind. "Would you come live with us? I want you to come live with us," Sammy demanded.

"Actually, I think I might be spending a lot more time at your house, Sam."

Sammy thought about that for a moment and then smiled. "Okay."

That night, long after everyone in the household was tucked in and asleep, Lila pulled on her only pair of shoes against the coolness of the autumn chill and wrapped a shawl around her shoulders before slipping out through the back door. Racing off to the smithy, she found a wooden crate and darted into the woods at the rear of her father's property. Anticipating that she could possibly encounter a problem at the end of her night journey, she had planned ahead for every eventuality. Since Daniel seemed determined to cling to some of his city ways, she was forced to think ahead.

She skirted the edge of town, keeping well to the rear of homes and shops until she arrived at Daniel's home. His was a pretty two-story house painted white with black shutters at all the windows. The house was not overly large when one first glanced at it, but it was surprisingly spacious inside.

Quietly, afraid she would awaken his neighbors and cause a stir, she gingerly attempted to open the back door. Locked. "Curse," she whispered and ran around to the front of the house. With little hope she mounted the front steps of the covered porch and gently tried the front door. *Locked.* "Daniel, thee and me have got to have a talk," she muttered. Retreating, she went to the back of the house, talking to herself all the way. "I should never have thrown that key away."

"Smart girl, bringin' your own box," she said softly as she positioned the thing, climbing up to test a window. "He locks the doors and not the windows," she scoffed in a whisper. The Briggses never bothered to lock their doors or windows. There was no need.

The first-floor windows of Daniel's house were higher from ground level than Lila had remembered. Even standing on her box, she had a ways to hoist herself. Having eased the window up a good way, she took firm hold of the window ledge, dipped down and then sprang upward . . . promptly banging her head on the raised window frame. "Shoooot!" she hissed, even as she shimmied the upper portion of her body through the opening. Once she was securely halfway into the house, she grabbed the top of her head. "Rattle brain," she whispered, cursing her own stupidity. With her legs dangling outside the house, Lila remained motionless until the stars cleared from her eyes.

Daniel had heard the soft bumps and the whispered commotion. At first he had thought some animal had wandered up on the porch, directly below his bedroom window. He'd heard the soft shuffling there and then only silence. Now, as he crept down the stairs, he knew it was no *animal* trying to get into his house.

The billowing curtains in the dining room were his first clue that whatever was amiss was happening in that area. Raising one hand to waist height, he moved silently forward.

Lila raised her head, and a sharp pain flashed behind her eyes. And then a light flared, and the pain intensified.

"For the love of God," Daniel muttered. "What are you doing?"

Lila dared to raise her head again, wincing before she managed a smile. "Hello, Daniel." Her eyes widened, however, when she noted the pistol in his hands. "You won't need a gun," she said. "I'm unarmed."

"In the wits department," he murmured, stepping forward just as his match sputtered against his fingers and died. "Shit!"

"Daniel!" she admonished.

"Oh, for God's sake, Lila, this is not the time for . . . just a minute."

She could hear him rummaging about, and a moment later the wick of a lamp caught the flame from another match.

She tried to smile at him as he advanced on her. "Daniel, I think one half of my body isn't getting any blood anymore."

He shook his head, not believing that she was dangling half in and half out of his dining room window. "Which half?" he questioned as he placed his hands under her arms. "The cerebrum, no doubt," he grunted as he pulled her up and inside.

Lila adjusted her footing and immediately began to rub her midsection against the deep dent in her flesh caused by the window frame. She grinned up at him. "Thank you, Daniel."

He stared at her in amazement and then shook his head, laughing. "You are unbelievable."

Lila nodded and immediately regretted the motion. Her hand left her middle and gingerly touched the top of her head.

"Have you hurt yourself?" Daniel asked as suddenly all the fun fled the game. "Let me see." He pulled her toward the center of the room and dragged a chair away from the table. "Sit," he ordered.

Lila sat quietly as he lifted the lamp and held it above her head. And even though his fingers were gentle, she couldn't help but cringe away when he came upon the sore spot.

"You've got a devilish bump," he said. "But the skin isn't broken."

"Your window smacked right into my head," she muttered.

"The *window* did that?" he teased and pulled out another chair, sitting to face her. "Couldn't be the other way around, Lee, could it?" He looked her over then, noting the night-dress and little more. "Where is your shoe?"

Stupidly she looked down at her feet: one shoe. "It must be outside," she said, and then twisted her head to look at both shoulders. "I had a shawl, too."

Daniel shook his head in mock disgust and laughed again. "I'll get them." He jogged around the back of the house because the ground was cold against his bare feet and the night air wasn't all that appealing to his exposed chest, either. Scooping up the shoe and shawl, he spied the wooden crate and took it with him, leaving it near the door before going inside.

Entering the room, Daniel walked up behind Lila and dropped the shawl across her shoulders before kneeling at her feet and presenting her lost shoe. "Are you ready to tell me why you've gone to all this trouble?"

"I'm compulsive," she said simply.

Frowning, Daniel raised questioning eyes as her shoe slid onto her dainty foot. "Don't you mean *im*pulsive, Lee?"

She grinned down at him then and asked, "Which is the least dangerous?"

He laughed shortly and settled back on his heels, resting the palms of both hands on his thighs. "So, what is this all about?"

"I think we've waited too long," she said bluntly.

That did not give him much to go on. "All right, love. Too long for what?"

"I was lyin' in my bed tryin' to sleep, and I realized if I soon didn't do somethin' I was goin' to wake the girls." She leaned toward him, and her voice, with her next words, became hushed. "Daniel, I got to thinking about what you said today, about *ultimate joy* and . . ."

Daniel propped an elbow on his thigh and hid his smile behind the palm of his hand. "*Enjoyment*, love."

"Right." She nodded her agreement. "Daniel . . . I got all feverish all over again," she added, as if she had just discovered a new wonder of the world.

Daniel reached out and smoothed her nightdress over her knee. "I know, darling," he whispered in empathy.

"Well, now that you've got me wonderin' about it, I think you'd better show me," she said earnestly.

Daniel's head dropped forward and his answer was a deep, single bark of laughter.

"Well . . ." she drawled, now acutely embarrassed. "What am I supposed to do about these feelings?" she pleaded. "They're worse now than what I had before."

"Come on," he said, easing her upward as he got to his feet. Once he was standing, he scooped her up in his arms and dipped her toward the table. "Take up the lamp, Lee," he said.

"Where are we going?"

"To my room."

Satisfied, Lila grinned and tightened her arm around his neck.

"To talk," he returned firmly. "Pick up the lamp, Lee," he said.

She did so, reluctantly. "We can *talk* any time," she muttered.

"Not this kind of talk." Daniel mounted the stairs.

"Are you angry that I came?" she asked. The small-voice act did not fool him for a moment.

"No. Not at all. But I hadn't expected to be rescuing you from a dining room window our first night together," he teased. "I'd planned something more romantic."

Lila smiled softly. "Did you, Daniel? What?"

"Oh, a nice dinner for two, candles, and wine."

Lila was rather sorry she had ruined that; it sounded wonderful. "Well, we've got the lantern," she said ruefully.

He entered the large master bedroom and lowered her to the center of the bed before relieving her of the lamp. "I think I can scare up the candle," he said playfully. He lit the candle on the table beside his bed and doused the lamp, setting it off to the side. Then he pulled the blankets over her and climbed onto the bed beside her, propping himself on his side. "So, my darling can't sleep," he said lightly. "It's called tension, Lee. It's a healthy reaction to being in love."

"I sure hope there's a cure," she muttered, burrowing more deeply beneath the blankets.

He grinned. "Oh, there is, never fear."

"Does makin' love make it go away?" she asked hopefully.

"For a time," he hedged.

She frowned. "You're not goin' to make love to me, are you, Daniel?"

He stopped teasing her and reached for her hand. "It's making me almost desperate with wanting, having you lying here in my bed. But, Lee, we've just survived one scandal, and we don't want people looking back in a few months and counting fingers. We've got three weeks, and then we will be together whenever, and as often, as we choose."

Now Lila was confused. "'Finger counting'? But you told me you knew how to prevent babies, Daniel." He'd better. She was counting on that.

Daniel's hand stroked slowly from her shoulder until he was holding her fingers again. "I do, love, but I can't guarantee that a baby won't happen."

Lila thought about that as she stared up at him. "Well, you could tell me how, and I could 'guarantee.' "

He dipped his head and whispered close to her ear. "It's another of *my* jobs." He raised his head, smiling at her rosy cheeks. "It's the man who has to have control, darling."

This was all very difficult to understand. "I suppose I shouldn't have come," she murmured, staring at the ceiling. "I'm gettin' all hot just talkin' about this, and I'm not learnin' much."

Daniel fell onto his back and hooted with laughter.

Lila rolled onto his chest and grinned at him. "Well, I am."

"I know," he said when he could speak. "Me, too, pet," he whispered, grinning as he raked his fingers through her hair. "I'm trying to be noble, and you're not making it any easier," he said lightly.

Lee dropped her chin onto her hands. "Do you really want me that much?"

Daniel nodded his head, watching her eyes as he gently guided her hand between their bodies to his erection. In a strangled voice he whispered, "That much, Lee."

It was the first time she had touched him there, but Lila

was far too open a woman to be startled or appear concerned. She had not failed to notice him in this condition a time or two, and she was satisfied with the message he was conveying. Well, if not 'satisfied,' Lila thought, she could sleep on it. "Maybe I should go?"

Unhappy at that thought, although he knew it was for the best, Daniel wrapped his arms around her and said fiercely, "Oh, God, Lee, I don't want you to." He truly did not, and he hoped he had been successful in putting her doubts to rest. If she had confused his nobility with a lack of interest, he certainly hoped she now understood.

Eventually they mutually agreed that they were strong enough to wait for their wedding night, and Daniel escorted her home.

They did not dare go by horseback for fear of making an easier target for the townsfolk to spot. Instead, Daniel pulled her behind him as they ran behind the houses and shops, within the confines of the edge of the woods.

When they stood at the back door of the small house beside the smithy, Daniel turned her to face him and pulled her hard against his chest. "Remember that I love you," he whispered.

"I know, Daniel," she whispered and then grinned at him. "But will you please learn to leave your door unlocked?" she teased. "Just in case."

He laughed softly and swept her into his arms, kissing her more fiercely than he had ever dared before, pulling her tight against his body as his lips demanded a return of pressure from her own. And then he was turning her to face the door. "In you go," he said simply.

Lila's cheeks were flushed with love and pleasure when she turned to wave him goodbye. She had never been so elated.

CHAPTER
15

 To say that Daniel Stone was distracted would be the understatement of the century.

 Once he had seen Lila safely home, he returned to his own house and prepared for a day of tending the sick. And while his attention was focused on a patient, he was fine. In between one ailing soul and the next he was prone to behaving more like a growing turnip—rooted.

Edmond stuck his head around the corner of the doorframe and found Daniel seated at his desk, star-ing thoughtfully at nothing. "There are sick people waiting patiently for your healing touch, Doctor," he said flatly.

Daniel started and peered up at his friend. "Sorry, Edmond," he muttered, jumping to his feet.

 "Sit," Edmond ordered and entered the room, taking a chair in front of Daniel's desk. "Would you mind telling me what the *sam hill* is going on?" he asked, knitting his fingers together over his slight paunch.

Daniel started to speak, hesitated, and shook his head. "I've talked with Jonathan Briggs," he said. "I have permission to marry Lila."

Frowning, Edmond questioned, "Isn't that what you wanted?"

Daniel stood, paced to the window, and stared out at the small shed that housed the doctors' horses during the day. "Edmond," he sighed, "I've got myself so wound up I can barely see straight."

Edmond briefly considered a number of possibilities that statement might cover and offered the first conclusion. "As in, *you need a woman*? That kind of 'wound up'?"

The younger man nodded.

"Well," Edmond drawled. "That's hardly any reason for shame in a man. Why don't you just do something about it before you become totally useless around here?"

Daniel laughed shortly and turned to face his friend. "I'm not interested in just *any* woman. And I'm not prepared to behave in any manner which could cause speculation about my devotion to Lila. I vowed, for her sake, this courtship was going to be of sufficient time to still the tongues of the gossips. I won't have them defaming her, Edmond. Besides, I love her so much no other woman could possibly interest me." He collapsed onto his chair, running splayed fingers through his hair. "The hell of it is, I've got the sexual appetite of a whole damned army."

"Horny," Edmond mumbled, and then he threw back his head and began to laugh.

Feeling a mild flush creep over his face, Daniel muttered, "Thank you."

Edmond found this enormously funny. "Well, that's what we called it in my day." But he was sympathetic, too. "I remember when I was a young man," he said, wiping laughter tears from the corners of his eyes. "I well remember having to keep my hands off Rachael," he added, sobering with effort.

"We're having the banns read this Sunday," Daniel sighed, as if he were sorry he hadn't carried Lila off and married her in some neighboring town away from Frankfort, the gossips, and her family. "I've been wondering if Rachael might be willing to give Lila a hand with the preparations for a wedding."

Edmond chuckled and nodded his head. "Oh, Rachael has had her heart set on this for weeks. In fact, I think she's already made some plans of her own."

"A *small* wedding, Edmond," Daniel said ruefully. "And the sooner the better."

That set off Edmond's laughter again.

Daniel had already formed the habit of stopping by the small house beside the smithy for supper whenever time and patients would permit.

Lila had, likewise, formed the habit of throwing an extra potato in the pot in hopes that he would be joining them.

And Daniel became an expected visitor around the table, as far as the family was concerned. The children enjoyed his attentions, and Jonathan appeared accepting, although quiet.

Daniel nodded from his place at one end of the table as the older man excused himself. He frowned, watching Jonathan leave the house.

Lila placed her hand on Daniel's shoulder as she set a cup of coffee in front of him. "I think our happiness is making him sad," she said quietly. "I think he's missin' Mama more and more. I guess he's rememberin' when they got married."

Daniel tried to mentally put himself in Jonathan's place, but he knew he could not begin to imagine the pain he would feel if he were to lose Lila. He sympathized with Jonathan's sorrow; he only wished he could somehow help the man before he drowned himself in rum.

Sammy eyed his sister as he spooned bread pudding into his mouth. "Tommy said you was goin' to get married," he mumbled. "I said he was a liar."

"Sammy!" Lila admonished.

But Daniel turned his attention to the boy in a much calmer manner. "Don't you want Lila to marry me, Sammy?"

The boy dropped his spoon into his bowl and rested his elbows on the table as he firmly shook his head.

Daniel's eyes were questioning as Lila eased herself onto the bench opposite her young brother.

Now the eyes of all the children were upon them.

"Why?" Daniel questioned softly as he returned his attention to the youngest member of the family. "I thought we were friends. You wanted me to come live here, remember?"

The child's eyes were troubled as he faced the man. "But you won't. Tommy said Lee's gonna live at your house."

Annie started to cry.

Daniel flashed Lila an apologetic look and reached out his hands. "Come here, Sammy," he said.

Sammy refused to budge.

"I'm sorry," Daniel said, his hands coaxing. "We should have made this very clear to you before now. Lila will still be here for you, Sammy." He looked around the table, ensuring that the promise he was making was clear to every member of this family. Particularly the youngest members.

Lila had tucked Annie under her arm, attempting to console the girl.

When Sam shuffled reluctantly toward the end of the bench, Daniel lifted him onto his lap. "Lila and I are going to get married," he said quietly. "But she will be here every day with you just like she is now."

Sammy clearly felt hope then. "Are you goin' to live here, too?"

Daniel shook his head and watched that hope die before he could speak. "I'll be here a lot more. Lila and I will only sleep at my house, Sam. The only time your sister won't be here is when you're sleeping."

Sammy gave that some thought and could come up with only one question. "Will she still make us cookies?"

Daniel laughed and hugged the boy against his chest as his eyes moved from one child to the next. "Yes, I'm sure Lee can be persuaded to make cookies now and then." Jon and Tommy were grinning knowingly, but Beth and Edward did not seem quite so satisfied. "I promise you little will change in your lives," Daniel said and reached for Lila's hand on top of the table. "I promise, if you allow me to wed your sister, that life will change hardly at all. Beth? Edward?" He waited patiently, hopefully, until both children nodded their consent, and Daniel knew he was at least halfway there.

Lila murmured something to Annie, and the small girl nodded, also.

"Well, Sammy?" he asked. "Do you think this will work out all right?"

"Will ya take me fishin'?" the boy asked hopefully.

Daniel smiled, squeezed Lila's hand, and blessed her with a look of love that branded her his forever. "In the spring, son. We'll do lots of fishing in the spring."

Jon and Tommy both rose, shook Daniel's hand, and kissed Lee on the cheek before they disappeared. The other children fell into their routine of clearing up the supper dishes as Lila and Daniel remained at the table, drinking coffee and staring at each other as they whispered words of love intermingled with plans for the days ahead.

Daniel had gone to bed, only to get up and wander about his lonely house. He could not remember any other time in his life when he had not been able to settle to things; not been able to concentrate for more than a few moments at a time. He was an educated man after all and should be in control of his thoughts and his body. But he had to admit that this matter involving his heart was a powerful force. *Lila* had become a powerful force in his life. His house seemed lonelier tonight because he wanted her to be there. He was starved for her happy chatter, her teasing and her laughter. Not to mention being hungry for her body. He needed her and wanted her, and shrugging into a coat, he eventually journeyed out to the back porch, wishing she were there beside him. It would be foolhardy for her to come again, but he had sensed something in her tonight at supper that he had never seen in her before. They had spoken with each other through silent communications and subtle touches, and he thought she must be suffering the same turmoil as he. And yet, he knew she would not have an understanding of that suffering. He knew, also, that they would not be waiting for the banns, the ceremony, or a wedding feast before they consummated their love. This thing between them had grown too immense, and the craving was now too dominant to be ignored.

He willed her to stay away.

Yet, he willed her to come.

Lila wondered only briefly about Daniel's reaction to her sneaking out of her house again a second night. He did not want her taking unnecessary risks. He worried about her being out on her own in the night. He had asked her to be patient for a few days, but the time for patience had passed. She had to be with him, and little else mattered. Little *else* even occupied her mind for more than a breath. Only being with Daniel mattered.

She understood that being with him tonight would be different. Tonight he would lie in bed with her, and it would be different. She willed it to be so. Instinctively she knew it was time for them.

Everything and everyone else in the universe became secondary as she skirted the neighboring houses, staying within the shelter of the trees. When she reached the trees at the back of Daniel's yard, she paused, remaining hidden as she watched a tiny red glow in the darkness. That red dot moved upward and flared, bathing his face ever so briefly in meager light. She smiled, emerging from her hiding place, and walked slowly toward him.

He sensed she had come before he actually saw her. And then his eyes focused through the darkness on the white of her nightdress moving slowly closer.

Daniel stepped to the ground and flung the remainder of his cheroot away as his heart began to beat a wild cadence. The red tip arched and fell, and then Lila was standing before him. Smiling up at him.

He stared down at her, his throat suddenly dry with anticipation. He was deliriously happy that she had come.

He smiled and reached for her hands, holding them between them. "Our good intentions didn't last long," he teased.

"Are you angry that I came?" she asked as she searched his face for the answer.

He shook his head and wrapped his arms loosely around her. "Didn't you hear me calling to you?" he asked quietly.

"Were you, Daniel?"

"In my thoughts I was, darling," he whispered before he dropped a sweet, chaste kiss on her lips.

"I had to come."

"I know," he said, pulling her more firmly against his chest.

"We have the consent of everyone who matters. . . ."

He nodded and lowered his head, his lips close to her ear. "The children."

"Somehow it doesn't seem right that we be apart anymore," she whispered fiercely. "And, Daniel, my heart is poundin' all the time because I can't seem to stop thinkin' about bein' with you."

The direction of those thoughts was clearly understood between them. "I know," he said again and backed away from her, pulling her along as he moved backward up the steps behind him.

Lila followed easily, her eyes focused only on his face until he turned, opening the door, allowing her to proceed him into the house.

Not a single word was spoken as he led her through the dark, silent rooms, up the stairs, and into the bedroom where she had rested next to him the previous night.

She stood beside the bed with her hands clasped together before her as Daniel stepped away. A moment later the room glowed softly with light from a lamp on a table near the large bed.

He turned and smiled, walking toward her. "Hello, my love," he said quietly.

Lila laughed uncomfortably. "I didn't think I would feel shy with you."

"You may be shy," he said as he ducked his head and pulled her firmly into his arms. "For the first moment or two."

"What happens after a minute or two?" she asked, grinning happily.

"You become wild and love-thirsty and ravish me."

"Really?" she questioned in well-feigned seriousness. "I thought that worked the other way around."

Daniel appeared distracted as he studied the glow in her eyes. "Remind me to teach you how it's done," he murmured.

"When?" she asked eagerly.

He laughed lightly and placed the palm of his hand over her heart. "When you're ready, love."

"I think I've been ready for days, Daniel," she said. "For weeks."

"That makes two of us," he said as he moved her hand upward on his chest. "Feel," he murmured as he pressed her palm over his own heart.

Lila tipped her head up and grinned. "Do you have a cure for these heart conditions, Doctor?"

"I believe I can help," he said before his lips moved close to hers. His lips met hers then, a warm, gentle pressure that was far different from that first kiss that night on her father's porch. That kiss had been desperate and needful. This kiss was gentle and coaxing.

Daniel paused long enough in their play to hastily pull his shirt over his head before he wrapped his arms around her again.

Lila felt the heat of him radiate around her and felt a sweet pressure where her breasts pressed against his chest. His body felt wonderful against hers; strong and warm and all encompassing.

She tipped her head back farther, pressing herself more firmly against him as Daniel's lips slanted across hers and his tongue played at the corner of her mouth.

His hand cupped her cheek and applied a gentle pressure.

"Open for me, love," he whispered, drawing away for a brief span of time. "Open," he said again and returned to her, surrounding her lips with warm moisture as his kiss became more urgent and his tongue sought to explore.

This was a kiss more potent than any he had dared before, and Lila felt a tiny spark of fear as she realized instinctively that the unknown was upon her. All her assumptions about physical loving were about to be revealed as right or wrong. All her imaginings about what they would do together were also about to be proved one way or the other.

Daniel abandoned the kiss and pressed his cheek briefly against hers, hugging her fiercely before easing his hold. She felt unbelievably *right*; all softness and curves. Diametrically matched to all those places where his body was hard and unyielding. Perfectly, wonderfully opposite. And he treasured her not only for the perfection of her body but also for the honest, earthy qualities she possessed. She could touch his heart, his mind, and his manhood with something as simple as one gentle little smile, and she was driving him to distraction as no woman ever had. "You know I'm going to take you, don't you, Lee?" he asked huskily before smiling down at her. "If you're feeling at all afraid of what is about to happen, darling, you must tell me."

She shook her head as any hint of teasing vanished between them. "I've been thinkin' about what we'd do," she said.

"Have you?" he whispered as he studied her expression and reached for the ribbon at the neck of her gown. "What have you been thinking?"

"That we would kiss," she said hesitantly.

He smiled and freed the first tiny button. "We've already done a good deal of that."

"And touchin'," she added as her fingers nervously gripped the material covering her thighs.

"We've done that, too," he insisted.

"*Naked*," she blurted.

He laughed lightly as his fingers proceeded to the last button. "And after we're naked?" he urged.

"Well, I guess you take me, and it must be pretty much over after that, Daniel," she said shyly.

His smile grew more tender as he raised his hand and stroked her cheek lightly. "You've missed a step or two," he said as he proceeded to push the gown over her shoulders and slowly down her arms. He *hoped* he would not cheat her of that "step or two" as he gazed at her firm, generous breasts. He was painfully hard and desperately in need as the palms of his hands covered her dark, taut nipples.

He seemed to search for something then; something he thought he might find in her eyes, and long moments passed them by. Finally he seemed to arrive at some conclusion. "You trust me to do right by you, don't you, Lee?"

"Yes," she whispered without hesitation.

"But there's that little tiny spark," he said knowingly. "That small fear of the unknown," he added, leaning close and whispering in her ear. "You will find pleasure, you know? I want you to know it and be free in it. I'm quite determined about that."

Lila smiled, even though she was confused by his words; she didn't know about this *pleasure* of which he spoke. Someone, somewhere, sometime had told her this was painful for women. But for men it was supposedly the height of pleasure. She couldn't recall who had said these things, but above all else, she wanted Daniel to have *that ultimate joy.*

He pushed the gown lower, past her hips, and allowed it to fall freely around her ankles. "I want to look at you," he murmured as his intense gaze met with hers.

Lila nodded her head slowly, once. Her complexion took on a healthy, rosy glow as an unfamiliar shyness crept over her.

He took his time and looked his fill.

Daniel drew in his breath as his gaze slowly roamed from her face to her neck to her breasts. This first complete sight of her was more powerful than he could have imagined. She was exquisitely porportioned with high, firm breasts and a small waist. Her hips flared gently, speaking of growing maturity and the promise of a woman who would carry her babies well and easily. Her skin was creamy white and the nipples of her breasts seemed to grow more taut as he stared. "So lovely," he breathed.

Lila breathed a sigh that could only be described as relief; she wanted so to please him.

Daniel knew he needed to take a step back. He had to go slowly, gently with her. He did not want to startle her, and yet, it was difficult. He wanted her wildly and passionately, and he wanted her to relax and enjoy. Time became his enemy and his friend.

It would be difficult.

But these first magical moments that would kindle a lifetime of memories between them would be worth any passionate agony.

He placed his hands on her shoulders, turned her and gently forced her to sit on the side of the bed before dropping to his knees to remove her worn, heavy shoes. He grinned up at the intensity of her eyes as she watched. And then he planted a quick kiss on her kneecap.

Lila smiled then, too.

"I'm going to kiss you all over," he teased.

"I think I might like that," she admitted.

Once her shoes were removed, Daniel whisked the quilts to the foot of the bed and eased Lila onto her back.

She felt no shyness about lying on his bed as naked as a jay while he remained partially clothed. In the next instant she smiled and her eyes focused clearly upon his as Daniel stood, attacking the buttons of his trousers. She studied the wide chest, the narrow hips. When he sat on the edge of the bed to remove his boots, Lila reached out and lightly ran her fingertips down his back. His muscles flexed in rippling spasms, and he grinned over his shoulder at her.

"You've found one of my most sensitive spots," he said huskily.

"I want to see you, too," she said as their gazes locked.

He stood and faced her, watching closely for her reaction as he shucked his trousers. It was important to him that she accepted what she saw and not be afraid.

Lila showed no fear as the object of her curiosity was revealed to her. She was a little surprised by this first sight of an erect male organ, but for the life of her she could not look away. "Daniel, are you really goin' to do what I think you're goin' to do?" she asked in a voice that expressed more awe than fear.

Daniel wasn't certain what he had expected, but it had not been that.

Once again, as he had experienced so often since meeting her, Daniel was struck by a sense of awe of his own. She was a natural wonder. A genuine, novel wealth of naïveté. A pure, curious, and open creature the likes of which he would never have believed existed.

And the last thing he wanted to do was cause her any anxiety. He stretched out beside her and propped his head on the palm of his hand. "Do you want to talk about this first, Lee?" he questioned softly.

Lila thought talking might prove embarrassing, and it would probably not be all that instructive. Besides, she was thinking too much, trying to figure how this was going to work. She trusted him; she had said as much. Now was the time. "No, I think you should kiss me again."

Daniel thought so, too; he could see by her eyes that she was puzzling it through. "Stop *thinking*," he ordered as he slowly lowered his head.

"I just don't see how you're goin' to fit," she said.

He grinned, holding back a delighted chuckle. "Thank you," he murmured as his teeth began to pluck lightly at her lower lip.

Lila put her arms around his shoulders and tried to read his expression. But he was too close; her eyes almost crossed. "I guess you're welcome."

He did chuckle then and turned his head to nuzzle her ear before he explained. "You just fed my male ego, love," he whispered.

"I did?" she gasped as his tongue circled the shell of her ear.

"Hmmm," he breathed. "I'll explain it sometime," he added. "Some *other* time."

He cupped the back of her head with one hand and a firm, young breast with the other, teasing her nipple for a moment before pressing his palm against her chest. "Your heart is racing again," he whispered as his lips moved toward hers once more. "That's what I've been waiting for." He kissed her for long, tender moments, feathering her lips with his own before he became more demanding. Eventually he felt her body tempo alter from the strain affected by doubt to the tension of anticipation. He abandoned her lips then, trailing tender kisses across her face and down her neck.

Lila sighed and moaned softly as his tongue and mouth and hands worshipfully worked down her body. What happened to her then reminded Lee of warm molasses. A slow-moving insidious *flowing* deep inside her. A methodical warm invasion that quickly robbed her of breath.

Daniel rested a leg between both of hers and pressed his lower body against Lila's hip; the firm contact of their bodies lessened the ache. He took the dark nipple of her left breast into his mouth and suckled slowly as his hand began to caress her thigh and hip.

The exquisite drawing sensation caused Lila to moan and press her head back into the pillow, raising her chest upward as she sought to be closer to him in her torment.

Daniel's hand inched upward over her hip, sliding across her flat belly while her hand traced light patterns over his back. Soon his breathless moans harmonized with hers, and he moved his head, devoting equal time to worshipping her other breast.

"Daniel," she breathed, her eyes closed as she turned her face upward.

"I know," he whispered. His fingers caressed her, moving downward until he touched between her thighs in response to her need.

Lila's entire body jerked in surprise.

"It's all right," he murmured, stretching up to look into her eyes as his caresses intensified.

She could feel the magic he was working as all her senses seemed to race from delicate pulsations to thundering madness. His lips played with hers, and Lila had difficulty determining which of the wonderful feelings he was promoting deserved the major portion of her concentration. Undecided, her mind went helplessly blank. In the next instant she was rocked by alternating waves of tension and release, and she was vaguely aware of Daniel pulling her hard against his chest while her body continued to quake.

"Oh, Lordy," she sighed as he eased her down.

And then Daniel was there again, the focus of her attention as he kissed her with mounting passion. He was gently demanding, and his hands seemed to touch every inch of her before he raised up and knelt between her thighs. He rested there but a moment, tilting her pelvis upward to receive him.

Lila stared at him, her breathing continuing its ragged pattern, as she tried to focus upon the look of sheer hunger in his eyes.

He moved forward, slowly entering her until he knew the moment was upon them, the moment he wished he could avoid. He also knew he could not prolong the unavoidable for her sake or his own. In his present state of desire it would not take much movement on Lila's part for it to be over and she still a virgin. He ground his teeth and lunged forward then, scooping her up in his arms as he heard her soft gasp. "I'm sorry, darling," he whispered against her ear.

The pain was fleeting and not even a memory a matter of seconds later. "I'm fine, Daniel," she murmured, and the tone of that sweet voice told him it was so.

All of Lila's thoughts and energies became redirected in that moment. She knew instinctively that now was the time that she could provide him the most pleasure; now was the time to concentrate on Daniel's needs.

Daniel had hoped to rest a bit, to give her time to become accustomed to him and then to elevate her once more to a second plain of passion and release. But his goals were undermined by the frantic kisses and caresses Lila was showering upon him. His frenzy grew until he feared his control would shatter, and then, as he felt the forces peak within him, he withdrew, shuddering within her arms and trembling over her body.

His climax was so intense that Lila actually feared for

him for a brief moment. But then he sighed into her hair, and she lovingly tightened her arms around his back.

"Oh, Lee," he groaned huskily, allowing his sated body to sag and rest upon hers.

Lila closed her eyes and smiled, pressing her cheek against his. "I guess I'm a bad girl now," she murmured.

Daniel chuckled softly. "You certainly are," he agreed and rolled to her side.

Lila turned her head, staring at him and grinning, simply for the sheer pleasure of it.

He smiled in return and kissed the tip of her nose before pulling her into the curve of his body. "My *bad* girl," he added. His hand stroked the length of her back to her hip as he stared down the length of their bodies. "You know I'll never hurt you again, don't you, Lee?"

Lila raised her head from his shoulder and waited until Daniel looked at her. "It didn't really hurt, Daniel. Just a bit and briefly. But I thought . . ."

When she hesitated, he frowned. "You thought . . . ?"

"Are you sure it will never hurt again?" she asked.

Daniel laughed shortly and continued stroking her back. "Positive, love."

"Somebody lied to me," she said with disgust and pressed more closely against him.

"Who?"

"I don't remember. It was a long time ago."

"So you came to me thinking I would hurt you every time I made love to you?"

Her head, nodding, bumped his chin.

"And still you came?" he asked in wonder.

Lila's arms tightened, and she pressed warm lips against his chest. "I love you and I want you badly enough to bear anything, Daniel," she whispered.

He buried his fingers in her hair and gently pulled her

head back. "You're an exceptional woman," he murmured, lowering his head. "Lila Briggs," he added before kissing her soundly.

Daniel settled them comfortably then; he had a few important matters on his mind, and if he continued to kiss her, he knew his mind would fail to nudge his memory. He had rehearsed the things he wanted her to understand.

He took her hand and enfolded it with his own, resting them on his belly. "We haven't talked about children," he said, smiling up at the ceiling. "Not really. Not about *our* children."

Lila was a bit taken aback by this opening conversation; she didn't know what she had expected him to say, but talk about babies was not a subject she wanted to pursue right now.

He stroked her arm from shoulder to wrist. "Should we make a plan?"

"A plan?" she parroted.

"Hmm. I suppose I'm asking whether or not you want me to prevent you from conceiving a child for a time?"

"Yes," she said softly.

The lack of hesitation in her response surprised him, and he looked down, trying to see her face. "I was inquiring about after the wedding as well as now," he explained.

Lila's head nodded.

His curious frown deepened. "Lila, look at me," he requested gently.

She did.

"Are you afraid to have a child?"

"What makes you think that?" she asked in surprise.

"Well, you seem to have thought about this . . . . I mean, you didn't hesitate. . . ."

"I'm afraid to get started," she said bluntly.

Daniel was feeling very stupid, and he was failing to connect with her meaning. "Started?"

It was clear enough to her. Lila nodded her head and sat up, bumping him in the side with a bent knee as she settled herself and faced him.

"I'm not worried about having babies, Daniel," she said forthrightly. She had simply made up her mind there wouldn't be any for a good long while.

"I'm happy for that," he said and waited patiently for her to continue.

"I don't mind waiting for a time if you're worried, though."

He smiled knowingly as he finally understood; she had watched her mother die from too much childbearing, too soon. She wasn't fooling him. He caressed her knee with the palm of his hand. "What's this fear of getting *started*?"

"How do you keep me from gettin' a baby?" she asked, blatantly ignoring his question.

Daniel thought she was being exceedingly evasive, a trait that was unlike her, but he told her what she wanted to know.

Lila listened carefully to his explanation, looking directly into his eyes. Her fingers plucked worriedly at the bed-clothes as he spoke, the only indication of her mild unease with the topic.

"Now answer *my* question," he said.

"What question?"

"What is this about fear of getting started?"

"Oh, that," she murmured and lay down beside him again. Once she was lying with her head on his shoulder, she said quietly, "Do you think I'll be like my mother, Daniel?"

"And have multiple pregnancies?" he questioned, beginning to see where her fear might actually lie. "I'll do my best to see that we have only as many babies as you want," he said with understanding.

"I don't know, Daniel," she drawled. "I'm afraid the women in my family could be a bit like rabbits."

He laughed at that.

Lila raised her head and frowned at him. "Well, my mother's mother had lots of babies, too."

He just smiled at her fondly and stroked a wisp of hair back from her forehead.

"You haven't had to cope with the load you're takin' on yet, Daniel. Not really. If we start adding baby after baby on top of what we've already got, we'll need so many rooms, we'll have to move into a castle."

"I think you're already deserving of a castle," he said quietly.

"Daniel . . ."

"I'm not worried about having too many babies around, darling, but I think I understand, and if you want to wait, we'll wait."

"You'll make sure you don't slip?" she asked seriously.

Daniel's head tipped back, and he laughed.

Lila's cheeks flushed. "Well," she said uncomfortably.

Daniel pulled her head down onto his chest and held her tightly. "I'll do my best not to 'slip,' " he murmured affectionately. "How I *love* you, Lila Briggs."

Lila thought *that* had gone rather well, having feared he might think she had no interest in having his babies. That was not the case at all. In fact, the exact opposite was true; she got all warm and toasty thinking about have his baby. But she also worried about Daniel having to adjust to the goings-on in a large family, and she feared he might not make the transition. He hadn't lived that sort of life, and she did not want to add to his burden while he adapted to the world of the Briggses.

She was cozy and warm and content now that she had extracted the promise she needed from him. As Lila felt herself drifting off to sleep, however, she was rudely disturbed when Daniel muttered something and jumped up from the bed. "What?" she asked in alarm.

Gloriously naked, Daniel padded across the bedroom floor and began searching in a chest near the door. "I almost forgot," he muttered. When he turned to face her, he smiled, hiding his prize behind his back as he advanced on the bed.

He wasn't nearly so alarming in his present state as he had appeared only a short time ago, but Lila felt he looked very funny wearing only a silly grin. She laughed. "What are you doing?"

"I have a surprise for you," he said. He stopped when his knees hit the side of the bed. "A gift."

All hint of laughter disappeared as she stared up at him. "A gift?"

Daniel had seen her look this way only once before; the night he had given Lila roses from Rachael Fraser's garden. It felt as if an unseen hand had reached into his chest and was painfully squeezing his heart. But he would not shame her by asking her to confirm that she had never received a gift before now. "It's just a small gift," he murmured and bent over the bed, reaching for her foot. He was almost reverent in his touch as he stroked her ankle and then her arch before he placed the first small, beige kid slipper on her foot.

Lila watched his movements with a catch in her throat, and his *gift* very quickly became blurred behind a veil of tears.

"There's a gown to match," Daniel said quietly as he fitted the remaining slipper. "You'll have to see Rachael about the fitting. . . ." He saw the tears in her eyes then and dropped down beside her. "Lee?" he questioned anxiously as he pulled her into his arms.

"They're beautiful!" she cried.

Daniel's heart was racing in concern over this reaction; he had not seen her cry since the day she had argued with that teacher over Edward. "Darling, I thought you would be happy."

"I *am*," she said as her tears dampened his neck and her arms tightened around him. She had been suddenly rocked by the wonder of him; the generosity and devotion she had never dared to even think about. Rocked by a love so overwhelmingly beautiful, she had a fleeting thought of having stepped into someone else's dream, and she was afraid to awaken for fear that dream would end.

Daniel smiled, relaxing back against his pillows as she cried. He had often heard of happy tears, but he had never known a woman to cry them without having a manipulative intent. But his Lila was more honest than most. And it had been quite a night for her, he supposed. "Remind me not to make you quite so 'happy' again," he whispered ruefully.

Lila choked on a dainty laugh, through her tears of joy.

CHAPTER
16

 LILA SAW THE WORLD THROUGH THE THREAT OF happy tears on several occasions over the next few weeks. Most of her nights were spent secretly in Daniel's arms, and her days were filled with the presence of friends and frenzied activities.

Rachael Fraser threw herself merrily into the finishing of the beige gown and coerced a few of her friends into the making of suits of clothes for the entire Briggs family. The girls were to have new dresses. Lila more than one. Each male Briggs received a new coat and trousers, and all were trouped off to Cuthbert's store in search of shoes.

 Daniel was very generous with his "potato" wages.

"So much, Daniel," Lila whispered as he presented her with a new winter cloak. She was genu-inely concerned for the state of his finances. "Too much."

Daniel had no such concerns, and he loved giving.

Lila had never even asked him if he had two pennies to his name. In fact, he possessed a modest fortune.

"I hate shoes!" Sammy complained as Tommy tried valiantly to dress the small boy in his new clothes.

"Ya gotta wear shoes to a weddin'," Tommy insisted.

Daniel easily detected the frustration in Tommy's tone and smiled at his bride-to-be. "Off you go," he said as he quickly kissed her cheek and then her lips. "You'd best get yourself ready."

He watched Lila turn toward her own room before he entered the bedroom occupied by Lila's brothers. Daniel knew that Jonathan would be of little help with the problem of a defiant Sammy. Sadly, the man had already dipped into the rum keg a time or two that morning; in celebration of his daughter's marriage, of course. He was sitting at the table staring morosely at the back door.

"Let me try, Tommy," Daniel said as he sat on the end of one bed. "You get ready."

Sammy was standing in the center of the room wearing a new shirt, a frown, and little else.

"I thought you liked your new suit," Daniel said as he reached for the small gray trousers.

Sammy shook his head but wandered unhappily across the room when Daniel beckoned.

"Well, you were sure proud of your new shoes when we picked them out," he said conversationally as the boy lifted one leg and then the other.

"They hurt my feet," Sammy said ungraciously.

Daniel smiled as he tucked the boy's shirt inside his trousers. "Your world isn't going to turn upside down, son," he said quietly as he fastened the first of three buttons. And then he sought to brighten the child's mood as he pulled

Sammy up on his lap. "And you have to wear shoes if you're going to a party," he said lightly.

Sammy watched as the first boot was laced. "What party?" he muttered.

Hooked him, Daniel thought. "Over at Dr. Fraser's house."

"But that's where—"

"What's your favorite kind of cookie?" Daniel asked as the second shoe found a home.

"Sugar cookies," Sammy said miserably.

"Mrs. Fraser's got some," he said. "I saw them."

"Why isn't Lee sleepin' here tonight?"

Daniel sighed and stood the boy between his spread knees. "Obviously I'm not as smart as I thought I was," he muttered.

"We told you why, Sammy," Jon said as he shrugged into his new coat.

"And she's not gonna be here tomorrow," the boy continued.

Daniel and Lila were taking two nights and one full day for themselves. Rachael and one of her friends had agreed to cook and see that the little ones would be entertained.

Daniel turned Sammy around and held his coat. "She'll be here the next day," he said as he directed one small arm into a sleeve. When the dressing was done, Daniel turned the lad to face him, knowing he had not succeeded in appeasing the child's concerns. "I love you, Sammy," he said.

After a long stare and a silence that seemed even longer, Sammy threw his arms around Daniel's neck. "I love you, too, Daniel," he mumbled.

Moments later Daniel stood beside a carriage, waiting anxiously for the first sight of his bride in her new finery.

Jon and Tommy had applied considerable wax and polish

to the best carriages the smithy had to offer so that the family could ride across town to the Frasers' home in style.

Lila proved well worth every minute of the wait, as far as Daniel was concerned.

She stepped into the October sunlight and became instantly aware that all eyes were upon her. She laughed nervously and completely out of character as Daniel walked toward her. Lee had swept her glorious chestnut hair high upon her head, leaving soft tendrils to curl around her face. The gown was the beige gown of Daniel's imagination that night they had danced Lila's first dance. "I bet they think Lila's gone missin'," she said lightly, staring around him at her brothers and sisters. "They don't seem to recognize me."

"I recognize you," he said as he stopped in front of her and took her hand. "I recognize you as the most beautiful creature I've ever seen."

Lila's head tipped to the side as she grinned up at him. "Maybe you should be borrowin' Edward's spectacles, Daniel."

"My eyesight is perfect," he murmured as he tucked her slender hand into the crook of his arm and led her toward the waiting vehicles.

News of the wedding was generally known, but none of the townsfolk had been invited; this was to be a family affair. Still, many smiling faces shouted words of happiness and waved friendly, exuberant greetings as the two vehicles rolled along the streets.

Annie and Sammy stood directly in front of Lila and Daniel in the Frasers' large front parlor while the remainder of Lila's family, accompanied by Edmond and Rachael, flanked the young couple.

Daniel gazed lovingly at his bride, his hand resting firmly on the shoulder of a fidgeting Sammy, while the preacher spoke the words that would join them together.

Annie stood as still as an angel's statue.

Beth silently dashed tears from her cheeks with her fingertips. Secretly Rachael did the same.

Jon, Tommy, and Edmond stood quietly with their hands at their sides.

And Jonathan tipped sideways when he started to doze off.

Daniel responded to the minister's words in a deep, reverent tone. "I do," he said.

Lila was radiant and happy, and when it came time to repeat her vows, she did so in a voice that was strong and did not waver. "I do."

Sammy grinned over his shoulder at the man who was now, somehow, related to him. "Now can we have the cookies?" he asked.

The preacher managed the final blessing around his smile. "You may kiss your bride, Daniel," he said at last and *did* laugh then at the expression of disgust on Sammy's face.

Rachael and her friends had outdone themselves with the meal; turkey, ham, breads, vegetables, and desserts weighted down the long dining room table. A sweet punch had been provided for the children, and the adults partook of whatever struck their fancy; Edmond had a good stock of wines and spirits, and Jonathan sampled a wide variety.

Sammy ate an unusually large meal and fell asleep and was put to bed in a guest room. He did not manage to stay awake long enough to wave his sister goodbye as she and Daniel departed to his white frame house. The house that Daniel had bought. The house that would now be *their* home.

Daniel unharnessed the mare and led her into the small stable behind his house with Lila on his heels. He felt her hand go into the pocket of his coat and turned a puzzled glance her way.

Lila smiled, holding up a folded square of paper. "Do you have a nail and a hammer?" she asked.

Daniel nodded, frowning in confusion. But he walked to the small bench where he kept a number of tools and gave her the items she had requested.

"Thank you," she said lightly, tipping up to kiss his cheek before leaving him alone.

The animals were no more than bedded down for the night before Daniel heard the tapping of the hammer. He followed the sound around to the front of the house and stopped in surprise. Lila was nailing the unfolded paper to the front door.

Their marriage document was about to be left to flutter in the midnight breezes.

When she had finished the chore, Lila stood back, giving a satisfied nod. "There! That should do it."

He stepped up behind her and placed his hands on her shoulders. "Do what?"

Lila continued to admire the piece of paper. "I can just hear Mae Belle Willoughby now," she said and began to imitate the older woman's scratchy voice. " 'We don't know they're married for sure,' she'll say. 'None of us was invited to the wedding, were we? We haven't seen a marriage paper, have we?' Now they'll all see it," Lila added happily.

Daniel laughed and turned her into his embrace. "And they can all go to the devil?" he asked lightly.

"To hell in a handbasket," she returned cheekily.

"Well," he drawled as he bent and swept her up in his arms, "that's enough of your deprecations. That poor, poor woman," he clucked.

Lila laughed and threw her arms around his neck. "Daniel!"

"Swept the woman right off her feet," he quipped. He

took the two steps needed to reach the front door and dipped his knees. Lila obliged by turning the ebony doorknob and swinging the door inward. "And for the next thirty hours or so, you are mine," he said, kicking the door closed with a booted foot. "No family, no friends, no enemies. Whatever. Mine!" he said happily as he mounted the stairs with her.

Lila simply stared at him, grinning happily.

"I'm so very happy you're here, Lila Stone," he said quietly.

Lila's expression turned seriously tender. "Me, too," she said. "With you."

"We are going to make love, sleep a little, and make love again," he said conversationally. "We might talk a bit in between."

"You've got this all planned out, have you?" she teased.

"Uh-huh."

"You know, Daniel, I get hungry now and again."

"There's food in the kitchen. Rachael saw to that, too."

When he entered the bedroom that Lila had come to know intimately, she was amazed by what she saw. "Oh, Daniel."

He let her slide to her feet and watched as she slowly inspected the room. A small, round table had been set before the windows, dressed in a lacy cloth and glowing in the flickering light from two candles. Lila smiled with pleasure as she walked across the room, beyond the dancing flames of the small fire that had been set, and stood admiring the setting of dainty plates, linen napkins, crystal glasses, wine, cheeses and fruit, jams and butter. She became suspicious when she lightly touched a tea biscuit and found it still warm.

Daniel walked up behind her and placed his hands on her shoulders as he, too, inspected the gift. "You see, we have some wonderful friends here in Frankfort, Lee. I suspect Mrs. Cuthbert was dashing out the back door as we were coming in the front."

"That's why the front door wasn't locked," she murmured.

"It's a shame we aren't hungry," he said quietly. "It looks so inviting."

Lila turned in his arms, laughing. "You'll be hungry," she bantered. "You are always hungry after you make love to me."

It was true. He frequently dashed to the kitchen to find them a snack after loving her half the night.

"That's because you drain all my energies," he returned. "A man has to maintain his strength."

"You'd better," she murmured and turned back to the table. "I think a glass of wine is in order," she said, reaching for the bottle. Lila thought she might need a little fortification, just to settle her nervous quivering. She had yet to initiate their loveplay, having always taken her lead from him. Daniel was a tender and considerate lover, teaching her well the means with which they could both enjoy separate or mutual moments. Lila had already planned that tonight would be different. Tonight she would show him, by word and deed, just how much she wanted to please him. Now that the moment was upon her, however, she was surprised to find she had a terrible case of jitters. What if she went too far? What if Daniel did not want her bold and brazen?

She struggled with the bottle cork for a brief space of time before Daniel stepped around her and relieved her of the chore. "Allow me," he said.

He grinned when she flashed him a happy smile.

"I'm a wife," she said, a little bit in awe, as if the reality had just hit her.

Daniel dropped a kiss on the tip of her nose. "Yes, you are, my darling."

She watched his strong hand wrap around the cork and pull. She looked around the room she would share with this man she loved; share forever more. She loved this place, she realized. She had quickly become comfortable here, feeling safe and cherished, surrounded by his things. Her own things now hung beside his in the cherrywood clothes press, and three drawers of the chest had been taken over by her. Her hairbrush resided next to his on the commode, just as she would reside next to Daniel. She felt as if she and her things belonged here and were welcome here. And she felt flushed with pleasure and love, right down to her toes. "I suppose I should act like a wife," she murmured as she returned her attention to her husband.

He laughed. "How does a *wife* act?"

"Reserved? Retirin'?" she speculated as she fingered the lacy tablecloth.

Daniel grunted over her remark as he pulled the cork free. He turned his head before pouring the wine and whispered very close to her ear, "*Not* in our bedroom, love, please."

That was exactly what she wanted to hear. "You're certain?"

"*Certain* is an understatement," he muttered as he concentrated on filling two glasses. "In fact, I don't want you to change one bit," he added as he handed her a glass and raised his own in a toast. "To my wonderful Lila. To your beauty, your smile, your infectious laugh, your generous and loving nature. Don't you dare change one bit," he said sternly.

This glowing tribute made Lila feel a bit shy. She quickly sipped from her glass and then set it on the table. "I love you, too, Daniel," she said before presenting him with her back. "Would you help with these buttons, please?"

Setting his glass aside, Daniel began the task of freeing the tiny buttons from her neck to her lower spine. "Do you like your gown?" he asked softly.

"I love it. It's exactly like the one you described that night at the school. When we danced," she murmured. "I especially love that you remembered and had Rachael make it for me. I didn't know men were so romantic."

"We have our moments," he returned ruefully.

"That night was very important to me, Daniel," she confessed.

"It was your first dance," he said as he dropped a sensuous kiss on her bared shoulder.

Lila turned to him then, placing her hands on his arms. "It was much more than that," she said tenderly. "I couldn't stop thinkin' about you after that." She explained no more but raised her hands to his shoulders and began peeling away his suit coat. "You'll be more comfortable without this," she said.

Daniel studied her eyes as she concentrated on her task. Something about the way she was behaving triggered his curiosity, and he raised his hand to test the pulse at her neck; her heart was racing, and it made *his* jump, inexplicably, in his chest.

She hung his coat over the back of one of the chairs that flanked the small table and gave Daniel his wine before quickly spinning away.

He watched silently as she stopped several steps away. When she reached for the shoulders of the beige gown, Daniel realized her intent and backed up, slowly lowering his buttocks to a chair as he freed his stiff collar.

She seemed hesitant, staring at him until an almost inconspicuous nod of his head and an ardent flash of desire in his blue eyes encouraged her to proceed.

Lila tipped her shoulders, and the gown fell forward. Her

thumbs guided it from there, slowly over her hips until it fell free and pooled at her feet. She bent, grasping a sleeve as she raised one foot and then the other, stepping free of the yards of material. The gown then sailed reverently to the end of the bed. She paused then, again watching her husband's reaction as she tugged lightly on the pink ribbon at her waist; her petticoat also fell away, and she stepped free of it, too.

Daniel did not so much as blink as he watched every slow, accentuated movement. She was lovely and graceful, and she was doing this to please him. Her sensuous movements were exciting him to the point he thought he might just have to free the buttons on his trousers any moment now. He drained his glass and set the thing on the table without so much as a glance as to where it might land.

"You want me, don't you, Daniel?" Lila said huskily as she raised the hem of her shift and eased her fingertips under the garters at her thighs.

He raised his eyes, his feverish gaze colliding with hers. "You're a perfect little minx," he said passionately.

Lila's smile turned completely seductive, and she rolled one stocking and then the other down her long, shapely leg. These, too, sailed off and out of sight. She was left with only a sheer chemise remaining, and that was raised slowly, inched up and over her hips, her waist, and her breasts until she was standing gloriously naked for his eyes alone.

And the fire in the hearth was nothing in comparison to the fire in his eyes.

Lila was greatly encouraged by his reaction and walked toward him, a single step at a time. She stopped before him, and his head was tipped back as they simply stared at each other for a long moment before Lila lowered herself to sit astride his lap. Her fingers disappeared into the thick, blond hair on either side of his head. "I love you so much,

Daniel. I think sometimes I'll burst with lovin' you," she whispered.

Surprisingly, moisture welled up in his brilliant blue eyes, and Daniel wrapped his arms around her as he buried his face in the hollow between her breasts. "Oh, God, Lee," he breathed. "I love you, too."

As soon as the words left his mouth, Daniel tipped his head back as one hand reached for the back of her head, forcing her to bend to him. He kissed her fiercely, passionately, with more tender force than Lila had ever known from him.

Their lovemaking became like a wild thing as each strived to reach into the other, needing like they had never needed before.

Daniel's clothing mysteriously disappeared before they fell on the bed in a jumble of frenzied arms and legs. They worshipped each other with hands and lips and fevered glances.

When his kisses caressed her from neck to lower limb, Lila's head tipped back into the pillows, and her eyes closed tightly as she endured the rapturous pain. "Please!" she cried softly.

He reared up over her then, entering her quickly, forcing himself into controlled motions that would give what she needed.

When her body quivered and snapped upward with the beginnings of her climax, Daniel pushed forward and then back, once, twice, before pulling free. He clung to her, burying his face in her hair as they rocked and trembled in a seemingly tortured dance. Their breathing was harsh in their ears, and as the apex of their passion slowly drained away, a molten glow permeated them both.

It was several moments before either could speak, and they absolutely refused to disentangle their bodies.

"That was something," Lila whispered before taking in a deep breath.

"You started it," Daniel accused huskily.

Lila's eyes closed briefly again as she memorized the feel of him along every inch of her body. "I know," she returned with quiet pride.

Daniel managed a weak chuckle before he rolled onto his side. "*That* was Lila's dance!" he quipped.

She giggled softly as she cuddled against his side.

His arm wrapped around her and pulled her close. "If there are many more occasions like that," he murmured, staring thoughtfully at the ceiling, "I don't think I'll live for another thirty hours."

Lila merely smiled and moved her cheek against his upper arm. "You know what else is nice?" she said quietly as her fingers toyed with the soft, matted hair on his chest. "We don't have to get up before dawn and sneak me back into my house."

Daniel rolled onto his side and shimmied down in the bed until they were smiling at each other, nose to nose. "That's true. And I can have my way with you any time I wish."

Lila arched a brow severely. "*Any* time?"

"*Any place*," he said emphatically.

"Really?" she questioned thoughtfully. "In the kitchen?"

"Uh-huh."

"You wouldn't."

"I certainly would."

"In the parlor?" she teased, warming to his game.

"On a chair," he said.

She laughed and pulled a hair on his chest. "Impossible."

Daniel winced but moved his lower body against hers suggestively. "It damn near happened on a chair tonight," he said ruefully.

They were silent then, staring into each other's eyes, grinning madly as if they knew some secret no one else could possibly know.

"I feel like a boy again," he said quietly.

Lila giggled meaningfully. "You're no *boy*."

"Well, I feel young and foolish. As if I could tackle the world and have fun doing it."

"Or reach the stars?" she whispered. "Me, too."

Her eyes suddenly sparkled with something more akin to mischievousness, and her hand disappeared between them. "You're warm," she murmured, snuggling against his chest as her fingers closed around him.

Daniel grinned. "I'll be more than warm if you keep that up."

Lila's lips twitched and she laughed.

Daniel felt himself responding to her caresses and drew in a ragged breath before pressing his lips against her cheek.

"We have hours to while away," she murmured as her hand traveled up his thigh.

"Lila . . ." he warned.

"I don't think I can leave you alone," she whispered.

He stared into her eyes for a moment, amazed that his body had responded to her so quickly. "I feel the same," he murmured, turning his head and pressing his lips against hers.

Daniel set the pace for the moment, desiring only to ease the need he knew she possessed deep inside her. He purposely forced her to lie back and allow him to minister to her.

At some early point she expressed her concern for *his* pleasure, but Daniel smiled and slowly shook his head. "This is for you," he murmured.

It was a difficult thing to accept, this first journey to

pleasure without him. Lila felt a pang of being alone, and the look she turned on him was troubled.

Daniel quickly set aside her distress as he propped himself on his side and covered and weighed her breast with his hand. "I want to watch you," he said. "There are many kinds of pleasures, Lee, and this is one of them." His hand moved downward, over her belly, and his head dipped, his lips very close to her ear. "I'll be right here beside you," he whispered.

Moments later Lila felt a tiny spark of a first spasm as his fingers played with her. She pressed her head back into the mattress, her eyes narrowing as she stared up at him. "Ohhh," she gasped fretfully. And then, suddenly, she was taking a long, deep breath just before her body became racked by forceful spasms. She rolled onto her side away from him, bringing her knees up and gripping her upper arms with her hands.

Daniel pressed his chest against her back, curled his legs beneath hers, and held her.

"Lordy," she breathed.

"All right?" he whispered.

Lila managed a nod of her head.

He eyed the two candles on the table, knowing there was a third, glowing beside the bed at his back. But Daniel did not want to remove himself from her to get up and extinguish any of the three. They would burn down and sputter eventually. He pressed his erection against the warmth of her and settled his head more comfortably on the pillow. "I want to hold you like this while we sleep," he murmured.

"But, you're . . ."

He knew exactly what she was thinking and pressed a sweet kiss against her shoulder. "I'm fine, darling," he whispered. "Sleep."

At some point during the night Lila turned in semi-sleep

to face him. A gentle smile tipped the corners of her mouth as Daniel eased inside her.

The following morning Beatrice Bundy slowed her pace when she noticed a piece of paper posted on the door of Daniel Stone's house waving in the breeze. Looking first left and then right, to ensure she was not being watched, Beatrice hurried along the walk and up the porch steps. She lifted a gloved hand to hold the paper down and read. "Oh, for *heaven's* sake!" she snapped.

CHAPTER 17

 DANIEL AND LILA DID NOT EVEN ATTEMPT TO dress that day. When they felt the desire to eat, he wrapped her in one of his heavy robes before they raced downstairs to raid the pantry. The rest of the time they talked and played. There were responsibilities aplenty awaiting them both; this day was theirs.

Late that evening a naked Daniel dashed across the cold bedroom floor and fed some logs to the hungry flames in the small fireplace.

Lila, equally as naked but with his robe over her shoulders, sat in the center of the bed daintily picking pieces of warmed chicken from the bones. "I'm feeling sad that this day is almost over," she said before popping a piece of white meat into her mouth. "I never had such a wonderful, lazy day."

"Lazy?" he questioned, pouring a glass of wine before joining her on the bed. "It seems to me you've been fairly active," he said as he folded his long legs and settled himself facing her, knees to knees.

Lila grinned wickedly and held out a piece of chicken.

He smiled in return before tipping forward and taking the offering in his mouth. "Good," he mumbled as he watched her separate more chicken from the bones.

"Everyone has been very good to us," she said, feeding him another bit of meat.

He nodded, chewing as he absently caressed her knee with the palm of his hand. "Here," he said and held the glass so she could drink.

She laughed when a little wine dribbled down her chin.

Daniel caught the droplets with the tip of his tongue.

She gave him a quick kiss before twisting at the waist, reaching for more food on the plate beside her. It seemed like heaven, being here with him like this, recipient of all his attentions. It had been like a dream that she had never dared to dream. But they knew that they would awaken a few hours from now and others would intrude upon their blissful world. The morrow would bring individual demands, and they would be separated for a time, until they could fulfill their daily obligations and turn to each other once again within the private confines of this room.

Daniel sipped some wine and then lowered the glass between them. "I imagine the children have missed you," he said. "Have they ever spent a day away from you?"

Lila shook her head and fed him a piece of cheese. "Rachael had great plans for keepin' them entertained," she said, smiling as she popped a small wedge of cheese into her own mouth. "They'll be full of tales and adventures to tell me about."

"I'm going to miss you tomorrow, Mrs. Stone," he said quietly.

Their serious glances locked.

"I'm missin' you already, Daniel," she whispered.

They awoke the following morning, made love, washed and dressed, and rushed across town to the small house beside the smithy before the sun was up.

Daniel remained long enough to join her in a hot breakfast before the remainder of the household arose. He was then off about his medical duties, but not without thoroughly, passionately kissing his young wife.

Lila stood in the open doorway with a smile on her lips and a tender promise in her eyes as he rode away. The *promise* would keep them both warm and blissful throughout the long day ahead.

The bliss, however, was not to last.

Moments after his departure Lila felt as if she had never spent a day away.

She could not waken Tommy to get him off to school, Jonathan was painfully hung over and bellowing for hot coffee, and Sammy followed her from room to room, verbally punishing her for daring to spend any time away from him. In addition, she discovered Beth curled up in bed, crying.

Lila shooed Sammy to the outer room and sat on the edge of the bed that had previously been hers. "What's wrong, Beth?" she asked softly as she forced the girl to turn toward her. It was then that Lila noticed the stains on her sister's nightdress.

"I'm bleedin'," Beth cried hysterically.

"Oh, Beth," she whispered and pulled the girl against her breasts. "It's all right, darlin', I promise. I should have told you sooner. I—"

"I have pains, too!"

Lila tried to get her mind past the fact that Beth had just passed her eleventh birthday. Surely *she* had not been so young. "We all have this happen, Beth," she crooned. "I promise you it happens to every woman."

The girl's fear seemed to ease fractionally, and she looked up at her sister, obviously questioning the validity of her statement.

"It does. It isn't a bad thing, I swear." They talked about it then, Lila explaining as best she could what was happening within Beth's young body and apologizing profusely for not having warned her sister in advance. "You just grew up too fast for me, darlin'," she said lightly and smoothed a few wisps of hair off the pale face. Lila kissed her sister's cheek a few moments later and left Beth curled up with a hot water bottle against her tummy to ease her aches.

Some hours later Sammy Briggs charged through the back door of the cottage and ground to a halt when he smacked into Lila's hip.

Jarred by the impact, she reflexively reached for his shoulder to steady him. "For pete's sake, Sammy," she snapped.

Sammy looked up, wary of her tone. But he was a man in need. "I gotta have some water," he said hastily.

Glaring, Lila said shortly, "Well, you know where I keep the dipper."

"I need more water than a dipper," he explained, backing away as it dawned on him that Lila was not in a very good mood. "I gotta have the bucket, Lee."

"What for?" she asked, frowning down at him.

"Annie and me need it," he said quietly, studying the scuffed toes of his boots.

Suspicious now, Lila bent at the waist. "Why do you need the water, Sammy?"

"We need the bucket," he said.

With growing exasperation, she grasped his bony shoulders. "Why?"

"We need to make the fire smaller."

Lila gasped, straightened, and ran for the back door.

Halfway down the yard, Annie was dancing around a healthy fire of twigs. But the dance wasn't in fun; her movements were frightened and jerky as the fire began to spread across grass that had been long baked in summer suns and further dried by fall winds.

Lila dashed back inside and snatched up the bucket, yelling "Jon!" as she raced toward her sister. "Annie, get away from there!"

Lila concentrated in emptying the contents of the bucket around the edge of the fire, wetting as much grass as possible before she ran toward the pump. "Jon! Fire!" she screamed.

Frightened now by all the frantic commotion, Sammy stood near the house and stuck a thumb into his mouth.

Jon came around the corner of the smithy, pausing only a moment before he, too, grabbed a bucket and ran for the pump.

Lila was back near the fire, wetting the area around the fire, when he joined her.

"How the hell did this start?!" he bellowed as he began to attack the flames.

Lila shook her head and ran for the pump once more.

After several more frantic dashes between the fire and the water pump, the flames were reduced to rising, billowing white clouds. It was then Lila looked up to see her clean sheets, blowing in the gentle breeze, directly in the path of the dying fire's puffs of smoke. "My laundry," she groaned.

Annie caught Sammy's eye across the distance, and it was understood between the two that it was time to remove themselves from their sister's presence.

But on the first movement of the children toward each other, Lila turned on them, her fear transposing itself into anger. "Get in that house!" she snapped. "Now!"

She marched toward the house in the wake of the scrambling duo, with Jon following.

Once in the kitchen Lila sat down before her shaking legs gave way. "What do you think you were doing?" she asked the children.

Sammy stood beside his sister, bravely facing Lila's wrath. "We was goin' to make horseshoes. Like Papa," he said quietly.

Seeing that Lila was too angered and astounded to respond in any manner approximating rational behavior, Jon knelt before the children. "How did you start the fire, Sammy?" he asked.

"Papa wasn't there, and you were too busy to help," he said nervously, "so Annie and me put a coal on a shovel."

"You took a coal from the forge?" Jon asked in disbelief.

Sammy and Annie nodded in unison.

Jon's head tipped forward briefly in dismay when he thought of what could have happened. When he looked at them again, his eyes were very troubled. "You mustn't go near that forge," he told them. "Don't you know you could be badly burned?"

"Not to mention burning the smithy and the house down," Lila muttered.

Jon winced at her tone but was forced to agree with the thought. "That fire was getting out of control," he told the children. "You must never play with fires."

Two small heads dipped forward, and Annie whispered brokenly, "I'm sorry, Jon."

Sammy studied a small hole in the thigh of Jon's pants. He remained silent because sometimes it was hard to say he was sorry; they'd only been planning to help after all. Sometimes he didn't think Lila understood how helpful he could be.

"Into the bedroom," Lila said wearily, rubbing her forehead with her fingertips.

Jon stood and watched them walk away in obvious misery. "There was no harm done, Lee," he said.

"No harm?" she questioned, moving toward the back door. "Would you care to do the laundry over again? And what if they'd been hurt?"

"Look, they're pretty scared. I think they've learned their lesson," he said logically as he followed.

Lila reached up and grasped a handful of white, cotton sheeting. Rather than remove it from the clothesline, however, she dropped her head onto her arm. "They scared me to death, Jon," she whispered.

Jon had never seen her quite like this and wondered if being a new bride had anything to do with it. With a teasing gleam in his eye, Jon dipped his head around until he could see her face. "Have you had any sleep, Lee?" he asked easily.

There was a moment's pause before she laughed and raised a red face from her arm. "Some," she said dryly.

He planted a wide, strong hand on her shoulder then and squeezed. "I know they scared you, but the kids are all right."

Bringing herself back under control, Lee reached for the first sheet and pulled it from the rope line. "If they ever do that again," she muttered, "I'll skin them both."

Jon laughed and squeezed her shoulder again before he, too, returned to his work.

Daniel experienced a very hectic day. With the loss of Indian summer, the onslaught of colder weather brought about a rash of sniffles and ague. Several families appeared to be hosting the influenza, and Edmond had simply not been able to keep up with the numerous calls for his skills during the time that Daniel had been unavailable to help.

"You should have sent for me," Daniel told the man toward the end of the day. He was secretly grateful, however, that Edmond had not.

Edmond stretched his legs under his desk and rested his knitted fingers on his belly. "Call you away from your bride?" He laughed. "Not likely. I value my hide."

Daniel hefted himself up from the chair in front of Edmond's desk and groaned as he stretched his weary back. "Speaking of my bride," he said, smiling. "I'm going to see if Lee can round me up a bite of supper."

Wearily Daniel entered the Briggs house to find Lila sitting alone at the table, staring unhappily at the stove. Only when she turned her head and saw him standing in the doorway did her mood lighten. "Hello, love," he said in response to her smile.

She said nothing but walked to him, raising up and wrapping her arms around his neck as Daniel bent his head and kissed her hungrily. "I think it won't matter how tired I am at the end of a day." He laughed softly and tipped his head to whisper, "I'll still be ready to make love to you."

"I should hope so," Lila returned lightly as she took his hand. "Sit and I'll fetch you some coffee."

"I missed you," he said before he let her go.

Lila's eyes reflected a happy glow as she looked up at him. "I missed you, too, my love."

Daniel sat and looked around each corner of the room. "Where is everyone?"

Lila filled a cup with black coffee and walked toward him. "Papa and Jon are still workin', Tommy's off somewhere, Beth is lyin' down, Edward's playin' up the street with Joey or somebody, and Sammy and Annie are in disgrace."

Daniel feigned an elaborate wince. "Again?"

"Yup," she said as she sat on the end of a bench and frowned at the tired lines around his eyes. "Are there a lot of sick today, Daniel?" she asked softly.

He told her about his day, and she listened in silence, offering only the occasional word of concern for this person or that when she recognized a name. Finally Daniel completed his list and shrugged out of his coat.

Lila got up and took the coat from him, hanging it on a wall peg near the door.

"And how was your day?" Daniel questioned as he lifted his cup. "Other than the little ones being in 'disgrace'?"

"Oh, things are pretty much back to normal around here," she said as she fetched coffee for herself and rejoined him at the table. "Tommy wouldn't get out of bed and was late for school. Then Beth became a woman today, and I feel terrible because I hadn't talked with her about it, and she was very, *very* scared."

Daniel could see that she did feel very badly, indeed, and reached for her hand. "Is she all right now, Lee?"

Lila nodded, sighed, and grinned the most charming, lopsided smile he had ever seen. "I kept her home and talked with her and fixed her a hot water bottle. A little comfortin' now and again helps a body when they're scared.

"And then Sammy and Annie decided to make horseshoes and built a fire that near burned up half the backyard. The smoke drifted all over my clean sheets, and I had to wash them again."

Daniel's eyes had been growing larger in disbelief as she talked. "Anything else?" he questioned hesitantly.

"I burned the stew!" she said and started to laugh. "See? Everything is normal!"

Daniel laughed with her, and then he helped her restart dinner . . . from scratch.

Supper was late but adequate, and as soon as Jonathan arrived at the table, Daniel could see that it was time to eat; Jonathan wanted his food when he wanted it—no two ways about that!

Annie and Sammy were allowed out of the bedroom just as Jon and Tommy sat down. Sammy cast Lila a worried frown as he approached the table, and Daniel lifted him to his place on the bench.

"I'm in trouble again, Doc." He sighed.

Daniel bit his lip to keep from laughing.

Lila had brushed Beth's hair and helped her into a warm, flannel robe before she emerged from her room.

Jonathan watched his pale-faced daughter cross the room and frowned as he reached for a slice of bread. "Are you sick, girl?" he asked.

Lila shot him a warning glare; Beth was already feeling self-conscious, certain that everyone would know that something about her had changed. "She's fine, Papa," she said, placing a platter of ham on the table in front of him.

"She don't look fine," Jonathan grumbled.

Daniel lifted Annie to her place and watched Beth surreptitiously; the poor girl managed to hold her head high regardless of the fact that she appeared acutely embarrassed.

"I'm fine, Papa," she said softly.

When she made to walk past him, Daniel stopped her with a hand on her upper arm. When she looked up, he winked comically.

Initially, the girl was stunned, but then she giggled and took her place at the table.

Jonathan's head swiveled, certain there was some secret being kept. "What's goin' on?" he asked his eldest daughter.

Lila moved behind her father on her way to her own place but paused long enough to whisper, "I'll tell you later."

Jonathan grumbled and reached for the ham.

The initial moments of every meal in the Briggs house passed with few discussions as bowls and platters circled the long table and plates were filled. Daniel had easily adopted the task of placing food on Sammy's plate, allowing Lila to sit through the meal and give her attention to Annie when needed.

Daniel cut Sammy's meat into bite-size pieces before picking up his own fork. He looked along both sides of the table, examining the bowed heads, feeling quite content that he was sitting amongst these people. They were a good family, these Briggses, and there wasn't one of them he didn't like. Jonathan had his moments, of course, but that was because of the drink, and Daniel was determined that there must be some way around that before the man killed his liver.

He ate a good portion of potatoes topped with Lila's savory red-eye gravy before he raised a topic that was of concern to him. "Lee, there's some influenza going about," he said, catching her attention. He looked pointedly at Sammy and then Annie. "It would probably be best if you went to the shops on your own for a few days."

Lila nodded her agreement. Daniel knew best, and she had heard that young children and the elderly were the most susceptible. She would work out some arrangement for the care of her youngest brother and sister whenever she had to go across town; she did not want them coming down with the influenza.

They didn't.

At least for a time.

Edward brought it home first.

Daniel and Edmond rushed from house to house. In the

space of a week they lost two elderly patients and one infant; and they did not even consider this a full-scale epidemic. Many families in town were struck, but the full rage of the illness was never realized. Edmond and Daniel ordered the school closed and declared that socializing with the ill was foolish.

Each night Daniel returned to the small house beside the smithy to find another member of the Briggs family had fallen ill; it was going to strike them all, he realized, and young Sammy appeared the hardest hit so far.

"How is he?" he asked as he entered the front bedroom of the house.

Lila was sitting in a rocking chair, holding the child in her arms. "He's havin' trouble breathin', Daniel," she said frantically. "And he's burnin' up with fever."

Neither of them had slept for two days, with Daniel racing from place to place as he was needed and Lila attending to her own loved ones. Unbeknownst to Lila, Daniel was growing very, very concerned about his young wife. Lila now had four sick children to tend, and he could see that she was approaching exhaustion. Still, the desperately ill came first, as long as they both were able to stand.

Daniel felt Sammy's brow and lifted the boy in his arms. "Let's put him in a tub," he said and turned from her, rushing toward the outer room.

Lila followed in stunned, blind faith. "Won't he catch his death?" Putting a hot body into water just went against all her experience.

Jon was sitting at the table, nursing a pounding head. When he looked up, Daniel issued a hurried order.

"Get the tub and fill it with cool water," he said. "Not hot," he added as Jon nodded.

Daniel sat on a chair and began to strip away Sammy's

nightshirt. "Build the fire, Lee," he said.

Everyone moved and fast.

Moments later Daniel was easing Sammy's small hot body into the cool water, proceeding to sponge the boy's head and face. "I need some water boiled," he said as he attended his task. "And the mustard for a plaster."

Sammy was sponged until his skin felt cool, and then the rubefacient plaster was applied to his thin chest. Once he was wrapped in an oven-warmed blanket, Daniel cradled the lad in his arms and sat before the roaring fire.

Lila moved hurriedly from room to room, cooling fevered brows and feeding water and warm broth to any who would take it.

Eventually she returned to Daniel's side and stood there for a moment, just silently staring at the pale face of her sleeping brother. Her fingers lightly touched Sammy's hair, as if just touching would relieve the illness. "The others seem to be getting better," she said quietly. "But not Sammy."

Daniel grabbed her hand urgently. "He will, Lee. He's strong, for all his smallness." Sammy would survive, Daniel decided on the spot, if for no other reason than he and Lila prayed it would be so. He touched the boy's warm cheeks. They were colored as if painted by a deep, red rose. And, disappointingly, the skin was dry.

Lila fixed Daniel a plate of bread and cheese and cold lamb and moved a stool beside his chair. She sat facing him, holding the food as an offering. "I'm sorry, Daniel, I haven't had time to cook for you."

He touched her cheek and shook his head. "I'm not all that hungry, love, and you're not to be doing anything extra. You've got enough to do."

Lila nodded tiredly and studied Sammy's face once again. "Is he any better, do you think?"

"His breathing has eased. If this fever would only break tonight . . ."

It was nearing dawn before Sammy's fever broke.

Lila had fallen asleep at the table with her head on her arms, and the night's blackness was giving way to gray when Daniel noticed the beaded sweat on Sammy's brow.

"Good boy," he whispered in relief and pulled the small body tight against his chest. "Good boy."

Jonathan and Daniel were the last to suffer through the illness. Lila considered most of the "suffering" was done by *her*, however. "There's nothin' worse than sick men," she muttered as she trudged into the bedroom that her father and her husband were sharing. All Lila's experience had taught her it was more efficient to keep the ill together in the same room, but in this case she seriously wondered that saving a step or two was worth the headaches of having two sick *men* so close together. They seemed to feed on each other's illness.

She set a tray on the table between the two beds and turned to help her father raise his head enough to drink.

"That's better," Jonathan croaked as she took the glass away.

"Papa, the last glass of water was just as cold."

Daniel was lying on his back, his eyes closed.

"How are you feelin', darlin'?" Lila crooned as she bent over him.

His aching eyes opened marginally, and he nodded, once.

Lila pulled the quilts down to Daniel's waist and reached for the shallow bowl from her tray.

"What are you doing?" he asked softly.

"I'm goin' to give you a mustard plaster."

She had his full attention with that!

"No, you're not, Lee," he whispered hoarsely as his fingertips pushed the bowl away from the area of concern.

Lila straightened her tired back and frowned at him. "Well, why not? It worked for Sammy."

"Sammy doesn't have hair on his chest," he explained firmly.

She thought about that for about as long as it takes to breathe. "What does that have to do with anythin'?"

Daniel closed his eyes again, just because they hurt so much. "Lee, you have no idea what it's like to have that thing dry on a hairy chest and then pulled off."

Well, isn't he the brave one? she thought as a smile tugged at her lips. "No, I don't, Daniel. Do you?"

"No," he admitted. "But I've removed a good number, and the men involved were not exactly friendly toward me after that."

"You're a baby," she teased as she smacked the plaster in place.

Daniel's eyes flashed open, and he glared his displeasure.

"I promise I won't let it dry to hardened," she said cheekily before she turned and sought to treat her father in a like manner.

"Don't let her do it," Daniel warned.

Jonathan clamped the quilt over his chest and narrowed his eyes. "Git!" he ordered.

Lila stood with the second soggy plaster draped over the palm of her hand. "Do you want me to call the boys for help, Papa? Do you want them to see how *brave* you are?"

"I don't need no plaster," he said forcefully.

"You do. You're wheezin' and coughin'. Now, I've got other things to do. . . ."

Jonathan turned his head on the pillow and frowned at Daniel. "She's got lots to do so long as it has *nothin'* to do with us," he complained.

As miserable as he felt, Daniel knew that was an unfair comment; Lila had waited on them just like a nursing angel. "No professional nurse I've ever known could have tended us better, Jonathan," he said in defense of his wife.

Jonathan could see his jest had not been taken the way it had been intended. "Well . . ."

Lila took advantage of her father's distraction, whipped the quilt away, and slammed the mustard plaster home. "There!" she said triumphantly. "See how you like *that kind of attention*!"

Jonathan frowned mightily as his daughter turned on a heel and stomped from the room. "So, you really *wanted* to marry her?" he asked conversationally.

Daniel nodded cautiously, not understanding the man's intent.

"You ain't sorry you did?"

"I will never be sorry," he said easily.

Jonathan grinned then. "You will! Along about the time she comes back in here to fetch these plasters!"

CHAPTER
18

 EVERYONE IN THE STONE AND BRIGGS FAMILIES bounced back from the influenza, and Lila found that she had learned a great deal more about her husband during the interval. One, his medical skills were obviously greater than she could ever have imagined. Two, he might be a great *doctor*, but he was a terrible *patient*. And she did not hesitate to throw that up to him whenever she thought his ego needed a trimming.

Life went on and she was happy.

It was late October when Daniel arrived home to find her wilted and exhausted, supporting her head on her fisted hand, sitting at their small table in the kitchen. He laid a paper-wrapped bundle down on the chest near the door and walked to her side. "Hello, my love," he said quietly, easing his fingers deeply into her hair, massaging her neck briefly.

Lila closed her eyes and leaned back against his hand. "Just what I needed," she murmured. "A knight with strong but gentle fingers."

Daniel hunkered down after a moment and stared into her weary eyes. "I think it's time to stop this, Lee," he said with obvious concern. He looked down briefly, taking her free hand in his own. "I'm going to find someone to help you."

"My knight wouldn't tire so easily," she quipped, guiding his hand back to her neck.

Daniel gripped her shoulder and squeezed. "Your *knight* is worried about you, stubborn woman."

The tired look in Lila's eyes was replaced by tenderness only Daniel could earn. "I'm fine, darling. The children were more active than usual today. That's all."

It was the same, every time he broached this subject with her. Angry, Daniel got to his feet and paced away. "In addition to the cooking and cleaning and laundry," he said in frustration. He looked around the tidy kitchen. "And a dust mote wouldn't dare set down anywhere in *this* house." He moved back to her then, his tone softening as he dropped to one knee. "I want you alive and healthy, sweetheart. You'll be an old woman before your time if you keep this pace much longer. Please at least let me find a woman to keep your father's house in order."

"Daniel, you're still not seein' life in a big family the way it is," she said patiently. "I've seen all the bustle tire you out. I'm used to livin' like this, but sometimes I'm bound to be tired."

Frowning, he disagreed. "That doesn't stop me from worrying about you, and the *bustle*, as you call it, doesn't tire me out."

"Yes, it does," she said, nodding her head as if that were the end of it.

"No, it . . ." He hesitated, studying her face and the set of her jaw as he reached for a nearby chair and drew it closer. "Are we going to argue about this?" he asked.

"We can if you want to," she returned.

Daniel rested an elbow on the table and scratched briefly on his upper lip. "This isn't the first time you've suggested that I'm not fitting in well with your family."

Lila gasped. "I'm not suggestin' anythin' of the kind, Daniel! I'm suggestin' a big family is a lot for you to cope with."

"Because I'm . . . ?"

"Not used to a bunch of children around all the time," she said hastily.

"What if I said I want *more* children around?"

Startled, she blurted, "From where?"

Daniel laughed. "I'm talking about making some." He leaned forward and took her hand, whispering conspiratorily. "You remember, darling, we talked about how it's done."

Lila's eyes suddenly found another target for her attention.

Daniel stared at her, but she refused to turn and give him her attention. They had only been married a few short weeks, it was true, but he was beginning to feel uneasy about Lila's reasons for disliking this particular topic. He certainly did not want to rush her into pregnancy, but he had naturally wondered if she would ever want to have his babies.

So, they had yet to resolve the matter of the housekeeper or the matter of making babies, and Daniel could see his young wife was not willing to discuss either matter any further.

Very well.

He got up from his chair and walked toward the parcel

he had brought home, as he suddenly realized he had been trying to impose his own will and desires on Lila before she was ready. If ever she might be ready. Lila was fiercely familial and exceptionally covetous of her position within the Briggs household; she might *never* allow another woman to set foot inside the small house beside the smithy. As for the subject of babies, he hoped he would never feel he was *imposing* that upon her; he wanted her *wanting* to make a baby with him.

In the meantime, he wanted only to pamper her, to ease her way as much as he could while they propelled through this novelty known as wedded life. He wanted to give her joy akin to what she gave to him every moment that he was with her. He wanted to spoon-feed her with happiness. "I've brought you something," he said as he returned to his chair and set the parcel on the table.

Lila looked from the bundle to his smiling blue eyes. "For me?"

He laughed at the wonder in her tone. "Of course, *for you*. To whom else would I give a gift?"

Lila shrugged as her gaze darted once more to the parcel. "It's not my birthday," she ventured.

"No. Your birthday is April third. I remember," he said gently, loving the look of growing expectation that brightened her eyes.

She turned her head and smiled at him then. "What is it?"

He laughed and said affectionately, "Well, open it, you little goose!"

Her hands seemed to hover momentarily over the knotted string that held the paper in place. And then she was attacking the knot with shaking fingers, cursing softly when the thing defied her.

Daniel laughed again and reached out, slipping the string

easily from the ends and sides of the parcel, excited now by her *excitement*.

Lila gently folded the paper away and flattened it on the table before her hand delicately covered her open mouth. It was yellow. Golden yellow. And there seemed to be yards and yards of it. "Ohhh, Daniel," she breathed as she dared to finger the fine material.

He could wait no longer and plucked the gown from its wrapping. "Let's see it against you, then," he said as he stood and pulled her to her feet. He held the dress against her shoulders and admired the exquisite contrast between the gown's golden yellow and Lila's rich chestnut hair. "Perfect," he muttered.

"Let me see!" she demanded happily, taking the material from between his fingers and holding the gown against his shoulders. "Perfect!" she chimed as she admired the daring neckline and the luxurious puffed sleeves. "Oh, Daniel," she said again.

He was delighted that his gift had pleased her so very much. "I'm certain I don't do it justice," he quipped.

Lila turned and reverently draped the gown over the back of her chair. And before Daniel could realize her plan, she flung her arms around his neck. "You spoil me," she murmured before pressing a tender, loving kiss against his day's growth of beard.

"You were born to be spoiled, my love."

She knew that was hardly true, but she loved the pretense. "I don't give you things," she whispered.

"Ho!" he countered and moved back, cupping her delicate face between his hands. When he was looking directly into her eyes, he murmured, "Don't you know you give me everything, Lee?"

She searched his face and his eyes then, knowing that

what he said, he believed. "Are you hungry, Daniel?" she asked at last.

He could not speak and ravage this perfect moment; he merely shook his head.

"Take me to bed," she whispered, drawing herself up against his chest. "Make love to me, Daniel," she breathed.

Sleepy and sated, Lila curled up in Daniel's arms some time later. "Where shall I wear my new gown?" she questioned softly.

"To the Harvest Dance," he said in a deep, mellow tone. "Next Saturday evening."

On the whole, life was very good now, Daniel thought as he ran down the stairs and moved toward the kitchen. He and Lila were even about to embark upon a social outing; their first together as husband and wife. The Harvest Dance was a party to celebrate the receiving of the earth's bounties, and Daniel Stone was going to have an opportunity to dance once again with his wife. The harvest was now complete, and it was time for folks to spend an evening in play. Daniel felt lighthearted and ready to participate.

He entered the kitchen to fetch warm water for washing but stopped dead in his tracks at the sight he beheld there. Lila had managed to drag the large copper tub near the stove and was lying back, enjoying the solitude of a bath. Grinning as a thought occurred, Daniel approached and hunkered down, resting his arms along the rim of the tub. "You took all the hot water," he accused.

Lila's eyes snapped open, and she bolted upright. "How do you do that?" she gasped. "Why do I never hear you?"

Daniel shrugged. "Maybe you were sleeping."

"I wasn't, Daniel."

"Perhaps you're going deaf," he offered blithely. "They say that can happen if you don't make love frequently enough with your husband."

Lila looked momentarily stunned, and then she laughed as she sprinkled his face with water from her fingertips. "I think you must have a very short memory. Why, just last night, as I recall . . ."

Daniel rested his chin on the back of his hands and raised his brows. "An entire day has gone by since then."

Lila giggled and kissed the tip of his nose. "You look just like a puppy," she said happily. "A very mournful puppy."

"It's just occurred to me that I have to dance with you this evening," he said with feigned seriousness.

Lila arched a well-shaped brow. "Is that goin' to pose a problem?"

His head nodded once. "The *entire* evening," he added. "And I have to hold you in my arms."

"That's how it's done," she said shortly.

"I don't think I can do that without embarrassing us both," he teased. He watched a healthy red glow creep up from her bosom and eventually reach her cheeks before he laughed and stood up. "You're just far, far too tempting, my love," he murmured, turning away and stripping off his heavy robe. He let the thing fall from his shoulders, caught it with a hand, and draped it over a high-backed chair beside the table before turning to her. His eyes were dark, his expression was serious, and his erection proud as he faced her.

Lila's breath seemed to catch somewhere between her heart and her throat as he advanced. "Daniel . . . ?"

He stood beside the tub, staring down at her, certain he had her full attention before he bent a leg and stepped into the water, one foot at a time.

Lila shrieked and began to giggle. "You can't!" she cried. "Daniel!"

Daniel grinned as he lowered himself into the water. "Yes, love?" he said softly as he reached for her.

Lila continued to laugh as she landed against his chest. "You can't do this!" she said.

Daniel looked down the right and then the left side of her, settled her between his bent knees and leaned back against the tub. "As you see," he said victoriously.

Lila couldn't seem to control her laughter and lowered her forehead to his chest. "This is embarrassing," she choked.

"Why?" he asked reasonably.

"Because I was taking a bath. This was *my* bath."

"Now it's *our* bath," he said reasonably. "We'll help each other get spanking clean." He raised her head then, staring at her pretty lips. Concentrating for a moment on the sight of her, the nearness of her. "In a minute or two," he added softly.

He gently nudged her chin then, coaxing her forward, toward his waiting lips. "I did warn you, Lee. Anytime. Anywhere. Remember?"

Lila moved upward on his chest, all laughter gone as she gave him her undivided attention.

Daniel moved his hand into the mass of hair she had coiled on top of her head and pulled, pressing her lips more tightly against his own. God, how he hungered for her. He was of the opinion, then and there, that he should not get her with a child. Not for a good long time. He could not stand the months of celibacy. "Oh, Lee," he murmured before deepening the kiss. She responded as ravenously as he, her tongue daring to duel with his until they were both breathless. Daniel forced himself to abandon the kiss, preferring to play with her and prolong this agony that was now promised a fulfillment. He traced a pattern across her cheek, worshipped her chin, and then teased the soft spot beneath her ear where he knew she was particularly sensitive. He pulled his head back then, staring at her, his fingers content to gently touch her face for a moment.

And then his hands wandered downward, skimming the surface of her water-slick neck and shoulders, pushing her lightly upward so that he could watch as he turned his fingertips inward and pressed his palms against her breasts.

Lila closed her eyes for a moment as she felt the warmth of his flesh against hers. It was something she knew she would never take for granted, his touching her like this. It made her feel as if they could just fold up within each other. But then Daniel was requesting something she did not fully understand, and she opened her eyes, staring at him through trancelike eyes.

"Raise up, love," he whispered, and his upper body moved close, his chest pressing against her breasts as he raised her with his hands under her buttocks. Daniel guided her downward then, allowing her to slowly take him inside her body. His head dropped backward briefly and his eyes closed as he simply enjoyed the feel of her moving cautiously to take him. He moaned something unintelligible as he wrapped his arms around her and simply held on. "You feel so good," he whispered, turning his head until he could feel the silkiness of her hair against his face. "I've missed you, Lee. It seems it's been a very *long* day."

"I've missed you, too," she breathed. "Daniel, I need you . . . to do something . . . please," she whispered brokenly.

He understood completely, because he felt the same. This quiet, peaceful joining had gone on long enough. Now their needs were great. Prolonged enjoyment would come again later, he knew, when their bodies were less demanding.

He pulled his chest slightly away from her and stared into her eyes as he felt her muscles contract around him. His breath hissed deeply into his throat and his eyes narrowed as he reached between them and sought the sensitive part of her where their bodies were joined.

Lila started, causing water to slosh over the edge of the tub, pulling up and unknowingly driving her husband close to the end of his restraint. But she realized very quickly what was needed for them both and placed her hands on Daniel's shoulders, raising her lower body upward and then settling back upon him again.

"Jesus," he breathed, when she began to shudder. He pulled her back into the safety of his arms just as she exploded.

Daniel held her there, even as she moved once more to take him with her on this, their ultimate journey. He moaned and rocked both their bodies in the small confines of the tub as he allowed his life to be drained within her.

Lila's arms were tight around him, her head ducked forward as she pressed her face against the pulsing spot below his ear. She felt him shudder again, unbelievably, and this time the fierceness of the movement frightened her momentarily. But she could feel him, inside her, and she knew instinctively all would be well. *That* was her first thought, reasoned in a haze of draining passion. Her second thought was a little more jarring. Lila placed her hands on his chest and jolted upright. "Daniel!" she said breathlessly. "You *slipped*!"

Daniel was basking in a warm, fuzzy glow and took a moment to catch her meaning. "*I* slipped?" he questioned lazily. "*You* are the one on top."

Lila immediately moved her lower body, freeing herself

from him. "Well, I didn't realize I was supposed to . . . I didn't know when . . . for certain," she stammered.

Daniel hooked an arm around her neck and pulled her back down onto his chest. "Relax, darling," he murmured.

Lila raised her head and frowned with concern. "Daniel, what if there's a baby?"

There was that big question again. The one that caused him to fear the true reason behind her concern about conceiving. "Would it be so very terrible?" he asked quietly.

Lila felt, instinctively, that Daniel had probably left a baby within her this night. It made her want to cry. And yet, it made her want to laugh with joy. Basically, it tore her between conflicting emotions. "What are we going to do with another child?" she questioned fitfully.

"Love it," he responded easily.

"Daniel, you already have a house *full* of responsibilities."

He managed to lift a hand and smooth an escaped strand of hair away from her face. "Do you feel I'm not handling my responsibilities well enough?" he questioned as his eyes searched hers for the *true* meaning behind all of this.

"Of course you are, but . . ." She faltered and wearily lowered her head to his shoulder. "*Another child*, Daniel," she moaned.

"I know it will be an additional burden for you, darling."

She raised her head in alarm, fearing he mistook her intent. "Your child would not be a *burden*, Daniel."

Now he was confused. "Isn't that what this is all about?"

"Well, yes. But not for *me*. For you."

Daniel shifted and moved them both upright in the tub. "Lila, I think this water is becoming too cold—it's affecting your thinking."

"There's nothin' wrong with my thinkin'," she returned

quickly and pressed him back again as she towered over him. "*I* don't want to burden *you* with another child. Can't you understand?"

Daniel ran his hands up her back as he studied her worried expression. "Let's get this straight, once and for all," he said softly, "because I'm beginning to believe you're making a lot of assumptions, and that's not fair."

Lila nodded her agreement.

"Now, tell me true, are you afraid to have a child?"

"No," she said adamantly.

"Is it fair to say you have nothing against having *my* child?"

Lila's expression altered in a blink. "Of course I would want your baby, Daniel. I love you."

"But you're afraid I'm not ready for the added responsibility?"

Lila nodded. "You already have a full herd of children to care for," she reminded him.

"That's the part that isn't fair, darling. What you fail to realize is that I would love to have a hundred children around me."

Lila was not convinced. "You would?"

"I would," he said, nodding his head. "*If* you allow me to find a woman to help you."

"I'm not worried about *that*," she said flatly.

"Pride," he said, smiling as he began to feel better about it all. "Foolish pride."

Lila's hands caressed his shoulders as she thought about what he had said. "You're not worried that you might have given me a baby tonight?"

"I've never been worried about it, Lee, other than wanting you to feel you're ready. And *once* often isn't enough."

"Really?" she questioned thoughtfully.

"It usually takes some time for most couples."

"Really?" Now she was frowning.

He laughed at her concern. "Are you going the other way now?"

"What?"

"Are you going to worry if you don't conceive immediately?"

Lila thought about that and then shook her head. "If I'm anything like my mother and my grandmother, I shouldn't have time to worry."

"I don't know that has much to do with it, love," he said, smiling because she seemed to have pulled a complete about-face. "Have you wanted to get with child, Lee? Have we been holding off because you were concerned for me?"

She did not respond.

"Be honest," he urged.

"I worried about you marryin' me because of the size of my family. I couldn't just walk away from them, and you've never lived in such a crazy household," she admitted.

"I love that *crazy household*." He laughed. "And all the world's children could not have kept me from marrying you."

Lila seemed to doubt that.

"I love you, my beautiful little goose. And I love to watch you with the children. Your mothering instincts are just part of the wonder of you."

She smiled then as a flush of pride colored her cheeks. And all of Lila's concerns seemed to vanish in the face of his praise. "Do you think you gave me a baby, Daniel?" she whispered hopefully.

Daniel laughed again, softly and with joy, as he wrapped her securely in his arms. "Ah, Lee," he murmured happily, "I do love you."

*   *   *

When Daniel and Lila Stone entered the large room that was the schoolhouse by day, heads turned and chatter ceased. Contrary to what the new Dr. and Mrs. Stone believed, the talk of their affair and subsequent marriage had not died but had spread far and wide. The crowd in the school that night was basically split into two factions; those overwhelmed by the romance of it and those with fingers ready to count upon.

Lila clearly disappointed the latter group as Daniel removed her dark, cloth cape and proudly displayed his wife's slimness in a dress of autumn yellow; the skirt was full but the waist and bodice were tucked nicely and it was clear that no advanced child resided within her womb. Rachael had made the gown at Daniel's request weeks ago. The yellow flattered Lila's coloring and the style her regal, slim figure; other women either envied her or hated her on sight.

Daniel, too, had dressed for the occasion, although his apparel was not of formal wear. Still, his dark suit complemented his fairness, and the whiteness of his shirt, tended to by his wife, would bring a glare to the eyes in a bright light. They made a fine couple.

Daniel dispensed with his short coat along with their warmer garments. Having attended to that duty, he turned to his wife and grinned wickedly as he offered his arm. "Are we ready for some fun?" he teased.

Lila stared up at him doubtfully. "I think that depends upon your meaning behind the term *fun*, sir."

Daniel laughed and lightly touched her hand as it rested on his forearm. "Trust me," he said quietly. "I believe your friend Beatrice is descending upon us."

Lila reached up and smoothed the shoulder of her husband's shirt in an intimate gesture that was meant to make a clear statement to the young woman who was fast approaching. "I see her," she said easily and tipped a smile upward in his direction. "I think I just might have some fun tonight, Daniel."

Daniel threw back his head and laughed. He knew that she was nervous and apt to say anything before the night was over, but whatever Lila felt she needed to say, many of these folk had justly earned. He wanted to dance and enjoy her, but if she wanted to make a point or two, Daniel had long since decided it was her due. He would be there to be her dragon slayer, if she needed him.

He quickly surveyed the room, noting that people stood on the periphery, awaiting either the musicians or some other form of entertainment, but he did not want that to be Lila.

Beatrice Bundy breezed around the room, dragging her poor clumsy husband, David, until they had reached the objects of her attention. "Well, Lila Briggs, you sly old thing. Where have you been for ever so long?"

Bathing with my husband, Lila wanted to answer. Instead, she said quite reasonably, "I've been busy, as most of us are, Bea. And my name is *Stone* now, you might recall."

Beatrice blinked, flashed a glance toward her husband, and pressed a gloved hand over her heart. "Well, you are correct," she said expansively. "I had heard that you are now married." She flashed a doubtful but becoming smile at Daniel. "Is it really true, Dr. Stone? Did you, indeed, marry our Lila?"

Daniel hated this nonsense. He bowed slightly, if insolently, and blessed Beatrice with something resembling a smile. "I sought the fair damsel," he quipped, "pursued her, and, at last, I won my heart's desire."

Beatrice, always a bit a-flutter when it came to theatrics, nearly swooned. She reached behind her for David's limp hand and breathed, "Oh, my."

Lila coughed behind a discreet hand and allowed Daniel to continue playing his game.

He tilted slightly toward the other woman and said confidentially, "I feared for a time that I would lose her, Mrs. Bundy. But, God bless her, Lila at last agreed to be mine."

Lila could see slow doubt stealing across the other woman's face and was grateful that Homer and Harmon Fielding had at last dragged Teddy Shoemaker to the front of the room.

The first dance would be a waltz, as would be the last of the evening.

With the first tuning of the fiddles, Daniel ignored the couple at their side and turned to his wife. "I believe this first dance belongs to me, my love," he said softly but just loud enough for Beatrice's attentive ears. "As shall be the last and all those dances in between."

Lila gave no further thought to her antagonists, other than to flash Bea a triumphant smile. And for those who gossiped and doubted . . . they could all *go to hell in a handbasket*, she repeated silently as she stepped into the arms her husband held out to her. Lila was about to dance the second dance of her young life. And as Daniel's arm went around her waist and his hand firmly held hers high, the moon and the stars moved right in under the high, gabled roof of the schoolhouse to bless *this* dance, as they had the *first*.

Her head tipped back as Daniel whirled her to the center of the room, and a warm, soft laugh escaped her. "This is Lila's dance," she said softly, for him.

They moved together as if they had practiced the steps a thousand times, so closely tuned to one another's bodies were they.

Daniel could only stare down at her, once more moved beyond human emotion by her delight. "This will always be your dance, my love," he whispered. "The *waltz* is for only you."

Lila could feel her skirts swirling around her, and the gentle breeze they created with their movements stirred the soft tendrils of chestnut hair at her temples. It was a feeling next to flying, she thought. Next to soaring with the birds. "It's wonderful, Daniel," she said, her eyes positively sparkling with happiness. "Our first dance made me fall in love with you, you know?"

Daniel's brow arched in doubt. "Really?"

"Oh, yes. It made me cry, what you did for me that night."

"I don't ever want to make you cry, Lee," he whispered.

"I cried because I knew you had danced with me out of pity."

He couldn't deny it. At the time he had probably felt that way. But he had been drawn to her, too.

"And I cried because I knew I would never dance again. And particularly not with you. It seemed impossible that you would ever be more to me than *Doc Stone*. There was just too great a distance between our lives."

"And too many people?" he asked quietly. And then he squeezed her hand, whirling her to a stop as the music ended. "But here we are, and you are *mine*," he added proudly.

Lila smiled with a little bit of pride of her own. "Yes, I'm yours, my dear Daniel. And this time I'm wearing *shoes*!" Pretty satin slippers that matched the golden yellow of her gown.

Daniel's arm dropped around her waist, and he pulled her against his side as he laughed.

"I have a confession to make," she whispered as they walked toward the side of the room. Lila turned to him, effectively halting their progress. When she tipped up on her toes, Daniel supported her with both hands on her upper arms. "I confess," she whispered for his ear alone, "that I liked it even better tonight."

Puzzled, Daniel pulled his head back long enough to see the sparkle in her eyes. "Liked what better? In the *tub*?" he whispered in return.

She giggled, her fingers digging into his shoulders as her lips moved close to his ear again. "I'd been dreamin' about what it would be like when you didn't leave me."

Daniel quickly looked around, just to be certain no one in the room could be close enough to overhear *this* conversation. The minx! "So you have little fantasies, do you?"

"Not so *little*," she whispered shyly.

Daniel was amazed, but he could actually feel his complexion darkening. "Lila, for the love of God . . ."

"I don't think I'll ever let you leave me again," she announced. Abruptly she set him free and tripped away.

In stunned silence Daniel watched her go. And then he tipped his head back and laughed before moving off to join his lovely little siren.

Daniel so loved this woman that at times her exuberance, her zest, her zeal, her very love of him, could move him near to tears.

Across the room Beatrice Bundy was scowling. "I just don't believe a man like Daniel Stone would willingly marry that woman," she whispered snidely.

David Bundy shrugged, sipped his punch, and offered, "Mae Belle Willoughby told you she saw—"

"Mae Belle didn't see it," Bea snapped the confession. "*I* saw that stupid marriage paper. What a vulgar thing to do, tacking it to the front door of Daniel's house."

David frowned at her. "What were you doin' skulkin' around Daniel Stone's front door?"

Having overheard a portion of the spiteful young woman's speech, Rachael Fraser stepped behind Beatrice. "I don't know that it was so *vulgar*, Bea," she whispered in passing. "It appears to me that Lila needed to make a statement, and she made it."

Bea's head snapped around, and her eyes narrowed as she scowled at the woman's back.

Rachael, dragging Edmond in her wake, headed straight for Daniel and Lila. "It might be nice for them to see a friendly face," she muttered to Edmond. "For a *change*."

"Oh, I think the majority of people here are happy for Daniel and Lila," Edmond countered. "Most towns have their share of busybodies, but we have more than our share of good folk, too."

Daniel opened the rear door of their house and stepped aside, allowing Lila to whirl into the kitchen ahead of him.

"It was wonderful, Daniel," she said giggling. "I could have danced forever. And Beatrice and Mae Belle have lost the objects of their idle chatter." She laughed again, delighted to have all the speculation about them put to rest. "It turned out to be a wonderful party."

Daniel stared at her askance. "I believe you may have sampled too much of that cider, love," he teased.

Lila was following her cloak in a circle while trying to be rid of the thing. He reached out with both hands and steadied her before removing the cape from her shoulders.

Lila tipped her head up and grinned. "I feel wonderful, Daniel."

She had reluctantly confessed, prior to arriving at the Harvest Dance, that she had been nervous about making her *social debut* as Mrs. Daniel Stone. Daniel suspected that her present state was due more to relief than it was to drink. Still, she did appear a little bit tipsy. Happily so. "I think we had best get up to bed," he said, laughing as he watched her eyes grow round and large.

"What a *wonderful* idea, Sir Knight!" she chirped and began to advance on him. "Maybe we should take another bath first, Daniel. I liked that," she said as she tried to push the coat off his shoulders.

"Did you now?" he teased. He shrugged and the coat fell to the floor.

Lila's head nodded as her hands worked his shirt up his chest and over his head. She let it sail off behind them as Daniel backed his way along the narrow hall toward the stairs.

When she reached for the buttons on his trousers, he stopped. "What are you doing?"

"Makin' you naked," she returned blithely.

His hand covered hers and he laughed. "It's cold without my clothes." But he didn't really care. He was enjoying her fun.

"I'm goin' to warm you, darlin'," she drawled.

He wondered where she had learned to do *that*. But he was, indeed, beginning to grow warm as she boldly touched him over the cloth of his trousers. "The party was fun," she said, raising her hands to his chest, forcing him to back up the stairs. "But it went on too long, Daniel. I just wanted to be alone with you," she added more seriously.

"I had the same thoughts," he admitted.

"The only thing I've ever regretted since marryin' you, Daniel, is that our lovemaking is interrupted by my woman's time," she said as she followed him into their room. "I miss you too much."

"And you call *me* bold," he teased. Daniel came to a halt when the backs of his knees touched the side of the bed.

"And I'm afraid there is little we can do about that, love," he said quietly.

"Oh, yes there is," she returned and playfully pushed him onto his back. "That much I do know."

CHAPTER
19

AS IT TURNED OUT, THEIR LOVEMAKING WAS interrupted again and again. As winter gave way to spring, Lila began to fret. When spring gave way to summer and there continued to be no sign that she had conceived, Lila was despairing.

With the first hint of summer, Daniel had ordered white furnishings for their front porch. The wood was solid, finely crafted, and the woven seats and backs were comfortable. Two rockers flanked a low rectangular table and, across from them, his favorite piece, was a chair wide enough for two . . . *two* who were either very good friends or *lovers*. He loved to sit on the porch with Lila of an evening, reading until the light turned bad or just contentedly watching Lila as she rested against him, sewing some garment or other for the children. He had convinced her over the months that funds were available for whatever the children needed. And Tommy, Edward, and Sammy seemed to be outgrowing everything they owned. What could be passed down from one boy to the next was passed down. Other than that, Daniel and Lila provided new. Occasionally Daniel felt that by doing this they were somehow robbing Jonathan of his masculinity. But Jonathan did not appear to object.

Everyone had fallen into a comfortable routine.

Lila reached into the basket at her feet and pulled out a single dark sock.

Daniel grinned at the three fingers she wagged at him through the hole in the sole.

"I don't know how he does it," she said as she reached for the darning yarn in her sewing basket.

"Sammy's, I presume?"

"Who else?"

He set his book aside and settled back in their shared chair; it was a sultry July evening, and he was content to just sit beside her and watch her slender, nimble fingers at work.

Daniel tended to watch her closely and frequently of late, knowing Lila was becoming increasingly anxious over their failure to produce a child. He worried, too, truth be known. But Daniel was experienced enough to understand that nature did not always respond as expected. Lately, he had tried to convince her that worry did no good; in fact, in his own mind, he wondered if *worry* could have a negative effect on what they were trying to achieve.

He sighed softly and tucked her under his arm as she continued the much needed darning. They were a loving, healthy couple, he told himself yet again. *It* would happen.

"Is it safe for Sammy to go swimmin' tomorrow?" Lila asked, successfully interrupting this thoughts.

"Certainly."

"I don't want him smackin' that arm around, though," she said as if she had considered tying the limb to the boy's body.

Daniel laughed and squeezed her shoulder. "He's fine, Lee. Let him be a boy again."

"That's what gets him into trouble," she said, turning her head to grin up over her shoulder. "Now you know why I married you," she teased. "We needed a doctor in the family."

Daniel laughed. It had been close to two months since this latest calamity had struck.

Annie and Sammy had engaged in a fight that had Annie falling to the ground, badly scraping a knee. Lila tended the cut and soothed the weeping child, but it quickly came to her attention that Sammy had been entirely too quiet for too long.

She went searching.

And found Sammy . . . up a tree. "What are you doing up there?" she asked, tipping her head back.

Sammy clutched the high tree limb, looking decidedly pale as he peered down at his sister. "I had to get my kite, Lee."

Lila could see the thing dangling by a string from his fingers. "Well, drop it down here and then get down yourself."

"Can't," he said. "It'll break."

"I'll catch it, Sammy," she said with mounting exasperation.

He thought about that briefly and then let the kite drop from his fingers.

Lila caught it easily and gently lowered it to the ground. She waited for a brief space of time, watching and growing curious as Sammy failed to move. "Come on, Sammy. I've got a lot of work to get done today."

"Can't," he said again.

"Why not?"

"I can't get down."

"Ohhh, Sammy," she breathed with exasperation.

"It was easy gettin' up," he said unhappily.

Lila's impatience dwindled now as she realized the boy was genuinely frightened. "You just hold on, Sammy. I'll get Jon to come and help you. Hold on," she said and turned to run for the smithy. Her first step came down square in the center of the kite.

When she paused and lifted her foot, Sammy could see the destruction she had caused. "You broke it!" he cried.

The next thing Lila knew, Sammy was on the ground and a sickening thud reached her ears mere seconds before his cry of pain. "Sammy!" she cried as she dashed to him and knelt at his side.

"My arm!" he cried. "My arm!"

Lila tried to roll the boy over but he resisted as he tried to clutch his left arm close to his body.

In the smithy Jonathan heard the commotion and walked outside. At the bottom of the yard he could see Lila kneeling on the ground. His heart skipped a worried beat when he saw her carefully pick Sammy up in her arms and turn toward the house. "Jezzuz, Mary, and Joseph," Jonathan mumbled and realized that he'd said the words, not as a curse but as a prayer. He took off at his best pace, sprinting toward his daughter.

"Papa! My arm!" the boy cried when he saw his father.

Jonathan looked from his youngest son to his daughter as they entered the house. It was apparent that he was totally lost as to what to do.

Lila motioned him toward his chair. "Sit down, Papa, and hold Sammy, would you? I'll have Jon run for Daniel. Again," she muttered as she spun about. "Lordy," she breathed, and hurried to the smithy.

Jonathan sat with Sammy on his lap. He was feeling quite foreign and awkward with this role of consoling father. He did the best he could, however, and pulled the boy against his chest. "What happened?"

"She broke my kite!" Sammy wailed.

Jonathan looked quickly toward the door, wishing Lila would hurry; clearly he needed her to perform some motherly fussing.

"We'll fix your kite," Jonathan offered.

Jonathan's intentions had been good that day, but once he realized his son would be fine, he quietly disappeared.

Daniel had repaired Sammy's arm and the kite that night.

The meandering creek was an excellent spot to bring small children. Frankfort was situated in the top half of the *S* created by the Kentucky River, but the waters there were too deep and too fast moving to make safe swimming for Sammy and Annie. Lila preferred the lazy, shallow waters of the creek. The area was well enough back from the main thoroughfare to be reasonably private, and the grassy banks were soft and well cushioned. It was their own little paradise, this place, and Lila felt safe enough in stripping off her own clothes for a swim, if the spirit so moved her.

Sammy and Annie loved the creek, and Lila frequently gave in to their demands for swimming and picnics each summer. The outing was a quiet, relaxing respite for her as well.

The children had run on ahead, and Sammy was struggling to be rid of his clothes by the time she arrived at the bend in the stream. "Nothin' shy about you." She grinned, setting the food basket aside before dropping to her knees. "Let me help, darlin'," she said.

"Danged shirt, Lee," he said with disgust.

"Don't use that talk, Sammy," she said firmly.

"Well . . ."

"Well, nothin'. Just let me help you." She pulled the fabric up and over his head while Sammy was trying to unbutton his pants. "Hold on a minute!" she said, laughing.

"Hurry, Lee!"

"That creek is not goin' anywhere, Samuel."

"Yes, it is," he said, giggling as he looked over his shoulder at the water. "It's running that way!"

Lila rolled her eyes. "*Very* funny."

Annie joined in the giggling as she, too, divested herself of her clothing. "I'm ready first!" she cried and ran toward the water.

"No!" Sammy bellowed with glee as he stepped out of his trousers. "Me, too!"

"You be careful with that arm, Sammy Briggs!" Lila called.

Naturally Sammy ignored her and immediately began scooping and splashing water with both arms.

Lila shook her head and folded their clothes, placing them far back on the bank, out of harm's way. She spread their blanket and pulled two squares of toweling from the basket before shucking down to her own shift.

"It's cold!" Annie laughed as her sister stepped gingerly from the bank into the water.

Lila shivered as the cool water shocked her overly warm skin and molded the shift to her body like a plaster. "Brrrr!" she said for benefit of the children.

"It's good!" Sam said, dipping down only to pop up again.

Lila eased herself cautiously into a sitting position and pulled him onto her lap. "Feels good, huh?"

Annie leaned on her sister's shoulders, wrapping her arms around Lila's neck. "You're fun, Lee," she said.

Lila was surprised by the suddenness of the comment, but it made her feel good. "Thank you, darlin'," she said.

Annie pressed harder against Lee's back and looked over her shoulder to where the skimpy white cotton ballooned outward. "How come you got tummies, Lee, and I don't?"

Lila smiled, unconcerned by the comment as she finger-combed Sammy's hair. "You'll get them too, when you're older."

Annie frowned at that. "I don't think I want to. They look kind of funny."

Lila laughed, tipping her head sideways to kiss the child's velvety cheek. "Thanks!"

Daniel had been standing close to their blanket, leaning against a tree while he watched them play. He chose that moment to make his presence known. "May anyone join this party?" he called as he walked slowly toward the edge of the creek.

Startled, Lila almost sent Sammy on his ear. "Daniel Stone!" she called, reproaching him with his own name.

"Hi, Daniel!" the children called.

"Sorry," he said sincerely.

"I want to see Daniel," Sammy said as he squirmed from Lila's lap.

"You said you wouldn't be able to join us," Lila accused. She was happy to see him, nonetheless.

"Well, it's hot today and I got thinking about you three out here having fun. I decided I needed a little fun for myself," he explained as he sat down to remove his boots.

It was true, Lila agreed. He worked very hard and deserved an afternoon to himself.

"The water looks inviting," he called.

Lila frowned as she watched him remove his shirt. "Daniel, I don't think—"

"You ladies had best turn your backs for a moment," he said, grinning, because he knew Lila would never turn away; but there was Annie to consider.

Sammy splashed and paddled out toward midstream, where he would await his friend.

Lila pulled Annie onto her lap, facing the child toward the opposite bank.

Annie giggled. "He's comin' in naked, Lee?"

Lila smiled. "Yup."

"We's naked, too," Sammy said.

"It's different for Daniel," Annie explained.

"It is not!" he said.

"Is too!"

"Stop!" Lila hissed as she watched Daniel tread cautiously into the water. She grinned when he shivered.

He eased himself down, sighing with delight as he rolled onto his belly and advanced toward her. "This feels good," he said. He swam to Lila's side and gripped her forearm to keep from drifting away. "Hello," he said softly and dropped a kiss on her upper arm.

"You're a devil," she said, but continued to smile with delight. She was very glad he was here with them.

Daniel's gaze darted pointedly toward Annie and then he returned his attention to Lee. "No harm done," he said. "And I'll take care."

Sammy waded across the short distance and threw himself onto Daniel's back. "We got a picnic," he announced. "Want some?"

Daniel laughed, his chin bobbing in the water. "After our swim. All right?"

The children moved away to play together shortly after that, completely at ease that Daniel and Lila were close by.

"Finally," he said when Annie was a safe distance away.

Daniel rolled up to a sitting position and wrapped his arms loosely around his wife as he faced her.

"I'm glad you came," she said.

"Me, too," he agreed and kissed her lips lightly.

Lila rested her forearms on his shoulders and Daniel pulled her hip tight against his under the water.

"We should be feeling guilty," she murmured.

She did not look guilty, however. She looked happy.

"I don't feel guilty and neither should you. There is always someone or something demanding your time or mine. It seems to me that we have very few private interludes."

Lila studied him closely as her fingertips wove their way through his hair. "Do you resent that, Daniel?"

"You know I don't," he said. "But I'm selfish enough to steal whatever time with you I can get." He grinned openly then and, with a well-concealed gesture, lightly caressed her breast. "And you should appreciate that, my darling, because I don't think your 'tummies' look at all funny."

Lila laughed and played the coquette, something she had been experimenting with lately. "That's the *only* reason I keep you around."

Daniel had realized weeks ago that she was practicing with her newly acquired feminine wiles, and he loved every minute of it. With her it wasn't trickery or pretending to be something she was not. With Lila it was *playful loving.* "I can think of at least one other reason why you keep me around," he whispered. "I might even come up with two. Shall I go on?"

"No!" She laughed. "Your point!"

Annie squealed then, and both adult heads turned in her direction. But, as usual, Sammy was tormenting the girl; this time he had a small, harmless snake.

"Sammy, don't you do that to your sister!" Lila called.

Daniel watched her as she was momentarily distracted by the children; she was so good with them. She was patient, attentive, and so very loving.

It was long moments later before she was satisfied that all was well with the little ones. She returned her attention to him then, and the wistful look he saw in her eyes almost broke his heart.

"I've seen this look before," he said quietly, stroking beneath her eye with the pad of his thumb. "But only recently and only after you've been watching various members of your family. What does it mean, Lila? What causes this little bit of melancholy I sense in you?"

She laughed, her gaze darting away for a moment as if she were too embarrassed to discuss these private feelings with him. "I don't understand it, either," she said. "Perhaps it has somethin' to do with growin' up or maturin' and *agin'*."

"Aging!" he hooted. "Darling, you have a long, long way to go."

Lila shrugged her shoulders and dared to face him with her fear. "I don't know why, but lately I look at my brothers and sisters, and I think about them bein' all grown. They'll be gone before we know it," she said. "Jon will probably marry soon, and then Tommy will be looking for a girl of his own and . . ."

Daniel pressed a forefinger against her lips. "They're not gone yet, Lee. And they'll probably live close by."

"I don't know what I'll do when Annie and Sammy—"

"Lila Stone," he said fiercely when the tears welled up in her eyes. "That is years away, darling. And we'll cross that bridge when we come to it."

But the tears spilled over, and he knew exactly what she was thinking, as if she had spoken aloud. He wrapped his arms around her and pulled her head to his chest.

Lila burrowed against him, now deeply embarrassed by her cowardly display. She hated crying women and rarely carried on so herself, but the pain she had been carrying around inside her for months just had to be released. "I'm sorry, Daniel," she choked. "I promised I wouldn't do this."

"You do whatever you must, my love," he whispered and pressed his lips against the crown of her head. "I don't want you keeping painful things inside."

"I'm such a mess," she cried.

"I think this is a little closer to home than brothers and sisters growing up and moving away," he said without doubt. "Closer to *our* home."

Lila nodded miserably. "First I don't want a baby and then I do and now I can't."

Daniel tried a little levity. "I have to admit, darling, it's seldom that you get yourself that confused."

"It isn't funny, Daniel," she said raggedly. "I didn't really *not* want a baby; I just thought we should wait. When we were courtin', I used to dream about havin' babies with you, and now it looks like I won't be givin' you any."

Daniel immediately forgot about teasing her out of her doldrums and demanded her attention. "Look at me, Lila," he said sternly and gently forced her head up until she could see his eyes. "*You* won't be giving?" he questioned. "Do you think this is only your problem, Lee? Tell me you're not blaming yourself," he added.

"Well, who else should I blame?" she cried.

She looked so wretchedly forlorn, with tears streaming down her face, that Daniel felt sympathetic tenderness well up painfully in his throat.

"Listen to me, darling," he said quietly. "Sometimes it takes years for couples to have children, that's just the way nature works. I would give you a dozen babies right now," he said, "right this moment, if I could and that was what you wanted. But, darling, you must realize that some couples never produce offspring. I hope, as you do, that's not the way with us. But I want you to understand, contrary to any old tales that you've heard, the problem is not always with the woman. Some *men* are simply not capable of fathering children, Lee."

This seemed to come as a surprise to her, and her tears began to dry on her cheeks as she studied him and thought about what he had said. "But, Daniel, we . . . you always . . ." Frustrated by her inability to voice her thoughts delicately, she blurted, "You always seem to leave a lot of your seed in me."

Daniel smiled his understanding when her cheeks flamed with color. "Quantity doesn't seem to be a factor, love," he said quietly.

Her eyes darted behind him, ensuring that the children remained a safe distance away. "I don't suppose you've got any little ones back in Boston?" she asked softly.

He laughed, happy that she seemed to be regaining her composure. "None!"

"You're certain?" she pressed. "Maybe there could be one or two you don't know about?"

God, she *was* resilient. *And* tenacious. "I'm certain."

Lila was finely in tune with Daniel's tones and mannerisms, and she sensed a discomfort that surprised her. "You can tell me, Daniel, and not be shamed. I'll understand."

"Will you?" He laughed and pulled her securely against his chest once more. "I confess to being a little unsettled by the discussion, Lee. It seems rather unusual to talk about the past in such a manner with one's wife. But I do assure you, I've left no children behind from a former life."

"Hmm," she sighed thoughtfully. "I thought we might put *that* concern aside, at least."

"There should not be *any* concern," he said quickly. "Not now, at least. If in a year or two nothing has happened . . . well, then we'll see. But not now, Lila. We're young and healthy and we have every reason to hope for the best. Please, promise me you won't fret over this."

She heard the plea in his tone and raised unwavering eyes to his. "I'll try, Daniel. I promise."

"We have so much," he breathed, stroking her cheek lovingly. "Let's not miss a moment of what we have by fretting about the future. We may not have a thing to worry *about*, darling."

She sighed wearily and flashed him a smile. "What would I do without you, Daniel Stone?"

"I hate to see you cry, Lee," he said simply.

"I hate you to see me cry!" She laughed brokenly as she dropped her forehead onto his shoulder. "I always look like someone popped me in the eyes!"

Daniel smiled and stroked her hair. "I love your eyes," he said, "popped or otherwise."

Seconds later Daniel had Lila in his arms and Sammy hanging down his back.

"How come Lee's cryin'?" the boy asked.

Daniel raised a hand and smoothed Sammy's arm. "Lee was feeling a bit sad, son."

"Why?"

Lila tipped her head back on Daniel's chest. "I was just bein' silly, darlin'," she said.

Sammy tipped over Daniel's shoulder to see her. "Are you better now?" he asked with obvious concern.

"I'm all right now." She raised her eyes higher and said to Daniel, "I really am all right now."

"I'm hungry," Sammy declared.

Daniel looked around, checking Annie's location. He did not want Lila to remove herself from his lap. "I think I'll drift over to shore," he said ruefully. "If you'll call Annie over here?"

Lila giggled at the comical wink he flashed her before he kissed her and then rolled onto his stomach.

"Why're ya doin' that, Doc?" Sammy asked as he watched Daniel's planned and cautious flight.

"Well, old man, we should get out of the water now and jump into our duds."

Sammy paddled alongside. "Why?"

Daniel turned his head and smiled at the lad. "Then we can move off downstream and give the ladies some privacy."

Sammy paused to give that some thought, looking momentarily puzzled. But he accepted Daniel's actions and whatever reasons might be underlying. "Daniel, how come spiders don't get stuck in their webs?"

Daniel grinned as Lila's laughter traveled the short distance across the water.

"I want to hear the answer to that one, too, Daniel!" she called.

For the journey home Annie chose to ride Daniel's horse while Sammy chose to ride Daniel's shoulders, and he and Lee ambled along the dirt road.

"So, what will you do tomorrow, sport?" Daniel asked the boy.

"Swimmin'!"

Lila smiled but shook her head. "Not tomorrow."

"I understand there's some preserving to be done," Daniel told the boy. "And that means you'll have to fit some berry picking into your schedule somehow."

Sammy barely took a second breath before he replied. "Ah, we'll cross that when we come to the bridge, Daniel." He laughed.

Lila stopped dead in her tracks; that was clearly one of

Daniel's expressions—a little tangled, perhaps, but Daniel's nonetheless—and she dreaded whatever additional *adult* conversation those little ears may have overheard back at the river. She turned a startled gaze toward the boy and her husband.

Now it was Daniel's turn to laugh.

CHAPTER 20

 LILA MANAGED TO SET HER CONCERNS BEHIND her by concentrating on her blessings each and every time Daniel walked through a door, or looked up and smiled, or kissed her or loved her. In all of these ways he made her life complete . . . he and her family. Still, she was honest enough to try and explain to Daniel that having his child went far beyond fulfilling her life as a woman. If she simply wanted to *fulfill* herself, she pointed out, she could make a baby with just any man. That brought about conversation of a different sort and another expla-nation on her part; Daniel teased her relentlessly over that statement. But clearly it was *Daniel* she wanted to make babies with, and everything else was secondary.

 Babies would come or they would not, she finally admitted, and they would have to accept what God was willing to give. Lila thanked Him regularly for the love with which she was surrounded, for it was much more than most people would experience in a dozen lifetimes. For that she was extremely grateful.

The summer passed them by with relative ease; Sammy did not break any more bones, at least. And suddenly the children were back in school. Edward, Beth, and now little Annie were off each morning, leaving Lila and Sammy to fend for themselves.

Sammy found this a very difficult adjustment and was clearly lost without his playmate. Tommy had taken up his apprenticeship beside his father and brother, and Sammy found that no one at the smithy had the time to play with him.

He turned to pestering Lila.

He had followed Lee back and forth from sink to stove at least six times before she tripped over him.

"Oh! Sammy!" she cried as a pan of spiced baked apples flipped from her hands to the floor. "Did you get burned?" she cried before she even considered the mess she now had to deal with.

"Can we go swimmin'?" he asked.

"Sammy Briggs," she muttered in disgust, now that she realized the boy was unharmed. "No, we can't go swimmin'." She moved away then to fetch her large spoon. When she turned back, he was standing beside the revolting mess on the floor with his hands riding his belly beneath his suspenders. "Get some water, Sammy, and help me clean this up."

"No," he said defiantly.

"Sammy," she gasped. "Don't you say no to me."

"I want to go swimmin'!" he cried.

Lila seemed to wilt when she saw his tears. After all, she knew what was troubling the boy, and she should have paid him more mind. At least until he learned to play on his own.

She also had a miserable mess on the floor.

"Which do I deal with first?" she muttered. There was no contest. "Come here, Sammy," she said softly and directed him safely around the brown, sugary globs on the floor. When she sat in her father's chair at the table, Lila pulled her brother up onto her lap. "I know you're missin' Annie, darlin'. But you'll get used to just us bein' here durin' the day."

"You don't play with me," he whined and pressed his face against her breast.

Lila sighed wearily. "I know. I can't do everythin', though, Sam, and cookin' for your hungry brothers and sisters has to come before playin'."

"I don't care about cookin'," he said firmly.

Lila smiled. "You care about eatin', though," she teased. "Look, Sammy, let me clean up this floor and start the supper, and then we'll play some pickup sticks." It was a weak bribe, but it worked.

Sammy nodded reluctantly and even helped clean up the lost dessert before he wandered outside to wait for Lila to play with him.

He was scuffing his way down the backyard looking for interesting bugs when he spied a tabby cat racing toward the bush. "Hey!" he called. The animal did hesitate and cast him a baleful look before sauntering forward toward her destination. "Come here, cat!" Sammy called and started to run toward the animal.

Concerned about this dashing bit of humanity, the cat took a leap and raced into the trees.

"Hey, cat!" Sammy called and followed.

Lila went to the back door to fetch her brother in time to see him charge into the thick brush. She frowned and stepped outside, calling, "Sammy!"

Sammy was beyond hearing by the time Lila had run halfway along the deep, narrow yard.

She had told the children a hundred times they were not to go into the woods. "Lordy!" she cursed as she increased her speed. "Sammy! No!"

Lila had no idea how large the stand of trees might be or what dangers the dense brush might harbor; she had always been too afraid to enter the place herself and had strictly forbidden the little ones from going in there.

Daniel's entrance into the small house beside the smithy was a bit disappointing that evening. Normally the smells of wonderful things cooking met him at the door, added by the welcoming arms of his wife. He always got that cozy, *I'm home* feeling when he heard the chatter and laughter of the children.

Tonight there was none of that.

Tonight, he was stunned to find no odors from cooking, no gentle female arms to greet him, and the laughter of the children had turned to tears and haunted frowns.

Annie was the first to jump up from the table and run to him.

"What's this?" he asked as the child threw herself at him. He picked Annie up and balanced her on his hip as he looked askance at the remaining children.

Beth dropped her head on her arms at the table and only Edward remained to explain.

"Sammy's lost," he said miserably.

Daniel instantly felt gravity pulling at the pit of his stomach. "Lost? Where?"

"In the woods!" Beth cried. "He's been in there for hours!"

With several long strides he was across the room and at

the back door. Lila was a good distance off but her posture, as she paced parallel to the line of trees, convinced him that the children had not exaggerated their tale.

Daniel set Annie on her feet and said quickly, quietly, "You wait here, sweetheart." And he ran through the door and down the yard.

Lila heard the thunder of feet on the dry ground and turned to see Daniel running toward her. Her only motion was to raise her fingertips to her lips.

"Is it true?" he asked breathlessly.

"I ran in after him and called and called," she said quietly. "He didn't answer, Daniel."

"Lee . . ." He looked her over, his concern for her almost equal to his concern for the lost boy. She looked dirty and ragged and tormented, but she was probably hiding the extent of her pain from everyone except him; he just knew her that well. He pulled her against his chest and just held on.

"I'm afraid he might have fallen and hurt himself and that's why he didn't answer. But I can understand how he might be lost, Daniel," she whispered. "I got confused more than once, trying to get out," she said evenly. "It's very dark in the thick of the trees. And he's only a little boy."

"We'll find him, darling," he assured her.

"I came to get Papa and Jon and Tommy to help. Papa made me promise to wait here. They wouldn't let me look with them."

She was telling him this in a steely voice that portrayed none of her emotions. Daniel knew she had reached inside herself and conjured up a remarkable facade that would see her through this and possibly hold her family together.

"There are the other children to consider, love," he said quietly. "They're looking pretty lost themselves, in a way."

She nodded, acknowledging only that she understood what he was trying to say.

"Go be with them, Lee. Wait at the house for us."

He turned toward the trees then, but Lila caught hold of his arm. "It will be dark soon."

He understood that statement expressed a variety of concerns; concern for Sammy, alone in the dark; concern for himself, her father, her brothers. He smiled and bent to kiss her cheek. "We'll be careful, darling."

"They're notching the trees, Daniel, on the east side. Watch for the notches."

He nodded and hurried away.

"Be careful. Please," she prayed.

Daniel had not taken too many steps before feeling he had stepped into an entirely different world; one foreign to a city-bred man, at least. It was cool amongst the trees, the odors of underbrush, growth and decay all striking his sense of smell simultaneously. The density of the trees increased as he continued, reducing the light in such a way that it was positively macabre. Hearing a noise ahead, Daniel called out, his determination bolstered; he did not want Sammy spending the night in this place.

He called out again and this time received a reply.

"Here!" It was Jonathan.

Daniel continued until he reached the older man.

Jonathan looked decidedly worried, and there was little point in speaking niceties. "What are our chances of finding him before nightfall?"

"There's always a chance," Jonathan returned gruffly as his eyes scanned the trees nearby. "Jon and Tommy have spread out, but if that boy kept walkin' north, he could be a good piece off."

"And if he didn't go north?"

Jonathan shook his head. "East, the trees thin out a ways. We can hope that he walked east." He shrugged his shoulders in resignation, however; clearly they had no way of knowing which way Sammy had gone. An adult could easily lose his sense of direction in a stand of trees such as this. For a small child, it would be almost impossible to recall in which direction he had come.

For Sammy, it would be very confusing.

And very frightening.

"I'll walk off to your right," Daniel said.

"Just stay even to me and keep hollerin'," Jonathan instructed.

It was the longest afternoon of her life, but Lila would have waited longer. Much longer, if it had meant finding Sammy. But night was threatening, and the men were forced eventually to abandon their search.

Lila saw Daniel first, but Jonathan, Jon, and Tommy were right on his heels. The grim faces of the men spoke a thousand words.

"He can't stay in there overnight," she said evenly as Daniel approached.

"Darling . . ." He reached for her, but Lila stepped away. All right, so tenderness would not help. He understood. Softness would break her down, and that was exactly what she feared most right now. He understood that, too.

"He can't stay there, Daniel," she said again. "It's dark and it will be cold. We have to find him."

"We're goin' to organize more help for first light," Jonathan explained. "More people fanned out and more voices have a better chance—"

"No!" Lila was shaking her head. She took a step around them, moving toward the trees. When Daniel gripped her arm, Lila pulled it free. "For the love of God!" she spat, her eyes narrowed and anointing each and every one of them with anger. "We don't know what's in there. We don't know what dangers."

They did. They all did. The numerous possibilities of what could happen to a vulnerable child were raging through all their minds. She simply failed to realize that they were all tormented.

"There's nothin' to be done now it's dark," Jonathan said gruffly. "I'm goin' to find some men for the mornin'."

When he began to walk away, Lila called, "Don't you go to that saloon, Papa! Not tonight!"

Jonathan stopped in his tracks and, after a long moment, turned an offended glare toward his daughter. "That's where I'm goin', girl. That's *exactly* where I'm goin'." But not for the reason Lila obviously believed, and Jonathan would be damned before he would explain it to her. His heart lurched painfully that his own daughter could think he cared so little for his son that he would go out drinking on this night, of *all* nights.

"He's not goin' for the drink, Lee," Jon said before he, too, walked away.

"We're all goin' to find help," Tommy added and then headed after his father and brother.

Daniel stood directly behind his wife, waiting as she watched the others disappear around the front of the smithy. He knew why she had said such a thing, of course. What bothered him most was that he knew she would regret it.

She faced him, raising her eyes beseechingly. "What have I done? How could I say such a thing?"

"We both know the answer to that," he said, not unkindly. He dropped his arm across her shoulders and moved toward the house. "So does Jonathan."

Daniel had intended to throw some sort of supper together for the children, but Lila walked right into that chore, if not by habit, then by design. "Let me help you, at least," he said.

But Lila shook her head. She needed to keep busy, and cooking required some thought in addition to the physical motions. "You've had a busy day, and I need to be doin' somethin', Daniel."

It was typical that she would think of him before herself, but Daniel also needed to be doing something. He was feeling useless and frustrated in his inability to bring about an end to Lila's suffering. He worried for her, he worried for Sammy, and then he turned and saw the naked fear on little Annie's face. Here was something he could do, at least.

While Beth took up her usual chores to help Lila, Daniel walked to his place at the end of the table and scooped Annie up in his arms along the way.

But the little girl did not collapse in tears or hysterics. She simply sat on Daniel's lap and looked to him for answers to her questions. "Is Sammy really bad lost?" she questioned quietly.

"Not so 'bad lost' that we won't find him," he returned confidently.

"How are we goin' to find him?"

Daniel's hand steadied her back as he smiled down at her. "We'll find him in the morning, sweetheart. There will be other people to help us then."

That seemed to worry her. "But it's so dark," she whispered.

"Is Sammy afraid of the dark?"

Well, no. There was that. Annie shook her head.

"Sammy's a pretty smart fellow, you know. He'll find himself a soft spot to sleep for the night."

"But he'll be scared," she said logically. "And I'm scared we won't ever get him back."

Daniel could see her tears beginning to threaten again

and wrapped his arms around the child. "I know, Annie." Daniel was afraid, too, but he wasn't about to admit it to this girl. He watched his wife's stiff, anxious movements as she worked at peeling potatoes. "And Sammy will be a little bit afraid, I suspect," he said. "But by tomorrow evening he'll be sitting here bragging to us about his adventure."

He spoke with such confidence that he caught Lila's attention, and she turned, stared at him for a long moment, and then nodded her agreement before returning her attention to her task.

When Jonathan, Jon, and Tommy returned to the house, they made a list of at least a dozen men and boys who would be arriving before dawn the following morning.

"We'll go lookin' again at first light," Jonathan said as he sat at the table.

Under normal circumstances the Briggs family, including Daniel, dug into their food with relish, but during this one meal there wasn't a soul who did justice to Lila's fine cooking. Every single person at the table was there for the purpose of being with the others, for the purpose of lending and receiving spiritual and emotional support. Such is the human condition to seek solace from those we love during times of distress. Food, at this table, was ancillary and eaten because sustenance was demanded by the human body.

Lila found, however, that every morsel that passed her lips turned immediately to acid, and her state was such that she was prepared to flee from the table as her stomach threatened to regurgitate its contents. She simply could not tolerate the thoughts of what Sammy might be facing out there, alone in the night.

She turned her attention to her father and realized he had aged in the span of one afternoon. She certainly had not noticed his pallor or the deep, dark set of his eyes before today. And the lines etched in his forehead expressed his mental condition more than words ever could.

There had been many occasions in the past when Lila had been on the brink of criticizing Jonathan for the lack of attention he paid to his children. Particularly the youngest. She knew that he loved them, but he had been stingy with demonstrations of his affections since the death of her mother. She wondered what he was thinking now, now that the welfare of his youngest was in jeopardy. Lila understood that Jonathan was fragile in many ways, and she worried that he could not tolerate another loss.

She wondered if *she* could tolerate the loss if something were to happen to Sammy. *That* thought brought her to her feet.

Daniel frowned with the abruptness of her movement, and as she turned toward the small table in the corner of the room, he followed her with his eyes. "Where are you going?" he asked as he watched her snatch up a lamp.

"I have to go outside," she said hastily and with equal haste quit the room.

She wasn't going to the privy. He knew that instinctively. Daniel cast his father-in-law a worried glance before he followed in Lila's wake.

He saw her hurrying along the length of the yard, her skirts flouncing wildly about her slim ankles in her haste. When Lila came to the stand of trees, she stopped and held the lantern high.

Daniel walked at a more sedate pace as he directed his complete attention upon her. Her back was straight, her stance determined as he approached her from behind and put his arms around her waist. He remained silent, staring into the blackness in front of them. The trees beyond the light from her lamp were like black silhouettes etched on a canvas of Satan's choosing. And Daniel was beginning to feel that those trees had been fashioned by Satan's hand. When she failed to speak and continued to stare into the forest, Daniel lowered his chin to rest on top of her head.

That one movement seemed to snatch her out of her daze. "Do you think he might see the light, Daniel?" she whispered. "Now that it's dark, perhaps Sammy will be able to see the light and walk toward it."

Daniel seriously doubted that; if the boy had been close enough to this side of the stand, they would have found him this afternoon. But the idea had merit in that it could certainly do no harm and might give her hope. "I think you're very clever, Mrs. Stone," he said. "In fact, a few lanterns might be in order."

Lila told him where he could find lanterns and fuel and remained in her place, holding the lamp aloft, as Daniel hurried off.

Moments later Jonathan walked to her side as Daniel lowered three lanterns to the ground near her feet.

Lila tipped her head up to look into her father's eyes. "I know he might be too far away to see," she said brokenly.

Daniel knew by her tone that speaking those words had nearly dissolved her control.

"But at least it's somethin', Papa," she added.

Jonathan nodded. "It's somethin', at least, Lila," he said quietly.

Daniel had fetched three lengths of wood from the smithy, and Jonathan offered a hand to wedge one end of each pole into the ground across the width of the yard. The lanterns were then suspended atop of these and the wicks turned up to increase the output of light. The radiance was considerable and the effect momentarily devastating; the hanging lanterns injected a festive air to a solemn occasion.

Lila began pacing.

"I know it's probably useless," she said as she approached Daniel, "but it's somethin'," she said again.

Daniel caught her elbow as she turned away again. "Come here," he whispered and pulled her back against his chest. "You're cold," he added as he wrapped his arms around her.

"Sammy's cold, too," she choked.

There was nothing to say to that. Nothing.

Daniel continued to hold her as the three of them remained within the circles of light. He marveled at the strength of her. She was quaking furiously within the shelter of his arms, but she would not cry.

At some point Edmond Fraser joined their vigil, advising the trio that Rachael was up at the house and would see to helping the children prepare for bed.

And while Daniel attempted to encourage Lila to go inside and join the woman, his effort was halfhearted because he knew she was not prepared to leave her post.

Edmond and Jonathan eventually drifted a distance away to talk quietly.

"I feel as if my own son is missing," Daniel said softly.

Lila gripped his forearm, digging her fingers into the sleeve of his coat. "I know." After a moment her head dropped back onto his chest. "This is a terrible thing," she whispered. "It's such a terrible thing, Daniel."

It was hours later, long after Edmond and Rachael had returned to their own home, that Daniel convinced Lila that she must at least lie down.

Beth had returned to sharing a bed with Annie for the night, leaving one bed vacant.

"I don't have a nightdress," she said woodenly as Daniel released the buttons on her gown.

"You can sleep in your shift."

"I won't sleep," she whispered.

In fact she did. It was as if she had been rendered unconscious by a mighty blow, so swiftly did sleep overtake her.

Daniel marveled at the resourcefulness of the mind to shut down in preservation of the body as he pulled a quilt up from the foot of the bed and smoothed it lovingly over her shoulders. With a sigh of fatigue, he removed his shirt and boots before he stretched out at her side and pulled her spent body close to his own.

Unfortunately, it is true that the mind will often become rejuvenated in a very short period of time, and both Lila and Daniel remained silently awake in each other's arms most of the night.

CHAPTER
21

 NEWS OF THE MISSING BOY HAD SPREAD FAR AND wide during the night.

 It seemed as if the entire town descended upon the small house beside the smithy the following morning. Before dawn was even a suggestion, men were gathering in the darkness of the yard. Women, too, accompanied their husbands, bringing food enough to feed this small army and then some.

 Lila found herself quite overcome by this show of support. The women took over the house, and soon the rich smell of coffee brewing could be detected beyond the back porch. The Briggs children were fed and pampered by others this morning as Lila wandered amongst the men. She spoke quietly, thanking each and every one as they prepared themselves for what lay ahead.

 Abigail Cuthbert had brought red-checked shirts

aplenty for those men who did not own such a thing; clothing that proved to be camouflage could be a dangerous thing. Each man carried water, a small sack of food, and his own rifle or pistol. It was agreed that three shots fired in rapid succession would mean that Sammy had been found safe and well.

Lila did not ask what a single or double report would mean. She did not want to know.

Daniel came to her side just as the men were positioning themselves to fan out to the east and west.

"I wish you could be in two places," she whispered. She wanted Sammy found, and it might take every man present, but how she needed him beside her for support!

Daniel kissed her cheek and squeezed her hand. "I find myself wishing the same thing." His gaze met hers and held as he willed her to remain strong. He had to go. He wanted to be a part of this effort, and he wanted Sammy safe and sound. But he would also worry about Lila every moment he was away from her. He smiled and touched her hair gently. "We'll be back with him," he whispered and then turned and walked into the trees.

Lila remained outside, pacing or standing until her legs and feet began to ache. When she could stand no longer, she simply lowered herself to the ground and sat . . . waiting for the glorious sound of *three shots fired in rapid succession*.

Beth and Annie joined Lila shortly after the men had left. They sat on either side of their sister as Edward hovered in the background.

"They'll find him," Lila told them as she tucked one sister under each arm.

Rachael Fraser joined them for a time, bringing with her a cup of steaming coffee that made Lila's stomach heave as soon as she placed the cup near her lips. Silently she lowered the cup to the grass in front of her.

"Come inside, Lila," Rachael pleaded. "You must be cold from sitting out here all this time."

Cold? She had been cold since the moment Sammy had disappeared from her sight the previous day.

"I'll stay a bit longer, Rachael," she said. And before the woman had taken a second step toward the house, Lila looked over her shoulder. "And, Rachael, thank you. Thank you," she said gratefully.

Rachael shook her head and turned away as tears sprang to her eyes.

The late September sunshine rained down upon them with little warmth as Lila, her sisters, and Edward continued to watch where there was little movement but for the flutter of leaves.

The day was threatening to cross over into evening when the first shot made Lila jump to her feet. A second shot felt as if the bullet had gone through her heart until, blessedly, a third report rang out from the distance.

What Lila did not know at the time was that the shots were being fired in relay over a greater distance. The first three shots were fired by one man and repeated by another who moved quickly to reach a lesser distance from the Briggs home.

Had she known, Lila would not have cared.

All that mattered was that someone had found her brother.

"They'll be bringing him home!" she cried happily. With her hands clasped together and held high, Lila tipped her head back and offered a silent prayer of thanks.

"Sammy's comin'!" Beth called as she ran to tell the women working inside the house.

Now that they were not searching the undergrowth for a

child, the men turned back with an increased pace. Still, it was over an hour before the first men materialized.

To Lila's disappointment, none of them had Sammy.

Daniel eventually appeared, running to her side as she swayed in indecision. "Where . . . ?"

Lila shook her head. "He's not here yet," she said as she moved a few paces to the east, searching the trees nervously. "I'm goin' to shake him, Daniel," she said softly as she stepped two paces west. "I'm goin' to shake him for scarin' us like this."

Daniel watched her move back and forth along the line of trees. "Lee . . ."

"My heart won't slow down," she said as she darted a hesitant smile his way. "It's beatin' like crazy."

A shout went up a few strides to the west, and Lila hurried beyond Daniel to the man who had spoken.

Teddy Shoemaker was grinning foolishly as Jonathan stepped out of the woods.

Lila saw him then. Her father had Sammy in his arms.

Jonathan had gone farther, moved faster, and tried harder than any man present. He had staggered through brush and stumbled over roots and climbed over felled trees, but he had found his boy. And no one, not even those closest to him, had any idea of how he felt about that. Jonathan had approached this day with fear and tension so extreme it had made his gut ache; he could not, *would not*, lose another person he loved. He had come to the realization the previous night of just how much his children meant to him. He had ignored them and taken them for granted for over five years now, but he would be damned if he would lose one. He had encased his mind in determination that morning at the same time he had climbed into his pants. He would find his son— or he would die in the trying.

Men and women milled about as Lila stood with one

arm clutching her midriff and the fingers of the other hand pressed against her lips as Jonathan took the few remaining steps toward her.

Sammy lifted his head from his father's shoulders when he saw her and reached out his arms.

Lila lunged toward them then and snatched her brother up in her arms. "Oh, Sammy," she whispered, her eyes closing against the tears that threatened as she pressed her cheek against his.

"It was cold in there!" he cried as he tightened his arms around her.

"I know, darlin'," she said as she tightened her hold. "We'll get you warm now."

The members of the Briggs family pressed close to Lila's skirts wanting to reach out and touch their brother. Annie's little face was wreathed in a lively smile, and Beth had tears in her eyes.

"I got lost," he said and pressed his face into her neck.

Jonathan swallowed heavily to rid his throat of a weighty obstruction.

Lila was looking around, looking for Daniel, who stood right by her side. Their eyes were gleaming bright as they stared at each other for that few seconds before Daniel's arms went around Lila and the boy.

Daniel hugged them with relief, kissed her cheek, and coaxed Lila to walk with him toward the house. "Let's get him warm and see that he's all right," he said.

Sammy's breath was warm against her neck as he said in a clear voice, "I'm hungry, mostly," he complained.

Lila smiled then, for the first time in more than twenty-four hours.

Daniel grinned. " 'Reason should direct and appetite obey,' " he said.

Lila cast him a curious glance, her attention momentarily

diverted from the warmth of Daniel's arm across her shoulders and the chill of the small body she held in her arms. "Who talks like that?"

"Cicero," he said. "A man who lived a long time ago."

Lila looked at where she was walking as they neared the house. "Funny name, too," she muttered. When she stepped up onto the porch, Lila turned toward the people who had followed. "Thank you!" she called and waved. "Thank you all."

The small house was warm and fragrant with the odors of food being prepared for those who chose to remain.

Rachael, Abigail, and Jane Rutledge appeared to be in charge.

Daniel endowed Mrs. Rutledge with a warm and tender look; he had not seen the woman since that night so long ago when her daughter, June, had died. "Thank you for coming," he told her quietly.

Jane nodded and smiled even though she was saddened by recollection at the sight of him. "We've got hot food ready and hot water for bathin' Sammy," she said.

Lila sat at Daniel's place at the table with Sammy on her lap.

The child was starving and reached eagerly for a piece of warm bread with butter that Rachael offered.

"That should keep you for a minute," she said as she smiled and gently touched the top of his head.

"For a minute," Lila returned weakly. Her heart had slowed finally, and now she was feeling physically drained by this ordeal. She thought what she would like most would be to lie down under a cozy quilt with Daniel. And she wanted Sammy between them; now that he was back, she was reluctant to give up her hold.

Daniel dropped to one knee in front of his wife and

grinned at the boy who was gobbling bread. "Not so fast," he said kindly.

Sammy nodded his head and continued to chew voraciously.

Daniel quickly determined that there was little wrong with Sammy aside from hunger and dirt. He had a few scratches and insect bites but other than that, the boy was in remarkably good condition.

"Ah, Lee! You're gettin' me all wet!" Sammy protested as he raised one hand to cover his hair.

Daniel had been in the act of removing Sammy's boots but quickly looked up to investigate the complaint.

Lila's arms were around her brother as he rested back against her chest, and tears were silently streaming down her face.

The dam had developed a crack in the past several hours, and Daniel speculated that this seepage of water would give way to a full-scale break at any moment. He stood, lifting Sammy easily. "Come on, son," he said as he turned to Jonathan. "You stay with your father for a few moments." There were plenty of hands willing to pamper the child, and right now Lila needed to be liberated.

Daniel led her by the hand into the girls' bedroom and closed the door, shielding them from the eyes of others and from the activity in the outer room. "Come to me, love," he whispered.

Lila seemed a bit bewildered about being there and turned in a circle before falling into his arms. "I promised myself I wouldn't do this," she cried.

"Now is the time, Lee," he said quietly. "You've gone on long enough."

"I've been so afraid!" she said raggedly.

"I know," he whispered. "Me, too."

He held her while she cried, while tears soaked the front of his shirt, and the intensity of her release brought moisture to his own eyes. When her knees went weak, he supported her against his body, and when she started to cough, he bent her over his arm and rubbed her back. "Easy, darling," he crooned. "He's safe now."

Lila gasped for air and eventually her stomach returned to where it belonged; the threat of its revolt had been much stronger this time than in the past hours. "I'm sorry, Daniel," she gasped and slowly straightened her back.

He led her to the bed and gently forced her to sit beside him. "All right?" he asked as he tucked her under his arm.

She nodded her head. "I guess I held a lot inside," she said ruefully and then took another long, cleansing breath. Her pallor was overtaken by a mild blush when she admitted, "I'm a bigger baby than Sammy."

"Not from what I've seen," he said firmly. "I think you're remarkable."

"I think Papa has been pretty fearful, too," she said quietly, wondering if her father might already be on his way to the saloon or searching for the rum jug she knew he kept in the smithy.

Daniel's thoughts just happened to be running in a similar vein. He, too, had seen the naked fear in Jonathan's eyes. He, too, suspected Jonathan would turn to rum.

Oddly, their thoughts were echoing similar matters but neither spoke of their concerns.

"I think you should lie down for a bit," Daniel suggested; he hated to see dark, purple smudges under her eyes. She worried him when she pushed herself so hard.

But Lila was shaking her head. She had regained her composure; her stomach was no longer queasy, and she had stopped shaking. "I want to see that Sammy doesn't eat too many sweets," she said. "With all those women out there coddling him, he's sure to eat every cookie they offer and end up not sleepin'."

Daniel smiled indulgently. "I'm certain the boy will sleep tonight, darling."

"And then I'll give him a bath," she added with determination.

And once the boy was settled in bed and asleep, Daniel intended to take her home to her own bed. They both needed sleep, and he wanted a bath of his own. More important, he was now impatient to have her to himself. They had spent a harrowing two days. They had been distressed and suffered concern. They had seen to the needs of others with little care for themselves. Lila had agonized alone while he had been active in the search. They were exhausted, to say the least, and to even *think* the things he was thinking about her was remarkable, given the way he felt. But he now felt it essential that they take at least a *brief* respite for themselves.

However, it was hours later before Daniel eventually was able to take Lila home.

A festive air developed inside and outside the small house beside the smithy. Having partaken of a generous meal and a rest, the many people who stayed on turned the gathering into a celebration. The September evening was cool, but not uncomfortably so, if one was active, and once Harmon Fielding removed his Jew's harp from his pocket, the fun got underway.

Lila was kneeling beside the tub, giving Sammy a good scrubbing, when Daniel returned from the back porch.

"I think Homer's gone home to fetch his fiddle," he said lightly as he knelt opposite her.

"How come there's a party?" Sammy chirped.

"Because a lost boy came home," Lila told him and tweaked his nose with soapy fingers.

Sammy plunged his hands under the water and squeezed them between his knees. "I wasn't much scared, you know?"

Lila laughed. "Oh, you weren't, were you?"

"There was this cat that kept purrin' around me all night."

Lila's startled eyes met her husband's briefly. "A cat?"

"Uh-huh. A orange one."

Almost afraid to ask, Lila mustered her courage. "Sammy, are you talkin' about a house cat?"

"I don't think he'd go much for houses, Lee," he said frankly. "He was pretty wild."

"Well, are you talkin' about a small cat or a *big* cat?" she demanded in frustration.

Sammy looked at her askance. "A small one. I chased him into the bushes."

Lila frowned at her husband before dropping her forehead on the edge of the tub. "Sammy, I swear I'm goin' to tie you to a chair inside this house until you're thirty years old."

Daniel laughed, but in sympathy, and went to retrieve the blanket she had warming near the fire.

Once Sammy was dried and wrapped in the heated blanket, it took only a matter of moments before he drifted off to sleep.

But Lila was reluctant to leave her brother right away, and Daniel drifted out back and stood on the porch, watching the partiers as he lit a small cheroot. Leaning against a porch post, he saw several men pass a jug amongst themselves, and he frowned as the thing landed in Jonathan's hands. But the man hesitated only a moment before passing it on.

Jonathan walked toward the house, knowing that Daniel had witnessed what had just taken place. But he was too tired to participate in the festivities any longer. His youngest children were in their beds and asleep, and he planned to be in his own very soon.

As he stepped up onto the porch, he smiled at his son-in-law. "I hope they'll forgive me for not stayin' and partyin'," he said.

"I'll make your apologies," Daniel told him.

Jonathan nodded. "I'm a little tired this evenin'," he said. He hesitated for a moment, as if he wished to say something, but muttered only, "Good night."

Daniel's hand snaked out and grasped the man's forearm. He knew he was assuming something that may not be, but he had to let this man know he was not alone. "Jonathan, if you ever need help . . . if you get to feeling shaky or bad . . . I might be able to help, and no one will ever know."

Jonathan's head bobbed again. "I don't need the grog," he said. "I need the love and respect of my family more."

Jonathan entered the bedroom he shared with his sons and found Lila sitting beside the bed, watching Sammy sleep. "Go to your husband," he said as he looped his suspenders over his shoulders and let them fall. "It's time you two went home and were gettin' some sleep."

Lila looked up at him, prepared to argue.

"No back talk from you now," he said. "I'm goin' to lie myself down right next to Sammy there. I'm tired. So, off you go."

Lila stood and walked to his side as he tackled the buttons on his shirt. "Hold on to him, Papa," she whispered. "Keep him safe while he sleeps."

Jonathan stared long and hard at his beautiful daughter before raising a work-worn hand to lightly touch her cheek. "I'll watch him, daughter," he said gruffly. "You go on with your man."

Daniel followed his young wife through the throng of partymakers as she thanked each and every person there for his or her contribution in bringing Sammy safely home. The very instant that responsibility was completed, however, Lila was ready for Daniel to take her home.

Lila insisted Daniel must be too tired to put a carriage horse to the traces and, instead, allowed him to lift her up before him on his saddle horse. When her buttocks were nestled against his thighs, she took the liberty of resting her back against his chest. "You're warm," she murmured and closed her eyes.

"Mmm." He turned the horse west, and they moved toward home.

"I'm beginnin' to dream about the softness of our bed, Daniel," she said sleepily.

Daniel laughed shortly. "We have like minds," he said softly.

"I forgot to give that boy a good shakin'."

He chortled at that. "Go to sleep."

Lila's eyelids fluttered upward. "On a horse?" she asked stupidly.

"I'm not going to let you fall."

"Mmm," she returned and snuggled firmly against him as her eyes drifted closed.

Daniel left his bride sleeping on a fresh mound of straw in the stables while he saw to his mount. And she did not utter a sound or open her eyes when he lifted her into his arms and carried her to their bedroom.

He stripped away her clothes and quickly washed her naked body before doing the same for himself. He did not have the strength to shave the two-day growth of beard that looked back at him from his reflection in the mirror; Lila would just have to see him ragged and scruffy in the morning.

Later, he would not remember lying down and moving against her as he settled under the quilts.

He could feel her warm breath on his lips, and Daniel thought that must have been what had wakened him.

"I think it must be midday," she whispered.

Lazily he opened his eyes.

Her face was very close to his, and she was grinning.

"I don't care," he returned and closed his eyes again.

"You might," she said impudently. "Edmond will be looking for you."

"No, he won't."

"Are you certain?" she asked.

"Positive. He said he would look after things today. And Rachael will be lookin' after things at the house. You're not to go over there today. Rachael's orders."

That was exactly what Lila wanted to hear.

Friends were wonderful, she thought.

A moment later Daniel asked drowsily, "What are you doing?"

She had her hand between their bodies and was groping around.

"Looking for you," she said blatantly.

He gave a bark of laughter before tilting his hips back fractionally away from her to give complete access to his body. "Don't you need more sleep?" he asked. His next breath was abruptly cut off when her hand closed around him. Daniel turned his head and pressed his lips against her shoulder, basking in the scent of her as she caressed his member.

"I might need more sleep," she whispered, "after you make love to me." He was erect and growing larger as she spoke. "Oh, Daniel," she groaned before ducking her head and teasing his nipple with her tongue.

He allowed her her freedom as long as he could; until his breathing became labored and his body felt as if it would explode without her joining him. "Damn," he muttered, rolling her onto her back and taking control. "What a wonderful little witch you are," he muttered. He kissed her then, ruthlessly arousing her as his mouth and hands moved everywhere upon her. His actions demanded her response, and quickly she gave it. In fact, she thought she would die when his fingers entered her body.

"Do it!" she cried. "Please."

Daniel's face appeared in front of hers then. "*Do it*, my lovely pagan?" he teased raggedly as his hand moved upward and his fingers circled. "What I'm doing now, Lee?"

"Dan . . . iel," she breathed.

"Uh-huh," he murmured heatedly. "I know." And he could not wait, either; the game had gone too far to allow for further tormenting. In less time than it took for her to expel another breath, Daniel was easing himself inside her.

Lila rocked and tilted her lower body against him as he began to move.

Daniel stilled his hips when he felt her shudder, slowly withdrawing in a way that drove her mad. And then he plunged deep inside her again, spilling his seed with a cry of pure elation.

He heard her wistful sigh as he rolled them onto their sides.

Lila was already asleep.

Lila had no idea of the time when she next awoke except that the light beyond the window did not appear as bright as it had when she had awakened her husband to play.

Daniel's side of the bed had already cooled when she rolled onto her side, but the scent of him remained and warmed her. She smiled over a fond recollection and tipped her nose toward the ceiling, breathing deeply of the aroma of brewing coffee from downstairs.

Suddenly her eyes flew open in alarm. Lila scrambled

up, seizing the chamber pot as she fell to her knees beside the bed. She had no more than positioned the porcelain container before her stomach carried out the numerous threats of the previous day. Lila had nothing in her stomach and tried desperately to control the painful retching that racked her. And she did not want to make any noise that would be heard by Daniel and cause him to be alarmed. She had honestly thought she was over her nervous reactions of the previous days, but that appeared not to be the case. She supposed the sickness had to occur before her stomach would completely return to normal. "But no use in worryin' Daniel," she gasped softly as she remained over the pot.

Moments later Lila felt better than she had in days. She replaced the lid on the chamber pot and returned it to its place under the bed. Once she had washed, rinsed her mouth and brushed her hair, she felt as if she could take on a breakfast fit for a lumberjack.

Buttoning a cozy robe around her nakedness, Lila hummed a gay tune as she ran down the stairs to join her husband in the kitchen.

Daniel turned his head and smiled as she entered the room. He had pulled on his trousers and little else and was in the process of whipping eggs in a bowl. "Hello," he said, dipping his head to receive her kiss.

"I'm starvin'," she said.

"Nothin' fancy here, ma'am," he drawled. "Coffee is made."

Lila turned her nose up at that, kissed his bicep, and wandered toward the stove. "I'll have tea," she said.

Daniel nodded his head knowingly as he reached back and grasped her hand. "Come sit with me for a moment, Lee," he said quietly. "I want to talk with you."

He sounded rather serious, and Lee did not want to be serious; they'd had *serious* enough to last them for a time.

She tried to divert his attention. "I'd like to go see Sammy," she said. It didn't work.

"Later, love," he said as he backed to a chair at the table and pulled her down onto his lap.

Daniel laid one arm across her thighs and warmed the small of her back with the palm of his hand.

Lila looked at him and frowned. "Is somethin' wrong, Daniel?"

He shook his head and smiled ruefully. "Not wrong exactly. But I think we should talk."

"About what?" she asked, clearly puzzled.

"The reason why you were ill a few moments ago?"

Lila's brows arched in surprise. "You heard!" She sighed. Clearly there was little she could put over on him. And now he would fuss. "I must be getting old and soft," she explained thoughtfully. She raised her forearm to his shoulder, and her index finger stroked his jaw as she defined her diagnosis of herself. "I was so worried over Sammy that my fear turned my stomach," she said. "The queazies hit me a few times while he was missin'."

Daniel was shaking his head.

"Well, I know he's home now and safe, but—"

"Lila," he said patiently. "Let's think about this. You were turning away from coffee before Sammy went missing."

So, that hardly made a case for anything, as far as she was concerned.

"Your cycle has changed," he added. "If I can count at all, you're long past your monthly."

Lila stared at him in stunned silence, her eyes growing large and round as she realized what he was telling her.

Daniel raised his hand and gently placed the palm over her breast. "Are you tender here, Lee?"

It took a space of time, but she eventually nodded her

head. Lila was almost afraid to hope . . . what if it wasn't so? "But they get that way sometimes, Daniel. Just before my bleedin'."

He was shaking his head again, and Lila's heartbeat picked up in pace.

"I don't think that's the reason this time," he said as his smile brightened.

"You don't?"

"No. I don't."

Slowly but surely the idea was getting through to her. "Oh, Daniel," she breathed. "Do you really think so?"

He was fairly certain; he'd been watching her closely for a few weeks now. "I do believe we've managed it, darling," he said proudly.

Lila's eyes began to sparkle, and then she laughed. "Oh, Lordy!" she said happily, wrapping her arms around his neck and holding on tight. "Oh, Daniel!"

CHAPTER 22

 RACHAEL AND EDMOND INVITED THE STONES TO join them for Saturday dinner. "Get you out for an evening," Rachael told Lila. "And away from cooking at least for one meal."

That was fine. That was nice. But there remained seven Briggses who would be looking for supper.

 Jonathan and Beth told her not to worry, they would fend for themselves. From Beth, Lee would expect such a comment. From her father, it was totally unexpected.

But Jonathan was slowly changing in a number of ways. He did not frequent the saloon at night, and Sammy could often be found in the smithy during the day, pestering Jonathan with a hundred questions; remarkably, Jonathan was patiently answering them all.

And a day or two after Sammy's return, Lila

had watched her father walk out of the smithy with a clay jug and a bottle in his hands. She had watched him from the house, curious as to his intent when he took the things into the privy. Less than a moment later he had emerged from the convenience . . . empty-handed.

"He dropped them down the privy?" she had whispered, puzzling over the event. As the idea took hold, she had smiled brightly. "Well, good for you, Papa!"

Lila had mentioned her father's behavior to her husband that night, and Daniel told her about Jonathan passing up the drink the evening Sammy had been found. He saw no reason not to give her hope. Jonathan seemed to have taken stock of his life and was making some changes. Daniel had reflected once again on the human condition; it was amazing how a shock could force people to stop and ponder the priorities in their lives.

The fall was grand, the sun brightening the spirits but not draining the body with its heat. Lila loved this time of year. She wrapped a light cloak around her shoulders and skipped off toward the smithy.

"I'm goin' to the shops," she announced as she entered the building of shadows. "Anyone wantin' to come along?" She looked pointedly at Sammy.

The boy stood facing his father, bent at the waist with hands gripping his knees while he studied the art of shoeing. "I'm busy, Lee!" he called.

Lila ignored the tiny pang of disappointment she felt. She had actually been missing Sammy lately. She was so used to having him at her skirts that she now felt as if something was missing when he wasn't there. But her brother was getting to know their father, and she was *very* happy about that.

Jonathan straightened away from the horse he had been shoeing, pulled a rag from his hip pocket and walked toward her as he wiped his hands. "Shouldn't you be gettin' ready for your evenin' out?" he asked.

Lila giggled. "Papa, there's hours before supper. How long do you think it takes me to get beautiful?" she teased.

Jonathan didn't laugh. Instead he reached out and touched her cheek briefly. "No time a'tall, honey. You've got the natural beauty," he said quietly. "Just like your mama had."

He'd been talking about Sarah lately, and Lila wondered if he was finally coming to accept the fact that his loving wife was gone.

"Thank you, Papa," she said sincerely. "I couldn't ask for more than that. Mama was lovely."

"Yup," he said, turning away abruptly as if he had suddenly become uncomfortable. "You should run along anyway," he said. "Go pamper yourself or whatever it is you women do."

Lila laughed and joined him at the workbench. "I'm goin' to leave you some supper, at least."

Jonathan reached for a large file and turned to smile at her. "We told you we can manage."

"Oh. You don't like my cookin'?"

He shook his head and laughed. A wonderful sound for Lila's ears.

"You're contrary," he said.

"Yup," she quipped and turned toward the open double doors. "I'll be back soon."

Jonathan grinned at the jaunty sway of her skirts as his daughter hurried toward the street.

Sammy stood beside his father with his hands tucked under his suspenders, riding his belly. He wanted baked apples for supper, but after the sloppy demise of the last batch Lila had made, he was afraid to ask. "Papa, could you ask Lee to bake up some apples?"

Jonathan shook his head. "Don't you be askin' Lila to be doin' anything today, boy."

That was disappointing, and he groaned, scuffing a boot as he turned away.

"Do you think we'll ever get her out of here?" Jon asked as he, too, watched his sister go.

Jonathan sighed. "We might have some scramblin' to do later on."

Lila's step was light as she moved along the streets. Life was good. She had a loving family and a father who was turning his life around and expressing some of his softer feelings. But most of all, she had Daniel. Daniel was everything. In spite a number of near catastrophes, she no longer worried about his adjustment to a large family and a small town; he seemed to thrive around the children. And that was good because they were now quite certain that she was carrying a child. " 'In the family way,' " she loved to quote to Daniel in her best imitation of Mae Belle Willoughby.

Lila had no sooner dispelled the quote from her mind than the woman appeared before her.

"Well, Lila Briggs," Mae Belle drawled.

"Stone, Mizzuz Willoughby. I'm Lila Stone now."

"Oh, yes," she tittered. "I quite forgot."

Lordy, it's a good thing I'm not showin' my condition, she thought. "Well, good day," she said and moved toward the door of Cuthberts store.

But Mae Belle blocked her way. "Have you heard about Beatrice Bundy?" the woman asked.

Lila wondered if something terrible had happened to Bea. "No. What's wrong?"

"She's *in the family way*," Mae Belle whispered, as if that were the most scandalous thing.

"Really?" Lila said cautiously.

"She won't admit it, you know?" the older woman continued in hushed tones.

"No," Lila breathed, biting her lip to keep from smiling. It was beginning to sound as if Bea was in for a time of it.

"It's the most scandalous thing," she said. "Why, Bea had made it very clear to all of us that children were not in her plans for the future."

"Guess David didn't know about those plans," Lila said lightly.

Mae Belle drew in a startled gasp. "Lila Briggs!"

"Stone," she corrected. But she was having a little fun with this. "Then again, it just might be that David had his own plan."

Mae Belle nodded her head repeatedly and tipped her short, round body close to her conspirator. "That's the problem with some young men," she whispered. "They just won't leave their wives alone."

Lila thought of her own child and murmured proudly, "I've got one of those at home."

Mae Belle's body jerked upright. "What?"

Lila felt sorry for dear Mr. Willoughby, but then she had for years. "So, how is poor Bea?" she asked. "Throwin' up merrily, I expect." Lila knew all about that and actually experienced a pang of regret for "poor Bea." Actually, when it came right down to it, Lila was bursting with the need to tell this woman of her own pregnancy. But she refrained, as she had refrained from telling anyone so far. She had also insisted that Daniel keep her condition a secret for a time, as if she were afraid to break the spell.

Mae Belle was incensed by this girl's crudeness, but she just could not seem to walk away. Not yet. There was more to tell. "Bea has forbidden her husband to come to her bed."

"A bit late for that," Lila observed. "Once you fall in the creek, you're already wet. Might as well enjoy the swim."

"Lila Briggs!" Mae Belle gasped. "You can't condone—"

Lila's eyes positively sparkled. "I *love* to swim, Mizzuz Willoughby," she returned and tipped her head in farewell before moving around the woman and entering the store.

"There's pork and peppers just needin' to be heated," Lila explained to Beth. "And the baked apples will be done once everybody's ready to eat."

Beth rolled her eyes toward the ceiling. "I *know*, Lee. You gotta get goin'."

Lila set the large iron pot on the stove and turned a suspicious eye on her sister. "Why is it everybody's tryin' to get rid of me today?"

"We're not," the girl insisted. "But you're goin' out tonight for supper, and you don't need to be fussin' over us when you should be home sprucin' up."

"*Sprucin'*," she muttered.

Daniel was already home and waiting for her with water heated for washing. And he was searching through his shirts.

Lila watched him for a moment and then pushed away from the bedroom door. "You're lookin' for your best one, I bet," she murmured and went to the clothespress. "I put it here."

Daniel grinned, walked to her side, and kissed her lips. "Thank you."

"Lordy, you would think we were goin' to the palace for tea," she murmured as she walked toward the bed.

Daniel left the shirt over the end of the bed and knelt at her feet. "How are you today?" he asked as he removed her shoe.

Lila giggled as she extended her other foot for similar attention. "Fine," she said. "I met Mae Belle Willoughby today and had a high old chat. You'll never guess who's havin' a baby."

Daniel raised his head and smiled. "You, for one."

She laughed. "Beatrice Bundy!"

"What's so funny about that?"

"I'm surprised poor David got close enough to get her that way."

Daniel was exceedingly happy he did not face that problem. He raised her skirt and eased a stocking down her leg. "So, did you tell Mae Belle about our baby?" he asked conversationally.

Lila grunted. "That would be one way to spread the news fast." She watched his hands as he gently touched her skin, thoughtfully appraising his good looks. "I really wanted to tell her," she said softly.

Daniel set her stockings and shoes aside and rose up on his knees, smiling as he planted his hands beside her thighs. "Then why didn't you, my love?" he questioned softly.

"Do you think it's safe?"

He laughed and shook his head. "You're a funny one," he murmured lovingly. He stood, pulling her to her feet. "It's always been *safe*, Lee. You're not going to put a curse on the baby by letting it be known that you're pregnant."

"Well, I think it's safe now," she said, as if he had not spoken.

Daniel turned her around and began to unfasten the buttons on her gown.

"I want to tell everyone!" she said happily.

Daniel refrained from releasing a relieved sigh. He suspected the subject would be raised tonight at dinner because he had already told Edmond, and Rachael was certain to comment. He hadn't meant to deceive his wife; he just had not been able to keep such wonderful news to himself.

He uncovered her shoulder and bent to kiss her there. "I have a confession to make," he murmured. "Edmond knows."

Lila whirled to face him. "You told?"

"I had to, darling," he said, grinning sheepishly.

She arched a brow, severely. "You *had* to?"

Daniel nodded, his delight unaffected by her apparent annoyance. "I was happy, elated, proud," he said. "I couldn't keep it to myself."

"Humph!" she said and turned away before he could see her smile. "You're a fine one," she added as she stepped out of her green winter day dress. "In fact, you're as bad as Sammy," she told him. "He can't keep a secret, either."

Daniel could have contested her statement; Sammy had apparently managed to do just that.

Lila looked and felt like a radiant princess that night. She had swept her hair softly on top of her head and dressed in her favorite yellow gown—the one Daniel had given her to wear to the Harvest Dance last year.

"Lordy," she said as he helped her down from the carriage in front of the Frasers' door. "Daniel, we've been wed almost a year."

"That's right," he said as he blocked her view of the house. Actually, he had been surprised she had not mentioned their anniversary before now. "I'm very happy that you mentioned that," he said as he reached into a coat pocket. "I have something I think you might like to use tonight."

Lila wanted to respond with something suggestive, but the comment flitted away when she saw the pretty package he held in one hand. "What is it?"

He laughed and extended the gift. "It's an early anniversary gift. Open it," he ordered lightly.

Lila held the small package in the palm of one hand and pulled the pink ribbon until it fell free. She loved the anticipation of opening a gift from him and always prolonged the process.

Conversely, Daniel loved to see the pleasure his gifts never failed to bring her, and he grew impatient. "For heaven's sake, woman!" He laughed and pulled at a corner of the paper.

A pair of single-stone diamond earrings appeared.

"Oh, Daniel," she breathed.

"Do you like them?" he asked anxiously. "You may have whatever stone you wish, if you don't."

"Diamonds," she said reverently and thrust the paper into his hand. Lila tipped her head and fastened the jewels in place. When she looked up, her eyes were sparkling in the moonlight in fine competition to the precious stones. "Thank you, my darlin'," she murmured and kissed him sweetly.

Daniel pulled her against his body and hugged her. "No. Thank *you*, Lila Stone," he murmured. "Thank *you* for the most enchanting year of my entire life."

Lila laughed and tipped her head back. "Well, it's been challengin'!" she teased.

"And we'll have a hundred more," he said lightly.

"Challenges?" she asked.

He laughed, also. "Those, too, no doubt."

Lila sobered then and stared up into his beautiful blue eyes; eyes that seemed to mirror exactly what she was feeling. "I love you, Daniel," she whispered.

He smiled softly. "I love you, too, my darling."

He kissed her then, not hard, but long and lovingly, and Lila came up laughing, flushed and a bit breathless.

"Let's go and show off my present!" she said cheerfully. She tucked her small hand in his as they walked toward the Frasers' front door. "I'm starvin'," she murmured.

Daniel laughed and hugged her against his side.

Rachael chose to be the one to open the door to them that night. And that was mainly because she could walk behind them as she ushered the young couple toward the parlor. Behind them was the safest place for her to be as Lila would not see her friend's expression.

Edmond was fussing about at the drinks cabinet when they entered the room. "Well, hello!" he bellowed and turned toward them. "Come in you two and sit."

Before Lila could smooth her skirts, Rachael was nervously wringing her hands. "I have to check my supper," she murmured and quit the room.

Edmond frowned at his wife's retreating back, and Lila looked confounded.

"Is something wrong with Rachael?" Lila asked their host.

Edmond shook his head. "There certainly is," he admitted. "And I think she's too old to get over it."

Daniel grinned and sat close to his wife, tucking her hands in his. "Rachael is fine," he said when he noted her look of concern.

"What will you have to drink?" Edmond questioned expansively.

Lila smiled up at her host, but before she could respond, a movement near the open doors to the dining room captured her attention. She turned her head, and her expression changed to complete surprise as Sammy stared back at her. "What are you doin' here?" she asked in amazement.

The boy grinned and Annie stepped from behind the door and stood beside her brother.

"Annie?" Lila questioned in a tone that said she was clearly confused.

Daniel squeezed her hand and turned to watch her expression as Edward, Beth, Tommy, and Jon appeared one at a time in the doorway. And all of them dressed in their Sunday best.

Stunned and feeling very silly, Lila turned a questioning smile Daniel's way. "What's goin' on?" she whispered.

"Keep watching," he said softly.

Lila turned her attention back toward the door. Her father was now standing behind his children. "Papa?"

Jonathan grinned and squeezed Beth's shoulder.

Rachael appeared beside him, and then Abigail Cuthbert was there. The crowd moved forward and fanned out into the parlor to make room for Jane and Harry Rutledge, the Fielding brothers, and Teddy Shoemaker. And on it went.

Sammy had received very thorough instructions about standing quietly, but he could obey no longer. He ran to his sister and threw himself toward her lap. "It's a party!" he cried.

Daniel laughed and scooped the boy up before he could do any damage. "Easy on your sister!" he said, but swung the boy high before settling him on his own lap. When he turned his head, Lila was staring at him suspiciously.

"A party?" she asked.

Daniel nodded his head. "For our anniversary. Our friends wanted to do this."

A slow smile tilted her lips. "And I said you couldn't keep a secret."

"Me, too!" Sammy said proudly as people began to mill about. "I didn't tell!"

A short time later Lila stood beside her father as Daniel helped some of the other men in moving the parlor furniture out of the way for dancing.

"I don't know how you managed to keep this a secret, Papa," she said with a smile. "Not with Sammy knowin'."

Jonathan laughed. "That was the easy part. The hard part was gettin' you out of the house so's all of us could get ready."

"That's why you all wanted to get rid of me today," she nodded, finally understanding.

"There's goin' to be some high steppin' here tonight," Jonathan observed as Homer and Teddy tuned their fiddles.

Lila smiled mysteriously and sipped her punch. "I'm only dancin' the slow ones tonight," she said softly.

Her father remained silent, staring down at the top of her head until she raised her smile to him. "I'm expectin' a baby, Papa."

Jonathan smiled, although perhaps a little more thoughtfully, and put his arm around her shoulders. "I was wonderin' when that would happen," he said.

"We've been tryin' for a while now," she said with unfamiliar shyness.

That was one thing he and Sarah had never had to contend with; it seemed every time he'd touched his dear wife, she came with a baby. But when a man loved a woman the way he had loved his Sarah . . . "Are you happy, Lila?" he asked, dispersing his sorrowful recollections.

She was and everyone knew it. They also suspected the reason behind Daniel's cautious attentions toward her and the reason she sat out a lot of the dances. But that did not prevent Lila from having a good time.

"Are you having fun?" Rachael asked as they watched the dancers from the sidelines.

Lila nodded her head and kissed her friend's cheek. "Thank you for this, Rachael. I'm feelin' a bit embarrassed by all this attention, though."

"Don't be," the woman told her. "You deserve this, and we wanted to do it. Everyone knows what an exceptional young woman you are. Particularly that husband of yours," she added fondly. "People naturally want to be around folks like you."

A single soft candle shed all the light Daniel needed as he slowly caressed his wife's flat stomach and examined the pattern his fingers were making. "I think you're getting a bit thicker here," he said softly.

Lila laughed. "Don't rush me, darlin'," she said. "I'll be *thick* enough, soon enough."

"I'm waiting for that," he confessed. "I'm waiting to feel our little fellow rolling around in here."

Lila smiled up at him as she rested on her back and let him explore her body. "Me, too," she whispered.

For a doctor who had witnessed this a hundred times before, Daniel appeared very much in awe of her.

"I understand you've been spreadin' rumors about me," she accused quietly.

Daniel's head popped up, and his gaze collided with hers. "Me? What rumors?"

Lila nodded her head slowly. "Rachael told me."

Daniel wasn't certain whether she was playing with him or not. "I don't know what you're talking about, darling," he said.

"Rachael said that I'm exceptional and that everyone knows that and you told them."

He stared at her in a moment of stunned silence, and then he laughed. "She's right. I'm guilty and I confess," he added lightly as he shifted himself upward on the bed. "You are *exceptional*," he murmured and lowered his lips toward hers. "But, darling, I didn't have to tell anyone. They all knew."

"I'm not anythin' special, Daniel," she said as she raised her hand and combed her fingers through his hair. "And if I am, it's because you make me feel that I am."

He shook his head and silenced her with a kiss. Such nonsense, he thought. The woman did not even understand her own worth. She had blessed his life and touched his heart, just as she did with everyone who entered her small world. Their friends understood that and wanted to be near her; she was a powerful, yet gentle, influence on all those around her.

Daniel felt a swell of tenderness surge through his veins and eased his body over hers. "I'm going to make love to you, my remarkable, exceptional little pagan," he whispered.

If you enjoyed this book, take advantage of this special offer. Subscribe now and get a

FREE
Historical Romance

No Obligation (a $4.50 value)

Each month the editors of True Value select the four *very best* novels from America's leading publishers of romantic fiction. Preview them in your home *Free* for 10 days. With the first four books you receive, we'll send you a FREE book as our introductory gift. No Obligation!

If for any reason you decide not to keep them, just return them and owe nothing. If you like them as much as we think you will, you'll pay just $4.00 each and save at *least* $.50 each off the cover price. (Your savings are *guaranteed* to be at least $2.00 each month.) There is NO postage and handling – or other hidden charges. There are no minimum number of books to buy and you may cancel at any time.

Send in the Coupon Below

To get your FREE historical romance fill out the coupon below and mail it today. As soon as we receive it we'll send you your FREE Book along with your first month's selections.